DEATH CHECKS IN

Praise for David S. Pederson

Death Comes Darkly

"Agatha Christie…if Miss Marple were a gay police detective in post–WWII Milwaukee."—*PrideSource: Between the Lines*

"The mystery is one that isn't easily solved. It's a cozy mystery unraveled in the drawing room type of story, but well worked out."—*Bookwinked*

Death Goes Overboard

"[A]uthor David S. Pederson has packed a lot in this novel. You don't normally find a soft-sided, poetry-writing mobster in a noir mystery, for instance, but he's here…this novel is both predictable and not, making it a nice diversion for a weekend or vacation."—*Washington Blade*

"Pederson takes a lot of the tropes of mysteries and utilizes them to the fullest, giving the story a knowable form. However, the unique characters and accurate portrayal of the struggles of gay relationships in 1940s America make this an enjoyable, thought-provoking read."—*Gay, Lesbian, Bisexual, and Transgender Round Table of the American Library Association*

By the Author

Death Comes Darkly

Death Goes Overboard

Death Checks In

DEATH CHECKS IN

by

David S. Pederson

2018

DEATH CHECKS IN

ISBN 13: 978-1-63555-329-1

This Trade Paperback Original Is Published By
Bold Strokes Books, Inc.
P.O. Box 249
Valley Falls, NY 12185

First Edition: September 2018

Credits
Editor: Jerry L. Wheeler
Production Design: Stacia Seaman
Cover Design by Jeanine Henning

Acknowledgments

I must start by thanking my husband, Alan Karbel. From reading drafts to being my publicist, and for believing in me, always. Thank you, Pookie, I love you. You're the key to my lock.

And always, thanks to my dad, Manford, who we lost in 1992, and my mom, Vondell. No matter what I do, Mom is my cheerleader. In large part, I am who I am because of the two of them.

I must also thank my sisters and their husbands, Debbie and John Kangas, Julie and Frank Liu; and my brother, Brian. Who else but family would put up with my shenanigans?

Unless it's my dear friends Jacques and Glenn, Steve W. and Mark B., Mike and Margot, Jeannie and Clif, Dave and Kathy, Justin Peters, Liz K. and Mike R., D.C. and Fern, Rick and B.J., Mike P., Randy and Michael, and Jennifer and Steve. They love me in spite of (because of?) my craziness, and I love each of them.

Of course, many thanks must also go to Jerry Wheeler, my editor, who I also consider a friend. He is a talent, and could have probably made these acknowledgments read much better!

Brenda T.S., Deb D., Beth H., Vicki S., Kathi B., Jeff M., and all the B.S. crew, thank you! For believing in me, for being my friend, and for making work more like play all those years.

And finally, thanks to everyone at Bold Strokes Books who have helped me so much. Special thanks to Sandy and Cindy; you two rock!

For Mary Fiedler, my champion and friend.

And for Margot Beckerman and Mike Macione, two of the most
non-judgmental, caring, wonderful people I've ever known.
Mike and I have been friends for over thirty years,
when back in the day he dragged me home down the sidewalk
after a night of a few too many cocktails!

Chapter One

June 12th, 1947

Late Thursday night, we were alone in my apartment, just the two of us. From the radio on the table came the sounds of Bing Crosby singing "Embraceable You," but other than that all was quiet and the lights were low. He looked up at me with those big green eyes and I could tell he wanted more, as I held him in my arms and danced him around the apartment, singing softly in his ear. He was insatiable, but I was done in. It had been a long day and a long night. Still, his eyes, his gaze, that adorable face were hard to resist. Finally, as the song ended, I set him down and gave him another scratch behind the ears as he rubbed up against my legs and weaved in and out between them.

"All right, Oscar, you've had a saucer of milk, a dance, a tummy rub, and an ear scratching. You are a sweetie, but I have a fellow with two legs whose ears I'd rather be scratching, and there must be a cat somewhere in all of Milwaukee who would be happy to see you, my friend."

He looked up at me again, blinked, and let out a soft meow, as if to say, "Maybe so." He walked with me to the door of my apartment, and I let him back out into the hall to continue his nightly roaming from door to door, looking for love and maybe another saucer of milk or two. After he'd gone, I picked up the phone receiver on the hall table near the door and dialed Kings Lake 5-2835. After a few brrrrrrrrrings, I heard Alan's deep, masculine voice.

"Hello?"

"I just let the cat out."

"Of the bag?"

I laughed. "That's a curious expression, isn't it? I wonder what its origins are. But no, our secret is safe, mister, at least for now."

"Good to know."

"You're good to know."

"That's good to know, too."

"All right, enough." I laughed.

"So whose cat did you let out?"

"Mrs. Ferguson's. She lives in 310 and lets him roam the halls every night. He goes from door to door and knows I'm a soft touch for an ear scratch and a tummy rub."

Alan chuckled. "Lucky cat."

"Indeed. Are you packed?"

"Packed, ready, and able, Detective. A long weekend in Chicago with you is just what the doctor ordered."

"I agree. I'll bring my stethoscope."

"You're in a mood, Heath."

"A good mood. As you may recall, our recent attempts to get away haven't exactly been successful."

He laughed harder this time. "To say the least. You have the hotel reservation confirmation letter?"

"I do. A double room, Edmonton Hotel, Chicago, Illinois, checking in Friday, June thirteenth, checking out Monday, June sixteenth. I have the train tickets, too. The morning train gets us into Union Station before eleven. It's just shy of two miles to the hotel from the station, so we'll grab a taxi."

"That's a bit extravagant, Heath. We could walk it."

"But we'll have our bags to lug. I think I can splurge on a taxi this one time."

"All right, big spender, it's your nickel. Of course, the way you overpack, your bag probably weighs thirty pounds."

I smiled. "Well, it's difficult to ascertain what one will need, you know."

He laughed again. "Very true, but not so hard for me. My wardrobe is a bit more limited than yours. Regardless, I can't wait."

"Well, you'll just have to wait one more night, Officer. I'll pick you up at your place at eight a.m. sharp."

"I'll be ready at seven."

"Good. Three days, three nights with nothing to do."

"Nothing?"

"You know what I mean, Alan, and by nothing, I mean everything to do with each other. Away from prying eyes, someplace where we don't know anyone and no one knows us. We'll just be two fellas out on the town, having a gay old time."

"I like the sound of that, Heath. It's not easy living behind a wall, having two faces."

"You're hardly the two-faced type, Alan."

"You know what I mean. My public face for friends, family, fellow officers, and the private face for you and maybe one or two others."

I sighed. "Yeah, I know only too well what you mean. This weekend will do us both a world of good."

"You know, I've never been to Chicago, Heath."

"So you mentioned. I still find that hard to believe."

"Just never had a reason to go, I guess. For me, growing up in Racine, Milwaukee was the big city. My folks never had much money, and vacations consisted of weekends at the beach or day trips to the zoo. We did go to the Wisconsin Dells once, when I was twelve."

"Chicago's nothing like the Dells, Alan. I think you'll like it."

"I can't wait. Dinner at the Pump Room?"

"On a police detective's salary?" I arched my brow.

"I'll order the melba toast and tea."

I laughed. "That's about all I could afford, mister, but we'll see."

"Thanks."

Then he got very quiet.

"What? You still there?"

"Hmm? Oh yeah, sure. I was just thinking, that's all."

"About the Pump Room?"

"No, about the nightclubs. I've heard and read about them my whole life—the Boulevard Room, the Empire Room, the Tip Top Tap, and Chez Paree."

"Swanky. Chez Paree is one of my Aunt Verbina's favorites."

"I want to meet her someday."

"Yes, we need to arrange that. Anyplace else of interest?"

"Well, there's the Sky Star Ballroom at the Edmonton, right where we're staying. Did you know Bing Crosby played there last year?"

"That should be an easy one. I'm listening to the Bing Crosby hour right now."

"Keen, me too."

"Nice. Well, we can definitely hit a nightclub or two while we're there, if you want."

"Sure, I know."

"But?"

"But we can't dance. That's one of the prices we pay for leading secret lives, isn't it?"

"I guess so."

"It doesn't bother you?"

"Of course it does. I'd love to lead you to the dance floor and waltz you about, maybe even do some swing dancing. That looks like a lot of fun. But we can't. Not in public, and you and I both know that."

"So, what's the point of going clubbing?"

"Because we can drink, listen to the music, and there will always be single ladies looking for partners. If we each choose a partner and dance close together on the floor, it will almost be like we're dancing with each other."

I heard him sigh. "It will have to do, I guess. But promise me when we get back to the room we'll push the furniture aside, put the radio on, and do some private dancing."

"That, Officer, is a promise. And the room's a double, but we can push the beds together at night."

"And apart again in the morning before the maid comes in."

"It's the way it has to be, unfortunately."

"I know, I understand. I really am looking forward to it, but I hope we're not courting trouble leaving on Friday the thirteenth."

I laughed lightly. "Always the superstitious one. You know it's the only weekend we could get off this month. And my buddy Mike, the dick at the Edmonton, got us a great rate because it's Father's Day weekend."

"That's another thing. What about your dad?"

"What about him?"

"Won't he want to see you on Sunday?"

"I'll buy him a tie down in Chicago and swing by the house for dinner with him and Mother Monday night after we get back to Milwaukee, just a day late."

"Your mother won't like that."

I laughed. "You're right. I phoned her earlier tonight and told her we were going to Chicago this weekend. She tried her best to make me feel guilty about it, and she kept making that clicking sound with her teeth, but I promised I'd be over Monday night for dinner. It's funny, you've never even met my mother and yet you know her so well."

"Well, you do talk about her."

"I suppose so. Still, she's my mom, and he's my dad."

"You're lucky you still have your folks."

"I know. You've been on your own a long time without your parents. It would be nice if you could come Monday night, get to know my parents, but…"

"I know, don't worry. I'll have unpacking to do, stuff to get ready for my shift on Monday night. It's fine. I'm just glad we're getting away."

"Me too. Well, I'll see you bright and early in the morning, then."

"I'll be there with bells on. Good night, Heath."

"Night, Alan."

Chapter Two

The next morning the skies were overcast, fog and light drizzle hanging in the air, and yet there was Alan, his battered tan suitcase in hand, waiting at the curb in front of his apartment building on the west side of town as I pulled up in my old Buick Century. He beamed at me from beneath the brim of his fedora, his Brownie camera about his neck. I got out and opened the trunk for him.

"Morning, Heath," he said with a wide grin.

"Good morning. How long have you been standing out here?"

"Only about ten minutes."

"You could have waited inside, it's cold and damp out here."

"I know."

He threw his bag into the trunk next to mine. I slammed it shut and got back behind the wheel as he climbed in beside me. "I was too excited to wait inside any longer."

I laughed. "Good, me too. Wish we had better weather, though."

"Let it rain," Alan said. "Nothing can ruin my mood today. I noticed you brought your umbrella."

"Yes, it straps right to the side of my suitcase. And good to be prepared, I'd say."

"You always are. I like that in you."

I smiled. "Good. No sense of ominous foreboding this Friday the thirteenth?"

"Not yet. I packed my lucky rock, though, just in case."

"Your lucky rock? Just when you think you know someone." I laughed.

"I never told you because I knew you'd make fun."

"Maybe I'd kid you a bit, but I wouldn't make fun, not of you, ever."

"Thanks. I appreciate that."

"So why is it your lucky rock and how long have you had it?"

He shrugged and looked a little embarrassed. "I've had it since I was a kid. My dad gave it to me after a trip he'd been on when I asked him what he brought me. I know he meant it as a joke, but I didn't see it that way then. Stupid, huh?"

"Not at all. I think it's sweet."

He smiled. "Thanks. And ever since he died, I usually carry it with me. It just somehow seems to bring good luck."

"I see."

"I know, you're a non-believer, Mr. Skeptical. But it works, at least for me. I was carrying it the day I met you, you know."

My heart flip-flopped a bit. "All right, you just made a believer out of me. Let's get going." I put the car in gear and headed east toward Wisconsin Avenue and the train station. I parked my car in the lot just beside the depot and we each retrieved our bags from the trunk, I with my monogrammed suitcase and matching train case and Alan with his dad's old case. I noticed he had added his initials at the end, A.K. A thought occurred to me that new luggage might be a good Christmas gift for him, and I smiled. It had been a long time since I had anyone special to buy Christmas gifts for.

The depot was bustling with people, heading to and from Chicago and points beyond. The train departed at five after nine, so we didn't have a whole lot of time. I bought a newspaper from the stand near the lunch counter and a pack of chewing gum for later as I waited for Alan, who had decided to get his shoes polished and shined.

He smiled at me as he stepped down from the shoeshine stand and gave the boy a quarter. "Better. Can't be seen in the big city with scuffed-up shoes."

I laughed. "Honestly, I hadn't even noticed. Let's go, though. We're short on time. Track two is this way." Soon the conductor was calling out the familiar "All aboard," and we climbed up the steps into the train. We found seats together in the third car, choosing window seats facing each other. Our bags and hats tucked in the rack overhead, we settled in for the relatively short journey. Once we rolled out of Milwaukee and the conductor collected our tickets, we felt like we were finally on our way.

As we watched the towns of Sturtevant, Racine, and Kenosha fly by out the rain-splattered glass, I looked admiringly again at Alan, so smart in his navy double-breasted suit, a white handkerchief tucked neatly in his breast pocket. "I hope my tuxedo doesn't get too wrinkled in my case," I said. "I probably should have gotten a garment bag for it."

"Tuxedo? Gee, Heath, you think we're going to need one?"

I nodded. "Well, sure, if you want to go clubbing. Chicago is the big time compared to Milwaukee. You packed yours, didn't you?"

He frowned. "I just brought my dark suit and this double-breasted for traveling. I don't own a tux."

"A tux in Chicago is *de rigueur*, I'm afraid. Maybe we can buy you one there."

"A tux is de what?"

"*De rigueur.*"

His frown became a scowl. "French again. For someone who only studied it in high school, you certainly use it a lot," Alan said, sounding annoyed.

"It's a beautiful language, the language of love. And besides, I had a remarkable French teacher."

"Coulliette something or other. Yes, I know, you've mentioned him before."

"Mss'r J. Coulliette, that's right. He and the handsome math teacher, Mr. Koos, were both bachelors, and they shared a flat, as I recall the rumor."

"People do talk, don't they?"

"Yes, they do. Or should I say *oui*?"

He rolled his eyes. "Yes works just fine."

"I remember running into Monsieur Coulliette and Mr. Koos once in the summer. They were walking their dog, a black border collie named Maddie. It seemed so odd to me to see them on the street, like normal people, with a dog and all."

"They *are* normal people, Heath."

"You know what I mean. Seeing teachers outside of school. You just don't think of them as leading normal lives. And seeing them together just reinforced in my mind the rumor that they were a couple."

"Did anyone ever find out for sure?"

"I don't think so, not that I ever heard, anyway. I know Mr. Koos went out with Miss Johnson, the English teacher, once or twice. But I think that was just to avert suspicion."

"The games we all have to play."

"Exactly."

"So anyway, what the heck does *de rigueur* mean?"

"It means necessary if you want to be socially acceptable, fashionable."

"Oh, well, I can't afford to be socially acceptable or fashionable. Not on my salary," Alan replied.

"I can help you. A good tuxedo is an investment, Alan, and should be about thirty or thirty-five dollars. A lot of money, I know, but I plan to do lots of clubbing with you over the next thirty years or so, so it's only about a dollar a year."

Alan laughed. "I see. I can't afford not to buy one."

"Exactly."

"Well, we'll see. I'll give it some thought and we can have a look in the shops once we get to Chicago. Anything interesting in the newspaper?" he asked, changing the subject.

I opened it up and perused the front page. "An article on Babe Zaharias. It says, 'Mrs. Zaharias Is First American to Win Women's British Golf Title.'"

"Wow, good for her. She's really an amazing woman."

"She certainly is."

"How about the horoscopes?"

"You're kidding."

"Hey, you believe what you want, I believe what I want. Besides, it's Friday the thirteenth, you know."

I sighed. "Okay, let me find them." I flipped through the paper to the Ladies section and scanned the horoscopes. "Your birthday's March sixteenth, right?"

"Yes, I'm a Pisces, sign of the fish."

I laughed. "Then you must love weather like this."

"Ha, just read, Detective."

"All right. It says, 'For you, magic will play a big part in your emotions in the next few days. A colleague, neighbor, or friend will give you the chance to seize some unexpected opportunity. Make the most of it.'"

"Hmmph. Well, all right then," Alan said, leaning back.

"What?"

"Well, you're a friend and a colleague, and you've given me an unexpected opportunity in this trip to Chicago, and I definitely intend to make the most of it, so I'd say it's pretty right on the money."

"And the magic part?"

"Hmm. Not sure about that yet, but let's see what the weekend brings."

I laughed. "Fair enough."

"What about yours, Heath? You're an Aquarius, right?"

"So they tell me."

"The water bearer. It's why we go so well together—fish and water."

"I won't argue with that, Mr. Keyes."

"So what does it say? Your horoscope, I mean."

I scanned the paper again. "'Don't be fooled by what you read in astrology columns today. Someone makes a good living writing them. A tall dark handsome friend or colleague will try to distract you. Be wary.'"

Alan folded his arms. "Very funny. You're lucky you're cute."

I smiled. "Sorry, just teasing. I just don't buy into astrology."

"To each his own."

"Very true," I agreed.

I finished reading the newspaper while Alan gazed out the window and fidgeted. Finally, I put the paper aside on the seat next to me and closed my eyes. I think at some point I actually dozed, but Alan was clearly too excited. When at last we pulled into Union Station, he was almost bouncing up and down in his seat. I checked my pocket watch and found we were right on time. Whoever wrote those timetables knew what they were doing. We put our hats on and hauled our bags off and then we walked down the platform into the station. Once inside, we made a brief stop in the men's room and made our way toward the Great Hall, its vast size and tall, barrel glass vaulted ceiling dwarfing us. Alan stopped, mouth agape, taking it all in.

"Golly, Heath, this place is huge. It makes the station back in Milwaukee look like a whistle stop."

"It is impressive, I agree. The first time I saw it I was taken aback, too." We stood for a while gazing about the room at the large number of people hurrying here and there, lugging cases, towing children, or standing in groups, couples, or by themselves. Uniformed porters went this way and that with large piles of luggage and trunks on their carts, and newspaper boys shouted out the latest headlines. The loudspeakers overhead frequently crackled to life, announcing the Capitol Limited to Washington, track three, and the Denver Zephyr, track eight, among other harder-to-understand bulletins about lost children, lost articles, and late departures.

Down the center of the hall, still more people were seated on benches, including a woman holding a crying newborn, and beside her not one, not two, but five other children, all of them talking at once, along with everyone else in the main hall. The great mass of voices made a buzzing sound in my ears.

"Which way?" Alan asked finally, ready to get going.

"There are some underground taxi stands, but let's go up to the main street. I think the rain has stopped."

"Lead the way."

We climbed the many marble stairs up to Canal Street, jostling shoulder to shoulder with the masses. Once outside, the car horns seemed to blare incessantly and the air smelled damp and smoky. The wind blew down on us, and we pulled our hats low as we made our way toward a line of cabs waiting for passengers. We loaded our bags into the first one available and gave the Edmonton as our destination to the driver. Soon we were off, and I sat back, enjoying just watching Alan staring out the window, craning his neck this way and that, and up, up, toward the many skyscrapers.

"Quite a city, isn't it?" I asked.

Alan turned to me, a big smile on his face. "I'll say. Even with the fog and drizzle, I can tell it sure isn't like Milwaukee."

"No, no it's not. For better or worse."

He turned back to the window then, and I gazed out the other side of the cab, watching the buildings and cars go by as the driver weaved in and out of traffic, making his way to the Edmonton on Michigan Avenue. On the sidewalks, people scurried here and there, some carrying umbrellas or packages as they sidestepped puddles, dashed in and out of shops and buildings, and waited at the corners for lights to change, cabs to come, or perhaps their dreams to be fulfilled.

Almost too soon, the taxi came to a stop in front of the hotel, its tires scraping against the curb. A uniformed doorman with a large black umbrella opened the cab door for us. A bellboy helped with our bags, and as I paid the taxi, tipped the doorman, and set aside money for the bellboy, I realized this would be an expensive trip. I was glad I had gone to the bank the day before to get a letter of credit and withdraw some cash. The two of us followed the bellboy.

I'd never been at the Edmonton, and I was impressed by the tall ceilings, marble columns, crystal chandeliers, and rich carpeting. The lobby was two floors high, a large marble staircase to the left leading up to a mezzanine level that wrapped around it on three sides. A coffee shop was behind the staircase under the north mezzanine, and the lobby bar was to the right under the south mezzanine. Cozy chairs, sofas, and tables were scattered here and there. The bellboy led us past the staircase to the front desk, which was opposite the entrance doors, tucked under the east mezzanine.

The bellboy deposited our bags beside the front desk, which had two banks of elevators flanking it. Behind the counter stood a small, bald fellow wearing pince-nez glasses, his forehead shiny but smooth. He looked up at us and smiled.

"May I help you gentlemen?"

"Yes, Heath Barrington of Milwaukee, checking in. This is Mr. Keyes, he'll be staying with me. I have a letter of credit from my bank and my reservation confirmation." I handed over the documents to the little man, who examined them and handed them back.

"Everything seems to be in order, Mr. Barrington, and we have your reservation right here. A double room, checking in today, leaving Monday morning, is that correct?"

"Yes, yes, that's right."

"Very good, sir. Any valuables for the hotel safe?"

"No, nothing to check, thank you."

"All right, then, if you'll just sign our register, Carl here will see you to your room." He nodded at the bellboy standing off to the side near a column.

I signed the register with my name, home address, and telephone exchange. "Thank you. By the way, is Mike Masterson working today?"

The desk clerk looked surprised. "Our house detective?"

I nodded. "Yes, that's right. He's an old friend of mine."

"I see. I believe Mr. Masterson is working an evening shift today, sir. Would you like to leave him a message?"

"No, that's all right. He knows I'm here, and a good house dick can always find his man."

"As you wish, sir."

"Thanks. Where's a good place nearby to get a tuxedo, by the way?"

"Blount's right here in the hotel carries tuxedos. Just past the south elevators and down the hall."

"Blount's, eh? Thanks for the tip."

"There's also Marshall Field's department store on State Street. Perhaps our concierge could assist you."

"We'll check out Blount's first, after we unpack. Sound good, Alan?"

He nodded. "Sure, that's fine. But I really could just wear my dark suit."

The desk clerk raised his eyebrows and adjusted his pince-nez, but didn't say anything.

"No, Blount's it is. A good starting point, anyway."

"Very good, sir. Should you need dinner reservations, club recommendations, or anything else, our concierge here in the lobby will be most eager to assist." He rang a bell, and Carl, who was still standing nearby, stepped forward. "Take Mr. Barrington and Mr. Keyes to 804," he said, handing Carl a brass key with a tag attached.

"Yes, sir." Carl, who appeared to be only about seventeen or eighteen years old, was dressed in a smart dark green uniform with brass buttons, matching green cap, and crisp white gloves. He put the key in his pocket, picked up our bags rather effortlessly, and with a nod to us, moved off toward the south elevators as we followed behind.

The ride up to the eighth floor was smooth and quick. "No operator?" I asked.

Carl looked up at me. "No, sir, the Edmonton automated last year. The elevators run by themselves. You just push a button and away you go."

"Another man out of a job."

"It's a changing world, mister."

"Yes, people keep telling me that."

"It was the strike in '45 in New York that did 'em in," Carl continued.

"Sad," Alan said. "I rather like the human touch."

"Automated is the way of the future. Someday they'll have self-driving cars, wait and see," Carl said.

I shuddered. "Now there's a frightening thought."

"Not to me, mister. Self-driving cars, picture phones, space travel, I can't wait."

"That'll be the day," I said. The elevator came smoothly to a halt, and we followed Carl out, stopping right next door at 804.

"Next to the elevator, huh?" Alan remarked.

I nodded. "Probably why Mike could get us such a great rate."

"Hey, it's okay, it's convenient," Alan said.

I smiled. "You're always finding the silver lining in things."

"Why not?"

"I'm with your friend," Carl said. Unlocking the door and ushering us in, he flipped on the overhead light.

The room was small but clean. Two twin beds against the right wall, separated by a nightstand with a lamp and a clock. The opposite wall held a dresser, upon which sat another lamp, an ashtray, and a radio. A small desk with a phone on it sat next to that, a metal trash can under it, and a luggage rack stood in the corner upon which the boy piled our bags. Above it was a wall-mounted fan.

Carl opened the curtains. "Not much of a view from this room, fellas."

I walked over and gazed out at the back side of another building. "It's all right. We're not here for the view. What have you heard about the weather this weekend?"

"Supposed to be in the seventies today, foggy and rainy. Cooler tomorrow with more rain." He turned back to us and gestured toward the front of the room. "The bathroom's near the door to the hall, and there's a closet there too. If you need anything pressed, just call the valet. Twenty-four-hour room service, also. Want me to unpack?"

I shook my head. "No thank you, we can manage."

"Sure thing." He moved toward the door and stopped, looking at me as I fished a fifty cent piece out of my pocket and handed it to him as he gave me the room key.

"Thanks," he said. I wondered if that was a sufficient tip in the big city, but he pocketed it easily enough and went out the door, leaving us alone.

"At last," Keyes said, setting his Brownie down carefully on the desk.

"Yes, indeed." I wrapped my arms around him.

"Very smooth, Detective, but not so fast. We have to unpack."

"That can wait," I replied, nibbling his left ear a bit.

He pulled back, laughing. "That's what you said in Lake Geneva, and I spent the weekend in wrinkled clothes."

"But they have a valet here."

"Nonetheless, I am going to unpack."

I sighed "All right, you. Better take off that traveling suit, too. It's looking a mite rumpled from the train."

He looked down at his suit, which was perfectly fine, and then at himself in the mirror and laughed again. "You, Detective, are a bit sneaky, and you have a one-track mind."

I smiled. "And you, Officer, are determined to derail me. Very well, let's unpack."

Together we opened our suitcases and put things away, setting aside my tux and both our dark suits for the hotel valet. I unstrapped my umbrella and placed it in the corner near the door. I called down to have the suits picked up, and they assured me they would have them pressed and back in about two hours.

In less than five minutes, a boy knocked on the door, and I gave him the suits along with another tip. I hung out the Do Not Disturb sign.

"Do Not Disturb?" Alan asked, looking at me.

"Unless you have something else to put away or unpack." I walked over to the windows and closed the curtains.

Alan grinned. "Not on your life, Detective. Let's try and get that train back on track."

"Woo woo," I replied. "All aboard." I took off my suit coat and hung it neatly over the back of the desk chair, Alan looking at me with an odd expression. "What?"

"You have your shoulder harness and service revolver on," he said.

"Oh, that. Well, force of habit, I guess."

"But Chicago is way out of your jurisdiction, and we're on holiday."

I shrugged and removed it, setting it on the dresser next to the ashtray. "I know. I probably should have left it in Milwaukee, but I didn't feel comfortable leaving it behind in my apartment. Do you mind?"

"No, it's fine, Heath, it just surprised me, that's all."

I smiled. "I have lots of surprises in store for you, Officer." I moved closer to him and ran my hands down his front. "Hey, I feel something hard down there."

Alan laughed. "Oh, I forgot. My lucky rock is still in my pocket." He reached in and pulled out a small, smooth stone, almost round, and set it on the dresser. Then with a grin, he turned off the light, allowing just the daylight filtering in through the drapes. "Now then, let's get this train rolling, Detective."

It had been ages since we had been alone like that, and it was over too soon. We lay together, entwined on one of the beds, listening to each other breathing.

"What time is it? "Alan asked quietly.

I glanced over at the small clock on the nightstand. "About twelve twenty. We should get dressed, I suppose."

"What for?" he asked, snuggling his head to my chest. "I can hear your heart beat."

"It does that. But we haven't had lunch yet, and we need to get you a tux."

Alan sighed contentedly. "Somehow, I think I'd rather spend the weekend right here in this room, never leaving until Monday morning. We could have our meals sent in."

"Romantic, but not practical. Why come all the way to Chicago just to stay in?"

He nuzzled me harder. "Because it's foggy, drizzling, and windy outside, and colder tomorrow. Why *not* just stay in? We could dance right here to the radio, then sleep, eat, and do it all again. Then I wouldn't need a tux, either."

I kissed the top of his head, smelling his hair tonic. "I thought you were the one who was so excited to see the big city."

He looked up at me. "I've seen it, and I'm so comfortable, and that was so nice."

"Me too, Mr. Keyes, but you haven't yet begun to see Chicago, and I don't want you to grow tired of me too quickly, so up with you. Besides, I packed my umbrella." I gave him a nudge.

He moved ever so slightly and gazed up at me again, his eyes so deep, so beautiful.

"Grow tired of you? Could I grow tired of the air I breathe?"

"You do know how to soothe my insecurities."

"You have nothing to be insecure about, Heath."

"We all have our demons."

"What are yours? I'll fight them for you."

I laughed. "Thanks. I was shy and chubby as a kid, awkward, clumsy, bad at athletics, and I had few friends."

"The ugly duckling, eh?"

"Yeah, I guess so."

"But you turned into a handsome swan."

"Sometimes when I look in the mirror, I still see that ugly duckling. I wouldn't call myself a swan, maybe just an okay-looking duck."

"And all this time I thought you were just admiring yourself every time you looked in a mirror, which, to be perfectly honest, is fairly often," he said, running his fingers through my chest hairs.

I laughed again. "Don't get me wrong. I generally like what I see, but like I said, inner demons, insecurities, you know. And I hadn't realized I looked at myself that often."

"Oh, it's not that bad. Just something I noticed. Well, anyway, we'll have to work on that insecurity of yours."

"Fair enough. And you've done wonders already, whether you realize it or not. Come on, let's get dressed and get you that tux, then we'll see the town."

We climbed out of bed and dressed, putting our traveling suits back on. I tucked my service revolver and shoulder harness in the nightstand drawer. "I guess that will be safe there. The maid won't be in until morning."

"True. But then you'll have to take it with you tomorrow."

"Unless I check it at the front desk and have them put it in the safe."

"If you're comfortable wearing it under your coat, it's fine with me."

"I'll leave it here for now." As I adjusted my tie in the mirror and smoothed down my hair, I glanced over at Alan and smiled. "Just making sure I look okay."

He laughed lightly. "You always look smashing, Duck, believe that."

"Duck? Is that my new nickname?"

"Maybe. Though you did pack your umbrella."

"It's true. Water and my wool suits don't mix too well."

"But water and fish do."

I grinned. "Very true. Ready?"

"If you're waiting for me, you're wasting your time. I've never shopped for a tux before."

"I like doing new things with you, and this is only the beginning."

"Careful, Detective, I may not look like it, but I can have expensive tastes."

"Thanks for the warning. Come on." I grabbed my umbrella from the corner, and Alan put his Brownie back around his neck and his rock back in his pocket.

Chapter Three

A bell jingled as we pushed open Blount's glass door, and a smartly dressed little man appeared from a doorway at the back of the shop. He wore a double-breasted blue pinstripe suit with a wide red polka dot tie, and a white carnation in his lapel. His fine dark hair was parted down the middle, and he wore an equally dark mustache above his thin lips, nicely waxed to narrow points on either side of his long, narrow nose. His eyes were closely set narrow ovals that reminded me of black olives.

"Bonjour, gentlemen, welcome to Blount's. Victor Blount at your humble service. How may I assist you today?" His voice was singsongish, his accent clearly French, and he waved his hands about with a flourish as he spoke.

I leaned my umbrella in a corner next to the door. "I'm Mr. Barrington and this is Mr. Keyes. We're just in from Milwaukee for the weekend and in need of a tuxedo."

"A pleasure to meet you both. You've come to the right place, monsieurs. I can fit you with a fine quality garment, alter it, and have it ready to wear within twenty-four hours, tops. I specialize in the design of handmade-bespoke as well as made-to-measure garments and high quality off-the-rack items for gentlemen."

"That's perfect, Mr. Blount. The tuxedo is for Mr. Keyes."

Blount walked closer to Alan and looked him up and down. "*Mais oui, mais oui.* Splendid, a forty-two long, easy. But we'd better make sure." He produced a tape measure from his pocket. "Take off your coat and hat, please."

Alan handed them to me as Mr. Blount wrapped the tape around Alan's waist.

"Thirty-three—hmm." He dropped to one knee and measured the inseam, Alan looking rather uncomfortable. "Thirty-five inches exactly, nice long legs." He got back to his feet, a rather queer smile on his face. "Arms out now. Thirty-four-inch sleeve, hmm. Now the neck. Just as I thought, sixteen inches." He walked to a rack off to the side. "This would look smashing on you, as you Americans say. Classic tailoring, Italian from before the war. *Très elegant*. Look at the turn back," he said, turning up the collar. "And notice the lapel roll, the cloth. For an off-the-rack tuxedo, this one is exceptional."

"How much?" Alan asked, looking unimpressed.

"Can one put a price on fashion, Mr. Keyes?"

"I can."

Mr. Blount looked somewhat indignant. "Forty-five dollars. And that's an absolute steal, monsieur."

"Ouch. What do you have for less?" I asked.

The little man sighed, rolled his eyes, and returned the Italian suit to the rack. "I suppose you could make do with this." He pulled out another tux that looked awfully similar to the first one. "It's made in New York, wool. Basic but functional, thirty dollars."

"Let's try that one," I said.

"Thirty dollars is still an awful lot, Heath."

"I can swing it. Where is the fitting room?"

"Through that curtain there, on the left. Put just the pants on first, then come out."

"Right." Alan handed me his Brownie, took the tux from Blount, and made his way into the office and fitting room while I waited up front.

"You may put those things on the counter, monsieur, while you wait for your friend."

"Thanks."

"Your friend is a photographer?"

"Just a tourist, Mr. Blount."

"Ah, the amateur. I do portraits, sittings, professional photography."

"Oh? Besides your men's store?"

"*Oui.* One must diversify, yes? In addition to the clothing, I do some portrait sitting in the back room of my store here, by appointment. Very private, discreet."

"How interesting," I replied, wondering why portrait sitting needed to be private and discreet. "Well, neither of us need our portraits done at the moment, Mr. Blount. Just a tuxedo."

"*Très bien*, that is good, too."

"You're French."

"*Oui*, monsieur. I came to the United States eleven years ago. The handwriting was, as they say, on the wall for me, but sadly for others they did not see, they were blind. The Nazis were rising to power, and I knew I could not stay any longer. I sold my tailoring business and came here, ending up in Chicago. I opened this store nine years ago."

"What about your family?"

"I have no family, monsieur, not anymore. They were fools who stayed behind, as were my friends. I am alone. I have no time for fools. I have my work, and I have done well, no?" He waved his arms about, indicating his shop.

"Yes, apparently so, Mr. Blount. It's a very lovely store. I would imagine rent in a place like this must be rather high."

"*Oui*, but it is a good location, and I diversify, as I said, so life is good." He went behind the counter then to fiddle with something or other and get his chalk and pins. I wandered over to a display of ties, realizing I had to pick one up for my dad for Father's Day.

The front door bell jingled again, and a lovely young woman entered, dressed in a red pleated dress, white shoes, and a wide-brimmed gray felt hat, beneath which flowed shoulder-length wavy blond hair. She walked briskly to the counter, carrying a garment bag in her left hand, clearly not even noticing me. Blount turned to her and smiled thinly. "Good afternoon, Miss Eye."

"What's good about it? This is the third order of shirts this month. Walter will never wear them, and I can't afford much more of this."

Blount glanced over at me and nodded. The woman followed his gaze and I tipped my hat.

She looked annoyed. "Excuse me. I thought you were alone."

"One should never assume, Miss Eye. This gentleman and his friend in the back are shopping for a new tuxedo."

"I see. I beg your pardon." Her tone was cold.

I nodded and turned back to the tie rack.

"Now then, mademoiselle, I have Mr. Gillingham's shirts right here, folded and pressed. Will there be anything else today?"

"Yes. I need my dress steamed and pressed for tomorrow night. How much is that going to cost me?"

"A simple steam and press, mademoiselle, for you, just fifty cents."

"I'll pick it up tomorrow afternoon before the show."

"Very good."

"Walter told me to tell you you'd better reconsider your pricing, Mr. Blount. And Walter is not someone you want to make angry, if you know what I mean."

Mr. Blount laughed. "Monsieur Gillingham is a big gorilla. He pounds his chest, he bares his teeth, but he does not scare me. I think instead I scare him, and I scare you."

"Then you think wrong."

"We shall see, mademoiselle."

"Yes, we shall. And so shall you. You've taken this too far, Mr. Blount."

"But, Miss Eye, our business relationship is so cordial."

"For you, maybe. Walter said to tell you he's had enough of your fancy shirts and expensive ties."

"Your fiancé, Miss Eye, is an idiot."

"Walter is *not* an idiot. He's just a little slow."

"Being engaged to you is proof enough of his idiocy, mademoiselle."

"How dare you."

"I don't dare. I merely state the facts, Miss Eye." He took the garment bag from her hand and hung it behind the counter.

In a small mirror next to the tie display, I could see Blount smile again, baring his teeth as he took her money and counted it out.

"I'm sure you will find my prices most reasonable, considering, Miss Eye," I heard Blount say. "Talk it over with your fiancé. *Au revoir.*"

"I will. But as I said before, you don't want to make Walter angry." She grabbed the package of shirts off the counter and turned on her heel. I tipped my hat once more as she nodded in my direction. "Try Wieboldt's on State, much better pricing," she snapped, then made her way quickly out the door, the bell jingling once more.

When she had gone, Mr. Blount laughed nervously and gave me a weak smile. "That was Mademoiselle Gloria Eye, one of my regular customers. She buys clothes for her fiancé, Walter Gillingham."

"It sounds like she buys quite a bit."

"Miss Eye is an actress and a singer. Her band is playing the Sky Star Ballroom again this weekend."

"I'm sure we'll see her there, then, Mr. Blount. We plan on going to the Sky Star tomorrow night, which is why we need the tuxedo."

"*Très bien.* Miss Eye sings for the Storm Clouds, funny name, no?"

"I've heard stranger names for bands."

"I suppose so. She is Gloria Eye, so she bills herself as the Eye of the Storm."

"Clever."

"*Oui.* She has some talent, and she is quite lovely. And she has good taste, of course. She feels her fiancé Monsieur Gillingham must present a certain image as a member of the band. He plays lead trumpet. Certainly my clothes are only the finest, most stylish."

"Of course. Are those two from Chicago?"

"*Oui*, yes. A local band, but I understand they are going to tour this fall. Perhaps the start of something big."

Alan emerged from the back room then, holding the tux pants up with his hand. "They're a little loose," he said.

Blount smiled again. "A minor adjustment is all that is needed. Please step over to the mirror." I watched as Blount pinned and chalked the pants. "The waist and seat will have to be taken in. As for the legs, no cuff, I say. Much more timeless, don't you agree?"

Alan nodded. "Sure, sounds good. Exactly what I was thinking."

I smiled, knowing that thought hadn't even crossed his mind. As Blount worked, I couldn't help but notice his wristwatch, which looked quite expensive.

"That's quite a watch you have there, Mr. Blount."

He glanced at his wrist, smiled, and took a pin out of his mouth so he could reply.

"*Merci*, monsieur. It is a Longines, of course. It keeps perfect time, to the second."

I nodded. "Of course. I use a pocket watch, myself."

"So old-fashioned, monsieur. A wristwatch is much more functional and highly accurate."

"Maybe so, but I like this one. It belonged to my maternal grandfather, Earl."

"Ah, sentimental, no? I am not a sentimental man."

"Yes, I rather got that impression."

"Sentiments do not pay the bills, monsieur, or keep you warm at night." He looked up at Alan. "All finished with the trousers, monsieur. Now, let's slip on the coat."

"Oh, I left it in the dressing room," Alan exclaimed.

Mr. Blount shook his head and then looked up at me. "Ah, Mr. Barrington, would you be so kind?"

"Sure, happy to oblige," I said. I went through the curtain and glanced about, as I've always been naturally curious. Nosy, some might say. The back room was smaller than I had expected, a basic narrow rectangle but not running the full width of the storefront, which seemed odd. To the far left was his photography equipment, set up in front of a platform covered in a plush black cloth. Red velvet drapes hung behind it, presumably as a backdrop. I wondered what kind of portraits Mr. Blount specialized in.

Immediately to the left of the doorway was a file cabinet and a desk with a telephone, ledgers, pens and pencils atop it, and just past that, a work table with scissors, pins, tape measures, bolts of cloth, and other tools of the trade. Behind the work table stood a large, free-standing wooden rack holding every color spool of thread I could imagine on dowels, and I chuckled as I read the names on the tops of the spools: Green Linen, Green Tint, Apple Green, Turtle, Oriental Blue, Orange Sun, Mango Gold, Orange Poppy, and more. I had to wonder whose job it was to name thread.

Next to the work table was a well-worn old pedal sewing machine. A metal door that must have led to the alley was behind it on the back wall, a small peephole in the center. Next to the rack of thread spools stood a headless dressing form, just a naked torso on a pole. The fitting room was on the right side of the room, behind a louvered door, and to each side of it were racks of clothes with shelves above them piled high with bolts of cloth.

I pulled open the louvered door of the dressing room, startled to find someone staring back at me. I quickly realized it was a full-length mirror mounted to the back wall, and I was staring at myself. The fitting room was surprisingly large, big enough for a client and the tailor, I supposed, and well-lit with an overhead light as well as side-mounted lights, all reflected in the mirror, which was somewhat dizzying. I grabbed the tuxedo jacket, closed the louvered door, and returned to the shop through the curtain.

Blount was running his hands a little too attentively up and down the pants Alan was wearing, smoothing out invisible creases.

"Here," I said. Alan slipped it on.

Blount's eyes lit up. "Ooh, it's almost a perfect fit, Mr. Keyes. You have such broad shoulders." He squealed delightedly. "The sleeves need to be taken down a bit, but other than that, a nearly perfect fit." He made some marks with his chalk inside the sleeves, checked the shoulders once more, and stepped back, smiling. "Beautiful, just beautiful. *Très bien*." I wasn't sure if he was talking about the tux or Alan, or both.

"You may go ahead and take it off again and get dressed."

"Sure, glad to," Alan said, padding off through the curtain once more as Mr. Blount turned to me.

"How will you be paying for this, Mr. Barrington?"

"A check. I have a letter of credit."

"Excellent. By the way, your friend will need a formal shirt and tie, too, no?"

I frowned. I had forgotten about that. "Ah, yes, I suppose so. How much?"

He smiled that thin weasel smile again. "Oh monsieur, I have a fine quality formal shirt for just four ninety-eight, and a silk black bow tie for a mere dollar forty-nine."

"What about a medium quality formal shirt?"

"Oh, monsieur, you joke, no? Surely you want your friend to look his best."

I sighed. "Of course I do. I assume you have a shirt on hand that will fit him?"

He shrugged his bony shoulders. "We could do a custom-made shirt, but that would take some time, which we do not have, apparently. So we can make do with one off the rack, still good quality, and the fit should be most excellent."

"All right, add them to the bill."

"*Mais oui*. Does Mr. Keyes have a stud set?"

I sighed. "Add those too," I said resignedly as Alan returned from the back and put on his coat, hat and camera, which were still sitting on the counter.

"Are we all ready?"

"Not quite. I forgot you're going to need a formal shirt and a tie, and a stud set with cuff links."

"Jeepers, Heath, this is getting expensive."

"Think of it as an investment, Alan."

"A very wise thought, monsieur." Mr. Blount opened a display case and took out a black velvet tray. "I have a wonderful mother-of-pearl set with gold inlay here that would look most excellent with Mr. Keyes's tuxedo. Or this fourteen karat gold set. Quite striking, no?"

"We'll take the gold inlay with mother-of-pearl."

"Heath, no."

"It's all right, Alan, this is something you'll have a long time. Consider it a late birthday present. Wrap it all up, Mr. Blount."

"With pleasure." He glanced down at Alan's feet. "Hmm. Size twelve?"

Alan glanced down at his feet, too. "Yes, that's right."

"Goodness, such big feet. But I have a pair of patent leather shoes in back that would look fetching with your new tux."

"Thanks, Mr. Blount, but these will do for now."

Mr. Blount tsk'd and rolled his eyes. "At least they are black and freshly shined. What about new socks and underwear?"

"I don't think anyone will be seeing my socks and underwear." Alan winked at me and I laughed.

"I think we've spent enough, Mr. Blount," I said firmly.

He shrugged resignedly. "As you wish. Please step over to the counter. That will be $50.30 with the alterations and tax. Half now, half when you pick it up."

Alan whistled, which I ignored. "How soon?" I asked.

Blount consulted his expensive wristwatch. "Why don't we say one o'clock tomorrow?"

"Fine. We're planning on wearing our dark suits tonight and the tuxes tomorrow, so that will work out well." I wrote out a check for half.

"Perfect, perfect. Here is a claim check, though I certainly won't forget you two fine gentlemen. Have you plans while you're in town?"

I shrugged, putting the claim check in my wallet. "Just some sightseeing, dining out, some of the clubs, the usual."

"Two handsome gentlemen on the town."

"Yeah, something like that, I guess," I said.

Blount turned to Alan. "You are lucky to have such a generous friend, monsieur. Perhaps you can do something special for him this weekend."

Alan looked quizzical. "Such as? I've never been to Chicago before."

"No? Oh, monsieur, you can have a very good time here, a very good time. If you are interested, I have certain connections for an evening's entertainment. Very beautiful women, very discreet. You both could enjoy yourselves immensely, unlike anything back home in your little town."

"What kind of entertainment?" I asked, curious.

"Oh, monsieur, the French have a saying, *vive la difference*."

"More French," Alan sighed.

Blount chuckled. "It just means to embrace the differences, monsieur. Try something new, *oui*? For a small fee, I could set you gentlemen up for the night with an experience you would not forget. Beautiful women, handsome men, all very discreet. Dark, secluded, private rendezvous in dark, secluded rooms. Music, drink, dancing, song. Together or separate. Enticing, yes?"

I glanced sideways at Keyes before answering. "Enticing, but we'll pass. We can find our own entertainment."

He shrugged his bony little shoulders again. "If you change your mind, I am always here, ten a.m. to seven p.m. except Sundays and Mondays."

"We'll keep that in mind. Oh, and Mr. Blount, wrap up that blue and white striped tie over there on the rack for me, too, a gift for my father."

"*Oui*, those are the finest quality silk, of course. I will box and wrap it and add it your bill."

"Fine. We'll see you tomorrow afternoon."

"It's been a pleasure, gentlemen. *Au revoir*."

I nodded. "Ah, yeah, thanks."

Chapter Four

When we left the shop we were talking about the slightly creepy Mr. Blount, not paying attention to our surroundings, and consequently ran into a small, frail-looking old woman. She wore a dark green dress, soiled gloves, and an old green velvet hat with an equally soiled ostrich feather, the hatpin protruding out precariously. Beneath the hat was thin, wispy hair the color of a stormy sky. Her fleshy neck was adorned with a sad-looking fox fur whose glass eyes stared out vacantly at no one in particular.

She lost her footing momentarily as we collided, and I grasped at her bony elbow to keep her from toppling over. She was clearly startled and frightened as she steadied herself. Once she had regained her composure, she pulled her arm away indignantly and looked up at me reproachfully. Her voice was gravelly, and she made noises like an old chicken clucking. "Bruck, bruck, bruck, watch where you're going, young man."

"My apologies, madam. I didn't see you." I tipped my hat. "I hope you're all right."

"Humph, you nearly knocked me over, bruck, bruck."

"I'm truly sorry. I hope you're all right."

She brushed herself off, then looked me up and down before turning and doing the same to Alan, all the while making those clucking noises. "Who are you?"

"I'm Mr. Barrington of Milwaukee. This is my friend, Mr. Keyes. We're just in town for the weekend."

"Hmmph. Bruck, bruck, bruck. Mrs. Gittings, Violet Gittings, Chicago."

"How do you do?" we both said, tipping our hats again.

"How do you do?"

"Not staying at the hotel, then?" I asked, curious.

"No. I live nearby. I like this place for lunch, which is where I'm going if I can make it the rest of the way without being run down or assaulted. Bruck, bruck."

"Well, Mrs. Gittings, we were just going to have lunch ourselves. Would you like to join us? I'd like to make up for running into you."

"Bruck bruck bruck. I take my lunch in the bar. It's late." She moved away from us and walked somewhat unsteadily toward the Acorn Bar off the east side of the lobby.

"Was that a yes, Heath? Are we supposed to follow her?"

"Your guess is as good as mine. She's a curious woman, all right. Let's lunch in the bar."

We followed her into the Acorn Bar. She took a table in a corner as we approached.

"May we join you, Mrs. Gittings?"

"Bruck bruck. It's a free country since we won the war. Sit, sit." She had pulled off the soiled gloves and placed them on the table. The seam on the left one had split.

I looked at Keyes, who raised his eyebrows. We removed our hats and sat down across from her as I placed my umbrella on the floor next to my chair. Almost immediately a waiter was at our side, a young fellow, neatly groomed, as all good waiters should be, in my opinion.

"Good afternoon, Mrs. Gittings. You're late today."

"Bruck, bruck. Fell asleep."

"I was worried about you. I'm glad you're fine. And I see you have guests today."

"Bruck, bruck. Two gentlemen from Milwaukee. I don't recall their names."

"Heath Barrington, and this is Alan Keyes," I said.

The waiter cocked his head. "Heath Barrington from Milwaukee. Why do I know that name?"

I shrugged. "I'm not sure. You don't look familiar. Do you get up to Milwaukee ever?"

"No, not really." He looked puzzled but then suddenly smiled. "Wait, I know. You were in the paper here not long ago. You're the detective that solved that murder case in Lake Geneva, aren't you?"

I was quite surprised but flattered to be recognized. "Why yes, that's right."

"I remember because I was hired to wait tables at a garden party at Dark Point several years ago. Mrs. Darkly, as I recall, was charming. I didn't see much of the old man."

"How interesting. It's a small world."

"Yes, I suppose so. When I read about the murder there, it stuck in my mind."

"Natural, I suppose, since you had a connection there," I said.

"Yes, of course. Well, it's a pleasure to meet you. What may I bring you?" He pulled out an order pad and pencil.

I looked at Mrs. Gittings. "Ma'am?"

"My usual, bruck, bruck, bruck."

"Of course, Mrs. Gittings. And for you gentlemen?"

"A tuna fish sandwich, please, and a vodka martini with a pickle, no olive."

"And for you, sir?" He turned to Alan.

"I'll have the tuna as well, and a Schlitz on tap."

"Very good. The tuna is excellent today." He put his pad back in his pocket and headed to the bar.

Mrs. Gittings stared at me. "Bruck, bruck, bruck. Detective, eh?"

"Police detective, yes ma'am. Mr. Keyes is a police officer."

"Bruck, bruck, bruck. I'm a widow. That waiter knew you."

"He recognized me, yes. From a case I worked on in Lake Geneva."

She glanced off then, staring across the room at nothing in

particular. "You're a detective. We are known by what we are, aren't we?"

"Ma'am?"

"Bruck, bruck, bruck. I was a girl once, you know."

"Of course," I replied, not knowing what else to say.

"Then I was a schoolgirl, then a wife."

"I see," I said, though I really didn't.

"Bruck, bruck. That's what I was, a wife. Now I'm a widow. We are known by what we are."

I nodded, understanding at last. "Yes, I suppose that's true."

"My husband was a field supervisor for the Chicago Gas and Power Company. He never made much money. I did sewing to help out, made most of my clothes, and I did repairs and alterations on the side, bruck, bruck."

"Very admirable, Mrs. Gittings. I'm afraid I can't even sew on a button."

"Bruck, bruck bruck. Men. My husband couldn't cook or sew, not that he needed to, he had me. You're not married?" she asked.

"No, ma'am." I was growing tired of that question in my life.

"You?" She looked sternly at Alan.

Keyes smiled. "Not yet, Mrs. Gittings."

"Bruck bruck bruck. Why are you here?" She looked at us suspiciously all of a sudden.

"In Chicago? We're on holiday," I replied.

"Bruck, bruck. Holiday. I see. Camera." She pointed at Alan's Brownie.

He smiled at her. "Yes, it's the new Brownie Reflex. I just got it. A splurge, but an investment, I figure. It even takes full-color pictures."

"Pictures. Happy pictures, sad pictures. Bad pictures. Evil." She brucked, shaking her head.

Alan looked confused, and I must admit I was a bit bewildered, too.

Mrs. Gittings looked away then, staring across the room at something we couldn't see. "We had a wedding picture taken, of course. He looked so handsome. Stanley and I never traveled, except to Michigan for our honeymoon. That was a long time ago. Bruck, bruck. Saugatuck and Douglas, stayed at a little cottage, no running water or electricity, but quite romantic."

"I'm sure. I've heard Michigan can be lovely," Alan said.

"Bruck bruck bruck. I don't remember much of Michigan, just that little cottage. It was blue with green shutters at the windows. And orange marigolds in flower boxes."

"A honeymoon cottage," I suggested.

"Bruck, bruck, bruck. Yes. Romantic. Just me and Stanley. We never had children. My brother did, two girls. They live far away."

"I see."

"Bruck, bruck. Stanley was an only child. What's Milwaukee like?" she asked, changing the subject abruptly and bringing her focus back to us.

"Oh, it's nice enough," I said. "Much smaller than Chicago," I offered.

"Bruck, bruck. People can get lost in Chicago. Swallowed up, and no one notices, no one cares."

I nodded. "Big cities are like that, I suppose."

"Bruck, bruck. Lonely places. Dark places. Alone in a crowd."

The waiter appeared with a tray and set a Bloody Mary in front of Mrs. Gittings, Alan's beer and sandwich in front of him, and my martini and sandwich in front of me.

"Anything else at the moment?"

"Uh, aren't you eating, Mrs. Gittings?" I asked, pointing to her drink.

She took a large sip and smiled contentedly. "Bruck, bruck, bruck."

The waiter looked at me. "Mrs. Gittings never does, sir. One or two bloodies, every day for lunch, like clockwork."

I stared across the table at the little woman, but only the milky glass eyes of the fox stole gazed back at me. She was ensconced in her drink now, and we were apparently forgotten.

Alan set his camera on the table and we ate and drank in relative silence, Mrs. Gittings clucking contentedly every now and then.

When she had finished, she motioned for the waiter and he brought her another one almost immediately.

She drank that one more slowly.

"Enjoying your, uh, lunch, ma'am?" I asked at last, finishing mine.

"Bruck, bruck bruck. Good. When Stanley died, I took a job at Blount's." She continued as if she had never stopped.

I raised my eyebrows. "The men's clothing store here in the hotel? We ran into you as we left there."

"Bruck, bruck. Yes. I was a seamstress. Didn't like it."

"No? It sounds like a job you would have been well suited for," Alan said.

She glared at Alan through glassy eyes of her own. "Mr. Blount is an evil man, bruck, bruck."

"Evil?" I said.

"The devil himself. Did you know vampires can't see their reflection in a mirror?"

I glanced sideways at Keyes, who looked back at me rather comically. Mrs. Gittings was an unusual woman.

"Uh, I've read that, yes."

"Bruck, bruck. Bloodsuckers." She drank again, now more than half finished with her second.

"But there is no such thing as vampires, Mrs. Gittings," Alan said.

She shook a bony finger at him. "Bruck, bruck. Don't you believe it, young man. What evil lurks in our reflections."

"Ma'am?"

"Bruck, bruck, bruck."

Keyes and I exchanged looks as the waiter appeared again.

"May I bring you anything else?"

"No, thank you, just the check," I said.

"Yes, sir." He turned back to the bar again as Mrs. Gittings finished her drink.

"So you don't work for Mr. Blount anymore?" Alan said.

"Bruck, bruck, bruck. I quit. That was several years ago. I don't see so well anymore. My eyes."

That's too bad," I said.

"Yes, too bad. I'm an old lady now. An old widow. Evil man, evil men in our midst."

"I see," I said, though once again I clearly did not.

"Bruck bruck." She pulled on her soiled gloves once more. "Remember, Detective, evil lurks in our reflections. Don't forget. Bruck, bruck."

"I won't."

The waiter returned with the check and I paid him, telling him to keep the change.

"Well, it was a pleasure, Mrs. Gittings," I said.

"Bruck, bruck. Nice that you two could get away down here. To get lost for the weekend."

"Uh, yes, yes indeed. We're here until Monday morning," Alan said.

"Come again, come again. Bruck, bruck. I'm always here, if you look."

"We'll look for you again, then," Alan said.

"If you look into a mirror hard enough, you can sometimes see the evil within," Mrs. Gittings said.

"Are you saying there's evil within all of us?"

"Bruck, bruck. Some more than others, Detective. Up to you to find out. Look deeply." She rose to her feet, more unsteadily than before. "Thank you for lunch."

We stood with her. "Our pleasure. We hope to see you again." Alan smiled warmly at her.

"Bruck, bruck. Like I said, I'm always here if you look. Though sometimes I can't be seen." Without another word she weaved toward the exit, still clucking.

"Golly, Heath, she was certainly something."

"Yes. Yes, she was. Yes, she is. I feel sorry for her, but I like her."

"Yeah, me too. What was all that talk about evil and vampires?"

I shrugged. "I don't know. Inner demons, perhaps. She's a lonely old soul, somewhat frightened, I suspect. I imagine she didn't fit well with the flamboyant Mr. Blount."

"She said he was evil."

"Indeed. I suppose she resents him for letting her go from her job, but he is rather creepy."

"Yes, I agree. All that talk about some different kind of entertainment for the night, for a fee. I wonder what he had in mind."

"I have my suspicions, but I don't want to find out. Why don't we get some fresh air and see a bit of Chicago? I have my umbrella at the ready." I picked it up as we gathered our hats and Alan put his camera back around his neck.

"I'm up for it. Where should we start?"

I placed my fedora firmly on my head and smiled. "This is your trip, Alan, but may I suggest a visit to the Art Institute? Perfect for weather like this, along with the Navy Pier, some shopping on Michigan Avenue, perhaps the Museum of Science and Industry or the Field Museum, and finally, the Garfield Park Conservatory."

Alan laughed. "Jeepers, that's quite a list."

"Did I miss anything?"

"Well, I would like to see the Wrigley Building and the Carbide and Carbon Building. Did you know it's got thirty-seven floors and is over five hundred feet high?"

I smiled. "I did not know that. Well, all right, then. On to Michigan Avenue we go. Some we can walk to, others we may have to take a street car or the L."

"The L?"

"The elevated railway system. It's pretty amazing in its own right."

"Oh, yes, I've read about that, too."

"Where did you do all this reading?"

He looked sheepish. "Well, I bought a guidebook last week, and I've been studying it every night."

I slapped him gently on the back. "That's great. I love your enthusiasm, now let's go explore."

Chapter Five

As promised, we saw all the tall buildings we could, in spite of the fog and drizzle, which did little to dampen Alan's enthusiasm. In addition to that, we window-shopped, peeking into all the fine shops and galleries along Michigan Avenue, including the Allegrae Auction House, Tiffany, Cartier, Louis Vuitton, and Wolford. Though tempted, we didn't buy anything except a few penny postcards Alan wanted to send home. Along the way we took turns taking pictures of each other with Alan's new camera, posing here and there around the city. After Alan treated us to an early dinner at a charming little Italian place on St. Claire Street, we wandered back to the Edmonton, tired, damp, and bedraggled but deliriously happy.

Back in the comfort of our room, we took turns taking hot showers. As I exited the bathroom in my towel, I noticed Alan at the desk writing out his postcards, some of the Water Tower, some of the Wrigley Building and the Edmonton, and some of Michigan Avenue.

"Who are you sending those to?" I said as I dried off.

Alan looked up at me. "I'm keeping a few for my scrapbook. The others I'm mailing to my landlady, my neighbor, Mrs. Heiges, my friend Bill, and my aunt and uncle in Lanesboro, Minnesota."

"And what are you telling them?"

"Just what we saw and did today, how the weather is, stuff like that. Can't fit much on these things."

"No, I suppose not. Did you mention me?"

Alan looked up at me with those puppy-dog eyes. "Just that I'm here with a good friend."

"Of course. A very good friend. Well, I think the front desk has stamps. We can drop them off later to be mailed."

"Good, thanks. Isn't there anyone you want to send a postcard to?"

I shrugged. "My mom and dad, my Aunt Verbina, and Mrs. Murphy. She'd get a kick out of that. Maybe my cousin Liz in Paris. But maybe our next trip."

"Suit yourself. I suppose I had better shower and change now, too. I'm pretty much finished."

"Go ahead. I promise I won't read your postcards."

Alan laughed. "I have no secrets. Not from you anyway. I won't be but a minute." He got up from the desk and padded off to the bathroom as I started to get dressed.

Once he was showered, he changed into his evening suit, which had been neatly pressed and hung in the closet by the valet while we were out, along with my suit and my tux for tomorrow night.

Feeling somewhat refreshed, we returned to the lobby and dropped his postcards off at the desk after purchasing stamps.

"You'll probably beat them home, Alan," I said.

"Maybe, but I wanted to send them anyway. I don't get out of Milwaukee much."

"This is just the beginning, good friend. What say we go in search of cocktails next?"

"That is a capital idea."

We found a seat at a table outside the Acorn Bar with a wonderful view of the lobby and watched the people go by, Alan still somewhat awestruck, which I found adorable. Presently a cocktail waitress came by, and I ordered a dry vodka martini with a pickle. Alan had a beer. She returned quickly enough with the drinks, and Alan again insisted on paying.

"It's the least I can do, Heath. Honestly."

"All right, buddy, since you insist."

"I do." He gave her a dollar and told her to keep the

change. After she walked away, Alan took a swig and looked at me. "Jeepers, twenty-five cents for a beer and sixty cents for a martini. That would have only been seventy-five cents total back in Milwaukee."

I laughed as I tasted my martini. "Everything's bigger and more expensive in the big city, Alan."

The drinks went down easily, and we were both feeling quite relaxed and happy when from just over our shoulders came a singsong voice we had heard before.

"Good evening, gentlemen, monsieurs," Mr. Blount said.

Keyes and I set our nearly empty drinks down and stood up. "Good evening, sir," we both replied. "We're just having a drink. We've had a long day out seeing the sights."

"*Oui*, traveling and sightseeing is always tiring. You mentioned earlier you just checked in today, yes?"

"That's right. We checked in, shopped, spent the afternoon being tourists, and had an early dinner. Then we changed and now here we are. It will be an early evening tonight."

"And when do you go home?"

"Early Monday morning."

"Ah, *bon*. So you have the rest of the weekend." He pulled out his wallet and extracted a business card, which he handed to me. "That is my private number, Monsieur Barrington, in case you change your mind about an evening of entertainment. I can arrange it for you with a moment's notice. All very discreet."

I took the card and glanced at it. *Victor Blount, Jackson Lake 3-4829.* "Thanks, but I don't think we'll need any other entertainment."

He shrugged. "Keep it just in case. One never knows."

I put the card in my wallet, just to be polite. "Right," I said.

He smiled his thin little smile. "*Très bien.*"

"That means 'very good,' Alan," I said, but Alan just rolled his eyes.

"May I join you, gentlemen? I've just closed my shop for the evening. and I'm waiting on someone."

"Of course," Alan said, though I knew he'd rather he didn't.

"*Merci*. Thank you so much. I hope I'm not intruding, it's just that I hate sitting all alone in big hotel lobbies. I feel so small." He took a seat across from us as we returned to our chairs.

"No intrusion at all, Mr. Blount," I said, quite insincerely.

He took out a gold lighter and a matching cigarette case, which looked expensive. He opened the case and held it out to us. "Cigarette?"

"Ah, no thank you. I don't smoke, neither does Mr. Keyes."

He took one out for himself and lit up, putting the lighter and case away. "To each their own, that is what I say, Mr. Barrington."

"I agree." I motioned for the waitress. "Cocktail?"

"Oh, but of course, *mais oui*. I'll buy this round, I insist. Gimlet, extra lime. And another beer for this gentleman, and for you, a martini?"

"Yes, vodka, with a pickle."

"A pickle? How eccentric, Mr. Barrington. You are a peculiar fellow."

The waitress took our order, returning presently with the drinks, which Mr. Blount did indeed pay for.

"Thank you, sir," Alan said, raising his glass.

"*Merci*," I said.

"You are both most welcome, my pleasure." He raised his glass as well. "Do you speak French, Mr. Barrington?"

I shook my head. "Not really. I studied it in high school and I know a few words and phrases. It's a beautiful language."

"*Oui*, the language of love, *amour*."

"*Mon petit chou*. I remember that phrase."

Blount laughed. "Ah yes, that is a French term of endearment. Do you have a little *petit chou* back home?"

I blushed. "No, no one back home." Which was the truth.

"What's a *petit chou*?" Alan asked.

"Little cabbage," I said.

"That's a funny term of endearment. I don't think I'd like being called that."

I laughed. "There was someone in my life once, a long time ago, that I called that."

Alan's look clearly said he wanted to know more.

"I'll tell you about it sometime, Alan." I pulled out my pocket watch. "It's ten to eight. Didn't you say you were meeting someone?"

"*Oui*, a woman I met just yesterday, in my shop. She is from New York and insisted on meeting for drinks this evening."

"You must have made a favorable impression on her," Alan said.

He shrugged his bony shoulders. "I am not a ladies' man, monsieur. But I have no objections to having a cocktail or two, and she was rather adamant." He glanced about. "Ah, there she is now."

He stood and gave a little wave toward a full-figured woman who had just stepped out of one of the elevators. She wore a red velvet cocktail dress, and her platinum blond hair had been twisted into curls and plastered close to her head. About her neck was a rather stunning and very sparkly diamond pendant. If I had to guess, I'd say she was about thirty. Thirty-five at most.

When she spotted him, the woman brightened and quickened her pace in our direction. The three of us stood once more to greet her as she approached.

"Ah, *bon soir*, Mrs. Verte. I would like you to meet Mr. Barrington and Mr. Keyes. They have just arrived from Milwaukee this morning and are in town for the weekend."

Mrs. Verte smiled sweetly. "A pleasure, gentlemen. You are friends of Mr. Blount's?"

"We just met him today," I said. "Mr. Keyes was in need of a tuxedo, which we purchased in Mr. Blount's shop this afternoon."

Blount smiled his thin weasel smile. "*Oui*, nice customers, Mrs. Verte. Mr. Barrington and Mr. Keyes are on holiday."

She took a seat at the table, and the rest of us followed suit. "Oh, how nice. I'm here on holiday myself, just for a few days. I grew up in Chicago, but I live in New York now. I'm in town here until Wednesday."

"Visiting family?" Alan said.

She shook her head, but her hair never moved. "I still have aunts, uncles, and cousins in the area, but no immediate family anymore. I still keep in touch with my uncle Fred. In fact, he sent me an article from the *Chicago Tribune* last month that they did on the Edmonton. Mr. Blount's shop was mentioned in it."

I looked at Blount, who was playing with his mustache. "How nice to get mentioned in the *Trib*, Mr. Blount."

"*Oui*, though it did not do much for my business. A few curious people, but nothing more."

"There's no such thing as bad publicity, they say," Alan said.

"It was a nice article, though they should have had a picture of my shop or me, or both."

We all chortled politely.

"Will you be seeing your uncle Fred this trip, Mrs. Verte?" I asked.

"Oh, yes. We plan to have lunch tomorrow. He's my mother's younger brother. My parents passed away years ago, and my younger sister died just before the war ended."

"I'm sorry to hear it, Mrs. Verte," Alan said.

"Thank you, Mr. Keyes. Life goes on, though, as all those families who lost loved ones in the war have found out. My husband was killed in the war, in Italy. The last time I saw him was over four years ago. His body was never recovered."

"My condolences, Mrs. Verte," I said.

"Thank you, but he left me quite well off financially, so I can't really complain."

"I see," I said. This woman seemed rather cold. "Did you just get in today?"

She shook her head once more. "No, yesterday. A rather nasty start, I'm afraid. My purse was stolen at the train station here in Chicago."

"Oh dear," Alan said.

"It was dreadful, it happened so fast. I had only set my handbag down for a moment, and the next thing I knew it was gone. I just caught a glimpse of a young ruffian running away with it under his arm."

"You notified the police, of course," Alan said.

"No, I didn't. I grew up here, as I mentioned, so I know the police have bigger fish to fry than tracking down purse snatchers."

"But still, Mrs. Verte, you should have reported it," I said.

Her head shook once more. "It was a bother, a nuisance, but nothing more than that. Unfortunately, I had my hotel confirmation letter in it along with my letter of credit. Beyond that I lost just a few dollars, some lipstick, and my compact."

"Gee, that's terrible, though. What did you do?" Alan said.

"Fortunately I keep most of my money in my train case, so I had cab fare. I came here to the hotel and explained my situation to this very nice assistant manager, Mr. Bennett. He couldn't have been more helpful or more kind. He took care of everything."

"The service here is very good," I said.

"Oh, I should say so. He was ever so charming. And I had my evening bag in my suitcase, so no real loss. Besides, it gave me an opportunity to shop for a new purse today, and I found not one but two."

"Then all is well that ends well, as they say. Mr. Keyes and I should let the two of you catch up."

Mr. Blount held up his hand. "Oh no, please don't go, Mr. Barrington. I would enjoy your company if you are so inclined, and I'm sure Mrs. Verte would, too."

"Of course, gentlemen, the more the merrier, isn't that what they say, also?" But her tone and the look she gave me seemed doubtful.

I glanced at Alan, but he gave me one of those "whatever you want" looks, so I agreed. I was curious to learn more about Mrs. Verte.

"Ah, and speaking of the more the merrier, look who is here," Mrs. Verte said.

A paunchy, odd-looking gentleman in a black pinstripe suit approached. His hair was thinning and gray, making him appear older, but I figure he was probably only in his mid-forties. His large nose was underlined by a gray, bushy mustache.

"Good evening, Mr. Bennett, *bon soir*," Mr. Blount said in that singsong tone of his as he, Alan, and I got to our feet.

The man he referred to as Mr. Bennett glared at him sternly. "Good evening, Blount. Gentlemen. How nice to see you again, Mrs. Verte."

"This is George Bennett, an assistant here at the hotel," Blount said.

"Junior assistant *manager*."

"Ah, yes, junior assistant manager—a jam, no?" Blount laughed. "This is Mr. Barrington and Mr. Keyes, from Milwaukee, and apparently you know Mrs. Verte, from New York. She was just singing your praises a few moments ago. I dare say she doesn't know you well." He laughed but Mr. Bennett just glared at him.

"How do you do? I hope you're all enjoying your stay." He shook hands with us. "Yes, Mrs. Verte and I met yesterday. I saw her here and thought I would just stop and see how she's getting along." He nodded politely at Mrs. Verte.

"Oh yes, Mr. Bennett, very nice, thank you," Mrs. Verte said. "I don't know what I would have done without you, you have been so kind."

"Always a pleasure to assist a damsel in distress, Mrs. Verte." He smiled and gave a little bow.

Mrs. Verte giggled. "Won't you join us, Mr. Bennett? We're just chatting."

"Thank you, but I just got off duty and it's been a long day. I should be getting along."

Mrs. Verte touched his arm ever so slightly. "Oh, of course. Your wife must be waiting for you."

He smiled at her again. "Actually, I'm a bachelor. Married to my work, I'm afraid."

She returned his smile, and I could swear she batted her eyelashes. "I see. Well, you *must* join us for a drink first, Mr. Bennett, at least one. I'm a widow, you see, and I always enjoy the company of nice gentlemen."

"Well…"

"I'm sure Mr. Bennett has other plans," Mr. Blount said.

Mr. Bennett looked at him sharply. "I was just going to go to

Frank's Diner for some supper and go home. I could join you all for a drink, if you don't mind."

"Wonderful, welcome," I said.

"Oh, I'm so glad, Mr. Bennett. Come sit next to me, and Mr. Blount, I want you on the other side of me."

The five of us sat down around the small table, Alan and I next to each other, then Blount and Mrs. Verte, with Mr. Bennett beside her and on the other side of Alan.

"Madam Verte, you look more lovely than the last time I saw you, *très charmant*," Mr. Blount said.

She blushed and laughed lightly. "Oh, Mr. Blount, you do say the nicest things. But the last time you saw me was just this afternoon. In fact, yesterday was the first time you ever saw me at all."

"*Mais oui*, and you look even more lovely now. As I told another woman today, I speak only the truth."

"Well, thank you, kind sir." Mrs. Verte fairly giggled, causing her ample bosom to rise and fall. Mr. Bennett looked annoyed, which was exactly the reaction I suspected Mr. Blount was hoping for. Until Mr. Bennett arrived, he'd been cordial to Mrs. Verte, but certainly not as attentive and complimentary as he was now. I wondered what he was driving at.

"I need that drink," Bennett said.

"An excellent suggestion, Monsieur." Blount held up his hand, his diamond rings and matching cuff links shining in the light.

When the waitress appeared, he ordered another gimlet and Alan and I ordered thirds. Mr. Bennett and Mrs. Verte both ordered martinis, dry.

"Put this on my tab, my treat," Blount said.

"You can afford it," Mr. Bennett said rather crossly. Then he looked at us. "So, what do you two do in Milwaukee?"

"I'm a police detective. Mr. Keyes here is a police officer. We're on a long weekend."

"How interesting."

I noticed Mr. Blount's hand shook, and he spilled some of

his remaining cocktail. He looked startled. "You are a policeman, monsieur?"

"A detective, yes. Mr. Keyes is a police officer. And the house detective here in the hotel is a friend of mine, Mike Masterson."

"Oh, I see, I see." He set his glass down and stubbed out his cigarette in the ashtray.

"Something wrong, Mr. Blount?" Mrs. Verte asked.

He laughed somewhat nervously. "Oh no, no, madam. Mr. Barrington just surprised me, that is all. You both looked like nice, respectable businessmen."

"Policemen and detectives are just normal people, sir," Alan said.

"*Oui, oui*, of course, of course."

The waitress brought the next round of drinks, and Mr. Blount drank almost half of his in one gulp. Mr. Bennett was not far behind.

"Do you enjoy working in the hotel, Mr. Bennett?" Alan asked.

"It has its ups and downs," he said, still grasping his glass. "One of the ups is meeting charming ladies like you, Mrs. Verte."

She touched his arm again. "Oh, Mr. Bennett, how nice of you to say. My husband was killed in the war, as I mentioned earlier before you joined us. I'm from Chicago, but I haven't been back in several years."

"Welcome home, then, madam," Mr. Bennett said with a warm smile.

"Thank you. New York is my home now, but it's nice to be back in Chicago. Have you been here at the hotel long?"

"Fifteen plus years. I hope to someday be the general manager here."

"How impressive, Mr. Bennett. I'm sure you'll do well." She looked at me and Alan. "Do you two visit here regularly?"

"This is my first time in Chicago, Mrs. Verte," Alan said.

"Oh, how nice. It certainly is a wonderful city. There are some things I definitely miss."

"Chicago has nothing New York doesn't have, Mrs. Verte," Mr. Bennett said.

"Oh, Mr. Bennett, I wouldn't say that." She laughed and turned back to us. "I'm in room 812, but the weather's been so dreadful, I can't hardly see a thing out the windows."

"What a small world, Mrs. Verte. We're in 804, and we got in this morning," Alan said.

She raised her painted-on eyebrows. "Oh my, such a coincidence. We're practically neighbors. Well, yesterday morning as soon as Mr. Bennett here helped me get everything straightened out with my letter of credit and hotel reservation and all, I unpacked and decided to pick up a little something for my uncle, who lives up on the north side. So I went down to Blount's store, and of course there was Mr. Blount himself, ever so charming."

"You are too kind, madam," Mr. Blount said, smiling his thin smile.

"Oh, and the clothes are exquisite. I picked up a lovely tie for my uncle, and Mr. Blount even wrapped it for me. The workmanship is outstanding."

"*Oui*, the finest silk, the best tailoring," Mr. Blount added, taking out his cigarette case and lighting up another smoke. "Cigarette, Mrs. Verte?"

"Oh, no thank you. I never do," she said, shaking her head.

"It seems the cheese stands alone, as you Americans say. I know you don't smoke, Bennett. And neither do these gentlemen."

"I'm sure you won't let that stop you," Bennett said dryly.

Blount ignored him and blew out a cloud of smoke almost directly at Mr. Bennett.

Mrs. Verte, who was seated between Blount and Bennett, waved the smoke away. "Have you been to his store, Mr. Barrington and Mr. Keyes?" She coughed just a bit.

I nodded. "Ah yes, we were in there today and made some purchases."

She giggled. "Oh, that's right. You said that earlier, didn't you? You bought a tuxedo. How delightful. As it said in the *Tribune* article, he really does have the most marvelous things, really exquisite taste. Do you shop there, Mr. Bennett?"

"Mr. Blount's clothes are rather expensive for me, Mrs. Verte, but I have purchased several things from him."

"Oh, Mr. Bennett, you can't put a price on quality and style," Mrs. Verte said.

"My thoughts exactly, dear lady. It is what I always say," Blount said, still smiling.

I glanced over at him beaming behind his cocktail while Mrs. Verte continued.

"Great minds do think alike, don't they?"

"Indeed, dear lady. Mr. Bennett, as a matter of fact, is a regular customer of my store, though you wouldn't know it. He always dresses so drably."

"Don't start, Blount," Mr. Bennett said flatly.

Mrs. Verte giggled again, her hand still on Bennett's arm. "Oh, I think you dress quite smartly, Mr. Bennett. An assistant manager can't be too flashy."

"Thank you, Mrs. Verte."

"Hmpff," Blount mumbled as Mrs. Verte continued.

"Anyway, I'm so glad I decided to come back after all these years. And the train trip was delightful. I always find long train trips to be so relaxing. Everything's just been wonderful, except for that nasty business with my handbag being stolen, of course."

"You should still report that to the police, Mrs. Verte," Alan said.

She waved him away with the flick of her wrist. "Oh pish posh, what's done is done. I'll never get it back, and besides, if it hadn't been stolen, I never would have met you, Mr. Bennett, would I have?"

He cocked his head. "Probably not. I don't mingle with the guests often."

"So you see? Having that old handbag stolen was actually a good thing. And then yesterday, I also met the charming Mr. Blount, and he invited me for cocktails tonight. And now here we all are, aren't we?"

"Actually I think you invited me, and such a kind invitation it was, Mrs. Verte." He laughed and so did she.

"Oh, Mr. Blount, do call me Vivian."

"Vivian Verte, a lovely name for a lovely woman. It is so lyrical, no? Perhaps I should call you VV, like Gigi. It's very French."

"VV, oh I like that. My maiden name was Dousman, so VV is definitely better than VD." She blushed as she laughed at her little joke, and we all tittered with her, except Mr. Blount. His entire expression and demeanor changed, and he looked rather ill.

Mrs. Verte looked over at him, somewhat alarmed. "Oh dear, I hope I haven't offended you, Mr. Blount. It was just my attempt at humor."

He stared at her for some time, his face blank, but finally spoke. "No, no, it is fine, Mrs. Verte, VV. It was a funny joke." But he sounded less than sincere.

She put her hand on her ample chest. "Oh good. Sometimes I speak without thinking. I only wish you carried women's fashions, but there are certainly plenty of other stores in Chicago for me. Though I suppose I really don't need anything new."

Blount shook his head and tsk'd. "Don't be absurd, VV. A woman such as you must have only the finest, the newest fashions. Of course, clothes only accent your beauty, really. You need nothing." He seemed back to his old self.

"Oh, Mr. Blount." Mrs. Verte giggled again like a schoolgirl, and Mr. Bennett looked slightly sick as he finished his martini. Again I had to wonder what Blount was doing. I didn't think Blount was interested in women in general, and certainly he wouldn't be interested in Mrs. Verte.

"I bought this dress just for the trip," she said, running her free hand across the fabric.

"You look lovely, Mrs. Verte," Mr. Bennett said. I got the impression he really thought so.

"Thank you, kind sir."

"Do you have children, Mrs. Verte?" I asked, changing the subject.

Mrs. Verte rolled her eyes. "Thankfully, no. They're a huge bother and a great expense. I never had time to be changing diapers, wiping snotty noses, or sitting through dreadful school programs and pretending to like them. For some reason or another, I never got the maternal instinct."

"Oh, I, uh, see," I said, sorry I had asked.

"I feel the same, Mrs. Verte. I go home to my cat at night, and that's enough children for me," Mr. Bennett said.

"Oh. I have a cat, too. Her name is Selket, and she's all black. Selket was an Egyptian goddess of magic, you know."

"I did not know that, Mrs. Verte. How very interesting. My cat's name is Kona."

"Oh, how nice. Please do call me Vivian, or VV, Mr. Bennett, like Mr. Blount does."

"Thank you, but then you must call me George."

"Well, all right, then. Aren't we all just getting along so well?"

I nodded politely but it certainly didn't seem that way to me.

Mr. Bennett smiled at her. "Very well. How did you decide on the Edmonton for your trip, Mrs. Verte, I mean Vivian?"

"I did my research, George. The Edmonton is right on Michigan Avenue, close to all the shops, the nightlife, the museums, everything, as you most certainly know. And the article from the *Tribune* that my uncle sent me helped, too. It all sounded so marvelous."

"And now you've discovered Mr. Blount," Mr. Bennett finished for her.

"Oh, George, you sound jealous," she said, her cheeks glowing.

Mr. Bennett's face was flushed. "Please, Vivian. Some men aren't worthy of being jealous over." He looked past Mrs. Verte to the little French man. "It's no secret I don't care for you, Mr. Blount, but it has nothing to do with Mrs. Verte, as you're certainly aware."

Blount took a sip of his drink and stared back at Mr. Bennett. "Perhaps, monsieur, the feeling is mutual, but I have what you need, no? Good quality tailoring is hard to find." He smiled that thin weasel smile. "And I pay the hotel good rent for my space."

Bennett scowled. "Yes, you have what I need, Mr. Blount, but at some point the well will run dry."

"Ah, well, until then we should drink, drink, drink." Mr. Blount took several swallows of his cocktail and laughed.

"As for your rent, we could easily lease that space to someone else for more than you pay."

"Ha. You make me laugh, Monsieur Bennett."

"It's not intentional, I assure you."

"Now, boys, please," Mrs. Verte said. "Let's not get unpleasant."

"There is nothing to get unpleasant about, VV." Blount took another sip of his drink and then suddenly narrowed his eyes and scowled.

"Something wrong with your cocktail, Mr. Blount?" I asked.

Blount shook his head. "No, monsieur, my cocktail, it is fine. It is her, that is all. Perhaps there is something to get unpleasant about after all. She is out late tonight."

Mrs. Gittings was making her way slowly and unsteadily out of the Acorn Bar toward us.

"Mrs. Gittings?" I asked.

Blount raised his thin little eyebrows in surprise. "You know her?"

"We ran into her outside your shop this afternoon," Alan said. "Literally."

He rolled his eyes. "Ugh. She haunts me. Every day she goes past my store, staring at me through the glass. She's a drunk, a sot, an old crone, with nothing to do all day but drink and annoy me."

"I understand she used to work for you," I said.

"Did she tell you that?" His tone was sharp.

"She did."

He shrugged his bony little shoulders and took another drink. "It is true, *oui*, a long time ago. She was a good seamstress once. Then the drinking, you know. I had to dismiss her, of course."

"How did she take it?" Alan said.

Another drink from his glass, which was now nearly empty. "Not well. She became angry, bitter. She blames me for her failure. She's even threatened me."

"Threatened you?" I said, surprised.

"*Oui*, monsieur. I don't take it seriously, of course, the ramblings of a drunkard. But still it is unsettling. She is in the hotel every day, as I mentioned, walking slowly by my store, staring in at me."

"Does she ever go in?"

He shrugged, took yet another sip, drained it at last, and then set the empty glass on the table. "Sometimes. Usually on Saturday afternoons when she knows I'm at my busiest. She comes in, clucking like a chicken, and gives me the evil eye. If I say something to her, it only makes it worse, so I ignore her as best I can. She is not someone you can reason with."

"If she's disrupting your business, you should talk to the house detective," Alan suggested.

"The leased shops are not the responsibility of the hotel, Mr. Keyes," Mr. Bennett said.

Blount nodded. "*Oui*, that is true. Besides, monsieur, I laugh at her, as do my customers. Or we ignore her, as I said. One does not take her seriously. Besides, I keep a gun in my desk in the back room, just in case."

"Speaking as a police officer, Mr. Blount, no threats should ever be taken lightly nor handled by the individual. I think you should report this to the authorities," I said.

"What I think, Monsieur Barrington, is that I need another drink." He motioned for the waitress. "And you gentlemen? VV? Mr. Bennett?"

"I've had enough," Mr. Bennett said. "Of everything."

"No thank you, I'm fine, too," Alan said.

"As am I," Mrs. Verte said. "I haven't had dinner yet."

"And I'm good as well, but let me get your drink," I offered.

"*Merci*." He smiled thinly again as I told the waitress to bring him another gimlet, extra lime.

Mrs. Gittings had stopped just shy of our table and was staring at us, or more specifically, at Mr. Blount. He nodded in her direction, staring back until finally she turned and wobbled off toward the exit.

"You see? She is harmless, but she watches me, no? Since she worked in my shop, she knows my routine. Sometimes when I leave through the back door at night, I even find her waiting silently in the alley. I park my car in the garage down the street as I don't trust the hotel parking attendants. So I must exit through the alley door to get to my automobile, and sometimes she is there. It is unnerving."

"What does she do?" Alan said.

"She watches me, monsieur. She never speaks, except for that annoying clucking sound. Sometimes she points one of her bony fingers at me and says 'Evil,' but that is it. I say, 'Go home, Mrs. Gittings, it's late and I'm tired.' And then I walk away. She doesn't follow me, I think. I don't look back."

"Do you live near the hotel?"

"I live in the Edgewater Beach Apartments on the North Side, by Lincoln Park."

"The Edgewater Beach Apartments is in a rather ritzy part of town, I understand," I said.

Mr. Blount nodded. "*Oui.* Though this recent housing crisis is getting out of hand. My apartment was once a single penthouse that has been divided, which is why I was able to get in. Many of my neighbors have divided their flats into two, even three units, but still the rents are very high."

"I see. That's a bit of hike up to Lincoln Park from here."

"I drive a 1947 Cadillac Convertible coupe, burgundy with a tan ragtop," he stated proudly. "It gets me back and forth quite quickly, as long as there is no traffic. I just picked it up last month."

"It's so nice to see new cars on the road after the war," Alan said.

"That's quite a car, Mr. Blount. A lot of power under the hood," Mrs. Verte said.

He smiled. "You have an appreciation for the quality automobile, VV?"

"Oh yes, I certainly do."

Mr. Bennett ground his teeth. "A brand-new Cadillac convertible coupe had to set you back close to three thousand dollars, Mr. Blount."

Blount laughed. "As I've said before, you can't put a price on quality, Mr. Bennett. What kind of car do you drive, may I ask?"

Bennett scowled. "A 1938 Packard. Very reliable."

Blount smiled his thin smile. "Ah, reliable and dull, just like you, Mr. Bennett. It's probably even beige." Then he turned to Mrs. Verte again. "Perhaps, VV, I can take you for a drive in my car along the lake with the top down sometime."

"Oh, Mr. Blount, that sounds lovely, but my hair would be ruined."

Blount laughed. "On you, touseled hair would only enhance, madam, and please call me Victor." The way her hair was plastered to her head, I doubted even a hurricane could move it.

She blushed and giggled, and I got the impression once again that Blount was trying to irritate Mr. Bennett by flirting with Mrs. Verte.

"Your shop must be doing quite well, Mr. Blount," I said. "An expensive car, an apartment in the Edgewater, a Longines watch..."

He looked back at me and shrugged. "I have an appreciation for the finer things, Monsieur Barrington. I do what I can to afford them. The shop does only so-so, as I mentioned before, so I diversify."

"You never hired anyone else after you let Mrs. Gittings go?" I asked.

"No. Hiring her was a bad experience, a bad idea. She was a nosy old busybody, always in my business. I am better off by myself. I am what some people call a loner, private, though I am sociable, of course. Mrs. Gittings hasn't worked for me in over three years, yet still she haunts me, as I said before. It's gotten worse lately. I think she is losing her mind, she is unstable."

"Mr. Blount, you really should report her behavior to the authorities."

"But, Heath, she's such a sweet old lady," Alan said.

I looked at Alan, who had those puppy-dog eyes that drove me wild. "I agree she seems to be, but if what Mr. Blount says is the truth, it can't be taken lightly no matter how nice she appears to be."

Blount shook his head and held up his hand. "No, no, Monsieur Barrington. She is fine. As I said before, she is harmless, I think. Perhaps I exaggerate. There is no need to involve the police. My, my, it's getting late, I think."

Mr. Bennett looked at his watch. "Nearly eight thirty. It *is* getting late. I should be off in search of some supper."

"Oh my, I should, too. I haven't had my dinner yet, either," Mrs. Verte said, clutching her diamond pendant.

Mr. Bennett smiled at her. "You're welcome to join me, Mrs. Verte—Vivian—if you like. I think I can manage to find someplace nicer than a diner."

"Why, George, that would be lovely, thank you. And I don't mind diner food." She stood up, and so did Mr. Bennett and the rest of us.

"Then let's go, shall we?" He looked at her admiringly. "You will excuse us, won't you, gentlemen?"

Mr. Blount laughed. "By all means. You couldn't be in safer hands, Mrs. Verte. Mr. Bennett is the strong, silent, dull, rather boring type."

"Look here, Blount—" Bennett started, but Mrs. Verte put her hand on his arm again.

"I'm ready if you are, George. I like your type."

"Very well, Vivian. Another time, Blount. That well will run dry, believe me," he said.

Mrs. Verte smiled. "It was a pleasure meeting you, Mr. Barrington, Mr. Keyes."

"Likewise, madam."

"Good evening, Mr. Blount. Victor."

"Good evening, VV," Blount replied, his eyes sparkling mischievously.

Without another word, Bennett walked away with Mrs. Verte on his arm, looking back at us once or twice.

The cocktail waitress brought Blount's gimlet, and I gave her seventy-five cents and told her to keep the change. When she had gone, I turned to Alan.

"I suppose we had better go as well. It is getting rather late."

Alan nodded. "Yes, it's been a long day. I'm ready for bed."

Blount took a drink from his glass, stubbed out his cigarette, then lit another and looked at us. "Mr. Bennett doesn't care much for me, gentlemen, as he stated. I think he thought I flirted too much with Mrs. Verte."

"I think he thinks something, Mr. Blount, but I'm not sure what. And I think you did flirt too much with Mrs. Verte," I said. "I can't really believe you are interested in her romantically."

He gave a little laugh and stroked his thin mustache, staring off in the direction they had gone. "For me, no. She is not my type. But for Mr. Bennett, ah, romance is in the air, no?"

I looked after them. "Perhaps. Perhaps two lonely people are a little less lonely tonight. But certainly no thanks to you, Mr. Blount."

"Maybe so, maybe not. Sometimes a man doesn't know he wants something until another man shows interest. You understand, no?"

"You don't really seem the Cupid type," Alan said.

"Cupid? Ah, *oui*, the little fellow with the bow and arrow, yes?" Blount laughed.

"You said you didn't care for Mr. Bennett, so why would you be interested in fixing him up?" I said.

"Fixing him up?"

"With Mrs. Verte."

"Ah, *oui*. Fixing up is exactly what he needs. I know a secret, Detective, about Monsieur Bennett. I wonder if you can figure it out." Blount smirked at me annoyingly. Clearly, he had had one or two gimlets too many.

"What kind of secret, Mr. Blount?"

"That's for you to discover, perhaps. But I will say it's juicy, very juicy."

"That sounds more like gossip."

"I assure you it's all fact, Detective, and facts are always juicier than mere gossip."

"You're an interesting fellow, Mr. Blount. You want me to discover Mr. Bennett's secret?"

"Let's just say I am curious to know if you are a good detective or not."

"Heath happens to be one of the finest, Mr. Blount," Alan said defensively.

"Ah, *bon, bon*. But then, some secrets perhaps are better left undisturbed."

"Then why bring it up at all?" Alan asked.

"It is no secret that Mr. Bennett and I are not friends. But surely your mind must wonder why."

"I think any man would object to another man flirting with someone in front of them," Alan said. "Especially if he was interested in that someone, too."

"Certainly, Alan, but there's something more, isn't there, Mr. Blount?"

He smiled thinly again. "Perhaps, but I don't think it is for you to know, and you will not know."

I returned his thin smile. "Perhaps, perhaps not."

"*Oui*, well, perhaps it is time for me to go as well. Tomorrow is another day, as they say."

"Good night, Mr. Blount. We'll see you tomorrow when we pick up the tux."

"*Bon soir*, sleep well."

"Thank you for the drinks, sir," Alan said.

"Hmm? Oh, my pleasure, gentlemen."

By the time we'd crossed the lobby, Blount had settled back in his chair and was ensconced in his cocktail and his cigarette, having apparently changed his mind about leaving.

Chapter Six

"Where are we going, Heath?"

"Away from him. He smells like trouble, and he sounds like it too."

"I thought so, too. Jeepers, Mr. Bennett sure doesn't like him. What was that all about?"

"I'm not sure. But there's a reason behind it all, and Mr. Blount is the type of man who likes to taunt people. He wants you to know he knows something and you don't, even if he doesn't want you to find out what. He wants you to know he's in control. Of course, I'm sure part of it was the alcohol talking."

"Mr. Blount sure didn't seem to care for Mrs. Verte's little joke about VD," Alan said.

"Some men find off-color humor like that vulgar in women, even if they may find it amusing if another man said it. Still, his reaction was curious. He had such a blank stare about him when she said it."

"Heath, don't go getting all curious on me again. We're here to enjoy ourselves."

I laughed. "I'm sorry, you're right, Alan, absolutely. Say, there's Mike."

I waved to Mike Masterson, who was standing near a pillar, smoking a cigarette and seemingly oblivious to everything around him, which I knew from experience meant he was fully aware of everything. Mike was the same age as me, but shorter. He was clean shaven, barrel chested and solid, with thin dark hair that accented his round face and brown eyes. He looked tough in his double-breasted pinstripe suit, as if he was someone you did not want to meet in a dark alley. And I knew from experience you didn't.

He greeted us cordially as we walked up to him, but he kept his eyes on his surroundings.

"Good to see you, Mike. I'd like you to meet Alan Keyes, my friend I was telling you about."

"A pleasure, Mr. Keyes."

"Likewise, and please call me Alan."

"I'm Mike, then. Any friend of Heath's is a friend of mine. We go back a long way."

I nodded. "We certainly do. You were still married to Kathy when we first met."

Mike grimaced. "God, yes. Seems a lifetime ago. I was young and foolish, and so were you. I could tell you some stories about your friend Heath, here, Alan."

Alan raised his eyebrows. "I'd love to hear them."

"Let's leave the past in the past, Mike."

Mike laughed. "Heath could be a bit unbuttoned, to say the least, especially when he'd had a cocktail or two too many."

"Oh really?"

"I'm sure he'll tell you about it sometime."

"I hope so. That's a side I've never seen."

"Well, like I said, that was a long time ago. I guess we grew up," I said.

"Yeah, I guess we did. I divorced Kathy, met the amazing, intelligent, blond bombshell herself, Margot Becker, married her, moved here, and got this job."

"A lot has changed," I said.

"It sure has. Listen, I'm about due for a break. Why don't you come downstairs to my office, and we can catch up for a bit?"

"That would be great, Mike, lead on."

He put out his cigarette in a nearby floor ashtray and turned toward a door marked *Stairs* next to the elevator. "My office is on

what I like to call the lower level." The three of us went down two
sets of fire stairs to a subbasement, then out to a narrow hall. "Just
me and the laundry down here, along with the housekeeping offices
and staff toilets. I'm over this way." We turned right and stopped at
the end of the hall while he unlocked a door marked *Security*. Once
inside, he flicked on the overhead light and I glanced about. It was
small, only about ten by twelve, half of which was taken up by a
large wooden desk and two chairs facing it.

"This is it, gentlemen. Welcome to my world," Mike said.

"Not bad, Mike. Very private," I said.

He laughed. "Always the diplomat, Heath. It's a dump, but it
suffices. I don't spend much time down here, most of my shift I'm
up patrolling the lobby or the halls. Sit, sit."

Alan and I both took a seat in the creaky wooden armchairs
facing the desk. The room smelled of dampness and stale cigarettes.
The ashtray on the desktop was full.

Mike pulled open a drawer and extracted a bottle of bourbon
and three glasses, which he filled generously before handing us each
one and lighting another cigarette. "You still don't smoke, Heath?"

"No, never started."

"You?" he asked Alan, holding out the rumpled package.

"Thanks, no. I don't smoke either."

"Figures. Sorry I don't have any ice for the drinks."

"It's fine, Mike," I said, though it certainly wasn't my drink of
choice with or without ice.

"Liar. But anyway, here's to old friends and new ones." Mike
raised his glass to us.

"Here's to," I said.

"Hear, hear."

We drank a good portion, and Mike leaned back and put his
feet up as he unbuttoned his suit coat and took several drags on his
cigarette.

"Enjoying your stay, guys?"

I nodded. "Great hotel, Mike. Thanks again for arranging the
rate for us."

"My pleasure. Your room okay?"

"We're in 804—clean and neat."

"Ah, they put you by the elevator. Sorry about that. Not much of a view from that room, either."

"It's fine. We're here to see the city, not the room," I said.

"I suppose. Too bad about the weather, though, but it's supposed to clear up soon."

"Can't do anything about it," Alan said.

"Very true, Alan."

"We met Mr. Blount today," I said.

Mike nodded. "Yes, I noticed you chatting with him in the lobby, along with Mr. Bennett and the jolly blonde."

"Right, Mike. That Blount is an odd fellow. Something doesn't seem right about him," I said.

Mike took another swig from his glass and took another long drag on his cigarette. "Yeah, I know what you mean. I don't talk to him much, but I've bought a few things in his shop, dealt with him a couple times. I don't think he's on the square."

"I agree, but I can't put my finger on it."

Mike blew a couple of smoke rings into the stale air. "He's French, you know. Maybe that explains it."

I laughed. "I know a few French people, and they're nothing like Mr. Blount."

"Maybe so."

"Mr. Blount told us he's had his shop here for several years," I said.

"That's right, he has. He keeps his nose clean, mostly. There was some trouble a few years back. A young girl killed herself over him, apparently."

I raised my eyebrows. "Oh?"

"Yeah. A young girl, just nineteen."

"How was Blount involved?"

"I don't know the details, but there was the implication he had taken nude photos of her and sold them to some seedy publication."

"Wowzer, so what happened?"

"The pictures got out, and she killed herself. But he was

absolved of any wrongdoing. Word is he bought himself out of serving any jail time."

"He mentioned he does portraits in the back room. How strange."

"Like I said, Blount's a strange fellow."

"I'm beginning to see that."

"Well, I wouldn't let him bother you. Just enjoy yourselves and have a nice weekend. You deserve it."

"Thanks, Mike," Alan said. "I seem to have to keep reminding Heath we're on vacation."

Mike laughed. "Doesn't surprise me."

I smiled. "You both know me too well. What's Mr. Bennett all about?"

Mike shrugged his shoulders and took a puff of his cigarette. "Buttoned up, straitlaced, dull, predictable. He's worked here quite a while."

"Fifteen plus years, he said," Alan replied.

"That sounds about right. He's single, lives alone, doesn't bother me, and I don't bother him. Why do you ask?"

"Just curious."

"You always are."

"Sometimes those buttoned-up straitlaced, dull, predictable ones can surprise you."

Mike laughed. "Don't I know it. We had a convention of school librarians in here a few years back. Damn, they really kept me on my toes. Noise complaints like crazy."

Alan and I laughed, too. "It's always the buttoned-up ones that come unglued."

"Or unbuttoned. So what all did you do today after you checked in?"

Alan grinned. "This is my first time to Chicago. We visited the Wrigley Building and saw the Carbide and Carbon Building today, a bunch of others, too. And we rode the L, did some shopping all up and down Michigan Avenue, and ate and drank a lot. Tomorrow we plan on going to the Museum of Science and Industry, and maybe the Field Museum and some nightclubs."

Mike whistled. "Sounds like a great weekend. Wish I could join you, but I have to work. Margot would love to see you, too. She sends her regards."

"How is Margot?"

"She's fine, getting prettier and smarter every day. One of these days we'll make it back up to Milwaukee to see you."

"I'd like that."

Mike stubbed out the cigarette in the already full ashtray and drained his glass before looking at his watch. "Guess I better get back to work, gentlemen." He swung his feet off the desk and returned the bottle to the desk drawer.

We finished our drinks too and stood up. "Right. What should we do with the glasses?"

"Just leave them on the desk. I'll rinse them out in the men's room sink later."

That thought did not appeal to me as I wondered how often they'd been rinsed out previously, but I didn't say anything. "We'll see you before we leave, then."

"You'd better. I'm working the night shift again tomorrow, but I'm on day duty Sunday and Monday. Those are the big checkout days, always problems."

"Sounds brutal, working Saturday night and then back again on Sunday morning."

He nodded. "It *is* brutal. I get home at two a.m., back here at nine a.m., but I just have that rotation once a month. Margot hates it only slightly more than me."

"I bet." We walked out of his office as he flicked off the light and locked the door. "I think we're going to call it a night, Mike. It's been a long day, and we have another one tomorrow."

"Sure, makes sense." He stopped a third of the way down the hall and punched a button. "Take the service elevator up to your room."

The elevator door slid open and we stepped in. "Thanks, Mike, see ya."

"See ya. Nice to meet you, Alan."

"Likewise. Have a good night, Mike."

We stood staring at each other briefly until the elevator door closed, then I pushed the button and we were off.

Alan glanced over at me as the elevator climbed up, creaking and groaning. "Mike seems like a nice guy."

"Top notch."

"Does he know?"

I shrugged. "I think so. He's a smart fellow, and I've known him a long time."

"And he doesn't mind?"

"Doesn't seem to. He's a live-and-let-live kind of fellow, and so is Margot. That's why I like them."

"The world needs more of them."

"I agree."

CHAPTER SEVEN

Saturday morning we awoke early, Alan actually crawling out of bed first. I lay there a while, feeling the warm spot on the bed where his body had been, smelling the pillow, breathing in the scent of his hair tonic, and feeling content. While he was in the shower, I got up and opened the curtains. Another gray day, but I refused to let the fog, rain, and drizzle dampen my spirits. I even found myself singing aloud a bit as I pulled the two beds apart, moved the nightstand back into position, and tidied up. Alan emerged from the bathroom, wearing only a towel emblazoned with *The Edmonton* in fancy script, and surveyed the room.

"It looks like we slept in separate beds all right. I don't see any indication they were ever pushed together."

"Good. The games we have to play, I guess. Sleep well?"

"Very, in spite of the occasional noise from the elevator. These mattresses are amazingly nice. They sure beat the one I have at home. And fresh, clean sheets every day, golly."

"You should invest in a new mattress for your apartment. A good night's sleep is important."

"Yeah, I should. I really slept soundly last night. How about you?"

"You snore," I said with a grin.

He laughed. "Take the good with the bad, mister. Better get showered. We have a lot to do today. What about breakfast?"

"How about the coffee shop here in the hotel? It's convenient, and then we can visit the museum. The weather doesn't look too good for the Garfield Park Conservatory, so maybe we can do that tomorrow."

"Sounds great, but you need to shower, shave, and get dressed first."

"I won't be but a minute, faster than you can shake a martini."

"That'll be the day."

"Very funny." I picked up a pillow and threw it at him as I scurried into the bathroom and shut the door. The hot water was invigorating, and soon I emerged to find Alan already dressed in his day suit and a spiffy red tie.

"New tie?"

"Yup, I bought it just for the trip."

"I like it—it matches your eyes." I grinned.

Now it was his turn to throw a pillow at me, which I dodged unsuccessfully, and we both laughed. He watched as I dressed. I liked sharing a morning like this, just the two of us. After what Alan said was an "eternity" of my primping, combing my hair, and shaving, I was finally ready.

"I think I could have shaken about four or five pitchers full of martinis in the time it took you to get ready."

"Wise guy. I just want to look my best for you."

"You always do."

"Better. Well, since you don't have any of those martinis, why don't we get this day started?"

"As I always say, if you're waiting for me, you're wasting your time."

We left the room for the day, my shoulder holster secured under my suit coat, the umbrella on my arm. Alan had his camera about his neck again and his lucky rock in his pocket, I was sure.

The coffee shop was opposite the Acorn Bar, behind the marble staircase and under the mezzanine. We slid easily into a booth across from a table for two who were apparently just finishing. The woman sitting there looked very familiar, a beautiful blonde with killer legs crossed neatly beneath a white pleated skirt. She wore a tight red sweater and a small white hat that looked like the top of an acorn.

She was seated across from an extremely attractive man wearing a dark suit and an eye patch that made him intriguing and mysterious. At his feet was an instrument case. As the waitress brought our coffees, I finally remembered where I had seen her before.

"Pardon my staring, but you're Miss Eye, aren't you?"

She looked over at me and smiled, obviously pleased to be recognized. "Why yes, that's right."

"We met at Blount's yesterday afternoon. I was the gentleman looking at ties. You suggested I try Wieboldt's on State."

She nodded. "Oh yes, that's right. Did you?" She pushed her plate away and crossed those killer legs in my direction.

I shook my head. "No, I bought at Blount's. It was just easier."

"Your loss, mister."

I smiled. "I'm sure. Foolish is the man who ignores advice from a beautiful lady, as my father always says."

"Your father is a wise man."

"Yes, I'm beginning to realize that. I'm Heath Barrington, from Milwaukee. This is my friend, Alan Keyes."

"How do you do? Gloria Eye, as you know. This is my fiancé, Walter Gillingham."

The man with the eye patch nodded in our direction as he swallowed his last bite of breakfast.

"Ah yes, the trumpet player, correct?" I said.

He looked surprised. "Gee, that's right, how did you know that?"

"Mr. Blount likes to talk."

"I don't like him much."

"With good reason, dear. He's rather a nasty little man," Miss Eye added.

"You don't care for him, Mr. Gillingham?"

"He isn't very nice to Gloria," he replied. "He needs to be cut down to size. I plan to pay that little weasel a visit." He slapped his fist into the palm of his other hand.

"Careful, Mr. Gillingham. He mentioned to us he keeps a gun in his desk in the back room of his shop," Alan said.

"Guns don't scare me much. I was a Marine."

"It's all right, Walter. We'll soon be done with him." Miss Eye reached out and put her hand on his arm.

"Mr. Blount gave us the impression you and Miss Eye were regulars, among his best customers, Mr. Gillingham," I said.

"Walter likes to dress well, Mr. Barrington," Miss Eye answered for him. "Good men's clothing stores are hard to find."

"Really? I should think a city the size of Chicago has hundreds of them. You yourself mentioned Wieboldt's."

"Blount's is convenient, as you said, Mr. Barrington. We live nearby and work in the hotel a lot."

"And yet I heard you tell him that you're basically through doing business with him."

"My, what big ears you have. You heard that from way over by the tie display?"

I smiled, somewhat embarrassed. "It's not a big store, and my hearing is quite good. I didn't intend to eavesdrop, I assure you."

"I see. Well, then you heard Mr. Blount has been increasing his prices to the point we can no longer afford it, so yes, Walter and I are, shall we say, discussing other options."

"Mr. Blount seems to think you will reconsider."

"That little weasel thinks a lot of things. He needs a good pop," Mr. Gillingham said, once more slamming his fist into the palm of his other hand.

"Walter," she said firmly, reaching across the table and touching his arm.

"Sorry. It's just that Gloria is a lady and deserves to be treated like one. Mr. Blount doesn't see that. He sees only dollar signs when he looks at her. He takes advantage, and I don't like that."

"Understandable, Mr. Gillingham," Alan said.

Gloria looked over at us and asked, "What do you two do in Milwaukee?"

"I'm a police detective. Mr. Keyes here is a police officer."

"Oh. I see. Just here for the weekend?" She uncrossed her legs and then crossed them the other way.

"Yes, a little time away," Alan said. "I've never been here before."

"Well, I hope you'll both come to the Sky Star Ballroom tonight. Walter and I will be performing there. We're rehearsing all day today."

"We wouldn't miss it, Miss Eye," I said.

She smiled, her red lips revealing lovely, straight, white teeth. "Good. I hope you'll enjoy yourselves. Walter plays a mean trumpet."

Walter cocked his head. "Oh, Gloria, I don't play anywhere near as well as you sing."

"Perhaps we complement each other, my love," she said.

"Well sure, that's what we were doing, weren't we?" Walter replied, looking a little confused.

"Yes, dear. Walter was in the war, of course, a Marine as he said. He was hit by a mortar shell and lost his eye. Rattled his brain a bit, too, but he's really a sweetheart."

"I wanted to knock the hell out of those Nazis."

"Yes, of course. I'm glad you made it home alive," Alan said.

"Me too. Mostly in one piece. Except for my eye, you know. But I can still blow."

"I'm sure," I said.

He nodded. "When I was discharged, I came back home here and looked up Mr. Storm—he's the bandleader, you know."

"Yes, I've heard of him."

"I played for him before the war, but I wasn't lead. He lost a few of the boys over there, so now I'm lead."

"And a very good lead trumpet player, Walter," Miss Eye said.

He grinned. "Ain't she something?"

"She is indeed, Mr. Gillingham. You're a lucky fellow."

"You got that right, mister. And she can sing like a nightingale. She's even cut a couple records with us."

"Golly, that's wonderful," Alan said.

Miss Eye looked at each of us and laughed. "Please, gentlemen, you're embarrassing me."

"It's all true, Gloria," Walter said.

"I'm sure it is," I said.

"Well, you can judge for yourselves this evening," she said.

"Fair enough," I replied.

The waitress dropped off their check. "Pay at the register, at the counter by the door. Enjoy your day."

"Thank you, miss," Walter said as she walked away.

Miss Eye picked up her handbag. "Well, we need to get upstairs and rehearse, gentlemen."

I nodded. "Yes, and we need to order and be on our way. It was a pleasure meeting you both."

"Likewise."

Alan and I slid over to stand, but Miss Eye waved us back down. "Don't get up, gentlemen. I look forward to seeing you both this evening." She turned and walked away, Mr. Gillingham following like a puppy dog, swinging his instrument case.

"The Eye of the Storm," I said, moving back over to the center of the booth.

"What?"

"The band she and Mr. Gillingham are in is called the Storm Clouds, so she bills herself as the Eye of the Storm. Blount mentioned it."

"Oh. Clever. I don't get why they shop at Blount's when they both clearly dislike him so. Sounds like they're going to try and finagle some better pricing, but still…"

"Mr. Bennett doesn't care for Blount either. Very curious indeed."

"There you go again, Heath, getting all curious. Forget I said anything. I'm starved, let's order."

"You're right, I'm sorry. Sometimes it's hard to turn off the detective part of my brain." I smiled and waved for the waitress, who came over and took our order and poured more coffee. I admit I was famished myself.

After a hearty breakfast of hotcakes and eggs, along with two orange juices and lots more coffee, I paid the bill and we stepped out onto Michigan Avenue in the mist and fog. "Perfect day for the museum, Mr. Keyes. Adventure awaits."

We rode the L to the Fifty-seventh Street station and walked the rest of the way under my umbrella, arriving at the museum only slightly damp. We spent nearly the entire day there, Alan snapping photographs, some of me, some of the exhibits, and one of us together that a nice lady offered to take for us. It was nearly six thirty before we got back to the hotel, as we had stopped for dinner at a little café we had stumbled upon on our way back to the L station.

As we entered the lobby and headed for the elevators, I stopped short and turned to Alan.

"Hey, we totally forgot to pick up your tux today."

"Jeepers, that's right. What time is it?"

"Almost closing. We better get it now."

"Right. Do you have your checkbook?"

"I do. Good thing we got back here when we did." I led the way back to Blount's, pushing open the glass door, the bell jingling. Mr. Blount was behind the counter folding a shirt. He looked up at us and smiled that thin smile of his.

"Good evening, gentlemen, I was beginning to wonder if you had forgotten."

"The day got away from us, sir. We've only now gotten back."

"I hope you had a good day."

"It was a wonderful day," Alan said, beaming. "This is a wonderful city. We've been on the go all day."

"I am so happy to hear that, monsieur. I have had a busy day, too."

"Good to hear," I replied.

"Yes and no, monsieur. Lots of last-minute Father's Day shoppers, and as usual on my busy days, especially Saturdays, Mrs. Gittings came in, clucking away."

"Oh my," Alan said.

"*Oui.* It was after lunch, so she no doubt had a few drinks in her. The store was full and I was busy trying to hem up a pair of trousers. She started sputtering about evil, the evil eye, and whatnot."

"Did you call the police?" I asked.

He shook his head. "No. As I said, she is a nuisance, but nothing I can't handle. I tried to ignore her, that is, until she went in the back room."

"What for?" Alan said.

"I have no idea. I didn't even see her at first. As I said, I was trying to hem a pair of pants for a customer. But suddenly I noticed she was no longer in view, and the bell on the front door hadn't jingled. I got up rather quickly and investigated, finding her talking to my dress form in the back room."

I laughed in spite of myself. "The headless one?"

"*Oui*. It can't talk back, and it has no ears, a perfect companion for Mrs. Gittings. Perhaps I will gift it to her. Maybe it will keep her out of my hair."

"Perhaps," Alan said with a smile.

"So you did indeed have a day, Mr. Blount," I said.

"*Oui*, yes. Mrs. Verte stopped by late in the day, too. She asked me to hem a dress she bought this afternoon. While she was changing in the back room, Mr. Bennett stopped by. I think he must have seen Mrs. Verte come in. Romance is definitely blossoming."

"How nice for them," Alan said.

"*Oui*, and nice for me. While Mr. Bennett was here, I got him to purchase a new suit."

I raised my eyebrows. "You are quite a salesman, Mr. Blount. I got the impression last evening that Mr. Bennett was through buying new clothes."

"Oh, he doesn't like me, nor I him, but it is a business relationship. You understand, no?"

"No."

He shrugged his shoulders. "As I said, some things you will not, cannot understand, monsieur. But he bought a new suit, tried it on, I will alter it, and it will be ready Tuesday along with Mrs. Verte's dress."

"Whatever works for you, Mr. Blount, and clearly it does work. You seem to be doing quite well, as I said last night."

He smiled thinly again. "I manage, I diversify."

The bell jingled behind us, and Miss Eye entered, looking radiant in a navy blue skirt and jacket with a white blouse underneath. Atop her blond tresses was a yellow hat.

"Ah, good evening, Miss Eye. It's ten minutes of seven, you know," Mr. Blount said.

"I can tell time. I sent you a message telling you I'd be late, didn't you get it?"

"*Oui*, I received your message, but I still close at seven."

Alan and I tipped our hats. "Hello again."

She glared at us. "Oh hello, the men from the coffee shop, of course."

"Yes, that's right. I'm Mr. Barrington, and this is Mr. Keyes."

"Forgive me, I'm terribly bad with names."

"No apologies necessary, miss."

"Well, I'm sorry to barge in like this but I need to pick up my dress. I want to wear it this evening."

Blount smiled his thin smile. "Of course, Miss Eye. I have it right here. I'm glad you made it before closing. Let me just finish with these gentlemen."

"I've been rehearsing all day, and I'm short on time," she snapped. "I'm going to try it on first, so finish with them while I do that."

Blount looked surprised. "I only steamed and pressed it, Mademoiselle. There is no need to try it on."

"Nevertheless, I am going to. I don't trust you and I don't like you."

He shrugged. "As you wish. However, these gentlemen were here first. Mr. Keyes needs to try on his tuxedo, and I close in less than ten minutes."

"And I go on at eight, so let's not waste any more time. Just give me my dress so I can try it on."

Alan smiled. "I'm sure the tuxedo is fine, Mr. Blount. I'll just take it and go, I don't need to try it on. Besides, it's late, so if something wasn't quite right, you wouldn't have time to fix it now, anyway."

"As you wish, monsieur. I will just bag it. I have your stud set, shirt, and bow tie here as well." He handed me the bill and then picked up a dress from the rack behind the counter. "And Miss Eye, here is your gown."

I wrote out a check for the balance as Gloria Eye took the dress and brushed past us into the back room.

Mr. Blount sighed. "Miss Eye, it seems, is more the storm itself rather than the eye of it."

"She does seem to have a temper," I said.

"*Oui*, and a short fuse, as they say. If there is a problem with the tuxedo, monsieur, please call me. I am closed tomorrow and Monday, but I will reopen on Tuesday."

"I'm afraid we're checking out on Monday, but if there is anything wrong, I can call you from Milwaukee."

"I am sure it will fit like a glove. I pride myself on my work."

"Of course." I handed him the check, and he wrote out a receipt, which I put in my wallet. Alan took the garment bag and the smaller bag containing the studs, shirt, and bow tie as Miss Eye came out of the back room, her gown in hand.

"It's fine. I need to get back upstairs and change. Here's fifty cents." She dropped two quarters onto the counter and swept by us toward the door before turning on her heel. "I'll see you gentlemen up top?"

"You can count on it, Miss Eye," I said, smiling.

"I hope you'll enjoy the show." Then she pushed through the door, the bell jingling once more.

"We'd better get changed, as well. Are you going to the Sky Star this evening, Mr. Blount?"

He shook his head. "*Mais non*. I have work to do, still. When one owns the store, one cannot just go home at closing time. But enjoy, gentlemen, *bon soir*."

"Good night."

He walked us to the door and let us out, then locked it, turning the Open sign to Closed. I nodded once more to him through the glass, and Alan and I made our way to the elevators, where we rode up alone and were able to hold hands. Maybe there was something to this automation after all.

Chapter Eight

Once back in our room, Alan undid the garment bag containing his tux, shirt, and bow tie and opened the stud set. "I might need your help with the tie, Heath."

"Happy to be of service, but we'd better hustle." I changed into my own tux, then helped Alan with his tie and cuff links before standing back to admire him. I whistled. "Handsome."

"You're not so bad yourself, mister. I only have my black oxfords I wore on the train to wear with the tux, though. I guess I should have bought the new shoes, too."

"They're fine, and they still have a nice shine to them."

"I guess so."

"With a handsome man like you, no one will be looking at your feet, believe me," I said.

"No one but Mr. Blount."

I laughed. "He's working late, he won't be there."

"I suppose so. The pants on my tux are a bit tight in the seat, though."

"Hmm, perhaps Blount did that on purpose."

Now Alan laughed. "I guess I should have tried them on, but he wouldn't have had time to fix them."

"Just don't bend over and you'll be fine." I chuckled. "Come on, handsome, the ball awaits."

"I'm coming, but I'm telling you this tux is definitely tight."

"In all the right places," I replied, and I let out a wolf whistle as

I stepped into the hall. I glanced toward the elevator and saw Mrs. Verte. I hoped she hadn't overheard our conversation or my whistle, but she probably had. She looked winded, and her hair was a bit out of place, a strand of it having come loose, but she was dressed to the nines in an off-white cocktail dress, long white evening gloves, and a beautiful sapphire blue necklace and earrings, her cheeks rouged and glowing.

"Good evening, Mrs. Verte," I said, somewhat embarrassed at the thought of her overhearing our conversation.

But if she'd heard, she did not let on. "Oh, good evening, Mr…" she responded, tugging up one of her gloves.

"Barrington."

"Oh yes, that's right. Forgive me."

"No forgiveness needed, madam. My name seems to have slipped the minds of many. Heading out?"

"Ah yes, heading *up*, to the Sky Star."

"How nice."

"I'm more than ready to start the night, Mr. Barrington."

"Planning on doing a lot of dancing?"

"Oh yes, I am. I want to dance tonight—dance, dance, dance. I've been dancing to the radio by myself in the room for the last hour, and I'm getting impatient for George."

"George?"

"Mr. Bennett. I ran into him in Blount's shop this afternoon. I invited him to the Sky Star tonight."

"He seems like a nice man."

"Yes, I told him to pick me up here at six forty-five, but I'm afraid I had to send him away when he arrived."

"Why?"

"Well, silly me, I broke my bottle of perfume in the bathroom when I was getting dressed. He was kind enough to go in search of a new bottle of it for me, but that was an hour ago. I decided I might as well go upstairs and have a drink and dance. He can meet me. Do you have the time?"

I took out my pocket watch. "It's nearly quarter of eight. We're heading up there ourselves, so we might as well ride up together."

"Certainly."

"Ah, but you've forgotten to push the elevator button, Mrs. Verte."

"What? Oh, so I have. I am so forgetful this evening," she said, laughing lightly.

Leaning over, I smiled and pushed the button for her as Alan joined us.

"You remember Mr. Keyes, Mrs. Verte."

"Oh yes, of course, good evening, Mr. Keyes. Don't you look handsome? You both do."

Alan smiled. "Thank you, Mrs. Verte. And you look lovely. Another new dress?"

"Yes. I bought this one in New York for the trip. I wanted something easy to dance in, not too tight. The weather was just dreadful today, wasn't it? I spent the day shopping. I bought a lovely day dress at a little boutique up the street. It needed a little altering, and they didn't do it on site, so I brought it to Blount's this afternoon. It should be ready Tuesday," Mrs. Verte added.

"Mr. Blount mentioned you had dropped off a dress to be hemmed this afternoon. He also said Mr. Bennett bought a new suit."

"Oh, that Mr. Blount—such a charmer, isn't he?"

"He does seem to be quite fond of you, Mrs. Verte," Alan said.

She laughed lightly. "Oh, I still have my feminine wiles, I suppose, though Mr. Bennett doesn't like the way Mr. Blount flirts with me one bit."

"Yes, I got that impression."

"It's harmless, I assure you. And I assured George, too." The elevator door slid open, and Mr. Bennett stepped out, clearly surprised to see us.

"Vivian. Mr. Barrington and Mr. Keyes."

"There you are, George. I had just about given up on you and was heading up to the Sky Star with these handsome men."

"You sent me out at a quarter to seven on a Saturday night, Vivian, to find Lavender Lilacs by Phillipe, not exactly an easy task, but I managed. Here." He handed her a small bag. "They were just closing, but I convinced them to sell me one bottle. It wasn't cheap."

"Good perfume never is, George. Thank you so much for doing this for me. I insist on repaying you."

He smiled. "Please don't give it another thought, madam. It was my pleasure, though certainly not easy to find."

She laughed. "Lavender Lilacs is my signature scent. I never wear anything else, George, so I really appreciate you finding it. Was it at Monique's as I suggested?"

Mr. Bennett shook his head. "No. I walked the four blocks up there, but they don't carry it. I finally found it over on Fairbanks Court at a place called Sheridan's, I think."

"It seems to me the ladies' boutique right here in the hotel has a display of Lavender Lilacs in the window, Mr. Bennett," I said.

He rolled his eyes. "Now you tell me. I've been up and down Michigan Avenue tonight, and it's not pleasant out."

"You should have looked in the hotel first," she admonished. "Now you're all disheveled and out of breath."

"I'm sorry, Vivian, but I didn't think to look here. You suggested I try Monique's four blocks north. I've been traipsing up and down the street, in and out of every women's boutique I could find. It's no wonder I'm disheveled and out of breath."

"Well, you'll have to put yourself together." She straightened his collar and smoothed out the lapel on his jacket. "Better. But you should run a comb through your hair once we get upstairs." She turned to us. "Say, why don't you join us in the Sky Star Ballroom this evening, Mr. Barrington, Mr. Keyes? Unless, that is, you have other plans. I'd love to have such handsome men to dance with."

"Well, we don't wish to intrude, Mrs. Verte," I said.

"Oh, George doesn't mind, do you, George? He would be happy to be able to sit out a few, I'm sure."

Mr. Bennett nodded. "It's true, I'm sure Vivian is more of a dancer than I am."

"Well, all right then. Okay with you, Alan?"

"Sure, it's fine," he said, but I couldn't really tell if he meant it or not.

"Splendid. This will be fun."

"Well, go put some of that perfume on, then, and let's get this evening started," Mr. Bennett said.

"I won't be but a moment. I've been dancing in my room, practicing my rhumba to the radio while I waited for you." She did a little rhumba step in the hall—"bump, bump, bump, bump, bump, BUMP."

"Good heavens," he said.

"Yes, indeed, and with such handsome dance partners, I intend to dance all night."

"Just don't ask me to rhumba," Alan said, feeling the strain of his pants, I was sure.

"Oh, I just might, Mr. Keyes. I just might." Her eyes sparkled.

"The band starts at eight, so we should hurry if we want to get a table by the window," Mr. Bennett said.

"I'll be right back." She hurried back down the hall and disappeared into her room.

Mr. Bennett shook his head again. "Women. Honestly, gentlemen, there's no need for you to wait here with me. Why don't you go on up?"

"We don't mind, Mr. Bennett."

"I get the impression that with a woman like her, the minutes could be more like hours." he said.

Alan and I laughed. "It's okay. We'll keep you company."

But it truly was only about three or four minutes before Mrs. Verte emerged once more, looking calmer and more refreshed and smelling softly of lilacs. The loose strand of hair had been recurled and plastered back in place.

"All right, gentlemen, I'm ready." She had switched to a smaller evening bag. "I thought George was going to bring me the perfume upstairs, so I was going to take my larger bag, but I don't need it now, do I?"

"No, ma'am. And you smell lovely, Mrs. Verte," Alan said.

"Thank you, Mr. Keyes."

Mr. Bennett stared. "Lovely isn't the word for it. I think I would have walked another fifty blocks to find that perfume."

Mrs. Verte giggled and smiled. "Oh, George."

I pushed the button for the elevator again.

The four of us stepped in, Mrs. Verte taking Mr. Bennett's arm, and I pressed the button for the Sky Star Ballroom. It was nonstop all the way up, and soon we stepped out into the vestibule of the ballroom, a small corridor with restrooms on either end. Through two open double doors, we glanced the famous ballroom of the Edmonton Hotel, the tables glowing with white linens and candles, everything sparkling and shimmering, the walls glittering behind gold sconces.

"Good evening, Mr. Bennett," the maître d' said as we approached. "How nice to see you here. You don't visit us often in the evening."

"I'm stepping out with this lovely lady and these two gentlemen from Milwaukee. We'd like a table for four by a window, please, Oscar," Mr. Bennett said.

The maître d' glanced at the tables behind him. "I am afraid, Mr. Bennett, our window seats are all reserved this evening."

Mr. Bennett sighed, took out his wallet, and handed him five dollars. "Yes, I have a reservation."

"Right this way, Mr. Bennett, of course," he said, seating us at a very nice table along a window.

The maître d' held Mrs. Verte's chair for her and handed us all programs for the evening, listing the various songs and numbers that would be played.

Alan gawked about the room, looking out the window. "Golly, Heath, look how high up we are. Look how pretty everything is down there."

I peered out the window but could only see dim lights below through the mist and fog. "Alan, you can barely see anything tonight."

"I know, but it's very pretty anyway."

I smiled. "Yes, everything is very pretty indeed. Some might say handsome."

He flushed but smiled back. "This whole place is pretty. The tablecloths, the candles, the windows, golly. And look at the ceiling, just like stars in the sky."

I looked up at the barrel-vaulted ceiling painted in midnight blue, with hundreds of twinkling lights set in it. "Hence the name the Sky Star Ballroom, I imagine."

"It's all so magical. Say, my horoscope said magic would play a part in my emotions this weekend, and it has."

I looked into his deep blue puppy-dog eyes, so big and wondrous, like a child's at Christmas, and I wanted to kiss him. "You're right, Alan. It is magical, just like your horoscope said."

Alan nodded again as he craned his neck this way and that. "And look at the people, all dressed up. I guess you were right about the tuxedo."

I glanced about the room myself, noting the many ladies in their gowns, gloves, and jewels of many colors, and the gentlemen in their black tuxedos and ties, all so handsome. "Yes, a tuxedo, as I said, is *de rigueur* in Chicago."

"And in New York, Mr. Barrington," Mrs. Verte added.

"Quite so, I'm sure. You really are looking quite radiant this evening, Mrs. Verte. That dress suits you well."

"Why thank you, Mr. Barrington. I wanted something easy to move in, as I said. Nothing tight fitting tonight."

"Unlike my pants," Alan said, shifting uncomfortably as we all laughed.

"I hope they won't impede your dancing, Mr. Keyes. I intend to get you and Mr. Barrington out onto the dance floor a great deal," Mrs. Verte said.

"It sounds like you will have us all worn out before the night is through," Alan said.

"That's my intention. It's not often I have so many eligible partners. I'm so glad you could join us."

"It's our pleasure, truly. Thank you for having us. I just hope we're not intruding," I said.

"Not at all, Mr. Barrington," Mr. Bennett said. "Vivian and I are just getting to know each other, but there's no reason we can't do that in your company as well."

"That's nice of you, but I'm sure you're just being polite. Alan and I will stay for a bit, but the night is young and we have many other nightclubs to hit."

Mr. Bennett laughed. "Ah, very well. But for now let's all enjoy ourselves together."

A waiter appeared and took our drink order, only to reappear a short time later with his tray.

When the waiter had gone again, Alan raised his glass. "To my first Chicago nightclub."

"Hear, hear," we all replied.

We drank our toast with good cheer all around. The night was festive, the atmosphere light and gay.

"George, you still haven't combed your hair," Vivian said.

He looked slightly embarrassed. "Oh, yes, I completely forgot."

"And what time is it? Shouldn't the band have started by now?" Mrs. Verte asked.

Mr. Bennett glanced at his watch. "It's 7:55, and they're supposed to start at eight. I guess I have time to freshen up now, if you will all excuse me."

"Go ahead, George, your hair is sticking up in places it shouldn't be." She laughed.

He grinned. "No wonder, running around all over Chicago in this wind. I'll be right back."

At six after eight, Mr. Bennett returned, looking more put together and relaxed. As he took his seat he remarked, "I'm not hearing any music."

All eyes turned toward the bandstand, where the bandleader and several musicians had gathered. Gloria Eye and Walter Gillingham were not in view. "Probably some delay or other," Mr. Bennett said.

We visited some more, Alan recounting with some relish his first two days in Chicago, and what we had planned for Sunday, our last full day. Mr. Bennett and Mrs. Verte, I noticed, listened politely.

"I could use another drink, George," she said, when Alan had taken a break between stories.

"Who am I to argue with that?" He finished his off and signaled for the waiter.

"How about you boys?"

"Thanks, Mr. Bennett, I'm still good," I said.

"Me too," Alan said. "I'm usually more of a beer drinker. I have to take it slow with these martinis."

"Suit yourselves." The waiter appeared again and Mr. Bennett ordered two more martinis before glancing at his watch once more. "This is getting to be a bit much. They're nearly twenty minutes late."

I glanced toward the bandstand again. "Looks like it shouldn't be too much longer, Mr. Gillingham and Miss Eye just arrived. He's looking rather disheveled and winded, too, must be the theme tonight."

"Where have they been, and who are they?" Mrs. Verte asked.

"Walter Gillingham is the lead trumpet player and Miss Eye is the vocalist. I guess they couldn't start without them. She seems rather out of sorts, as well. I wonder what happened," I said.

The bandleader took to the stage, above which hung a banner that read *John Storm and the Storm Clouds, starring Miss Gloria Eye, the Eye of the Storm, with Maynard Henning on the piano.* "Ladies and gentlemen, our apologies for the brief delay in this evening's festivities, but we promise to make it up to you. I'm John Storm, bandleader for the Storm Clouds. We're going to kick things off this evening with the Lindy Hop and the song 'Goody Goody,' vocalized by our own Eye of the Storm, Miss Gloria Eye."

The ballroom applauded politely as Miss Eye took the stage and stepped up to the microphone, looking stunning in the long, sleeveless, low-cut champagne-colored gown she'd picked up at Blount's earlier. A large emerald glittered around her neck. Even from a distance I could tell she had hurried to get onstage. Her makeup was off a bit, and her hair was tousled, but still attractive. She smoothed it into place behind a pearl comb as she began to sing and swing.

In an instant Mrs. Verte was on her feet. "George, let's dance."

"To the Lindy Hop? Gee, Vivian, I think that would give me a heart attack. Perhaps one of these young pups is up to it."

She laughed. "Very well, but you can't sit them all out. Gentlemen?" she said, turning toward Alan and me.

I looked at Alan, and he looked at me before getting resignedly to his feet. "Sure thing, Mrs. V, but I'm not very good at it."

Mr. Bennett and I watched from the sidelines with a mixture of admiration and humor as Alan turned and twirled her every which way. When at last the song ended, they both returned to the table breathless but smiling.

"Oh my, Mr. Keyes, you are too humble. You're a very good dancer."

"Why thank you, Mrs. V, but you make me look good. And my pants, I believe, are still in one piece."

We all laughed as they took their seats once more and Mr. Bennett ordered a bottle of champagne, 1936. "We're celebrating tonight, aren't we?" he said.

Mrs. Verte looked at him. "We certainly *are* celebrating, George. Let's all drink up, for the night is young and so are we, relatively speaking."

"What are we celebrating?" Alan asked.

Mr. Bennett smiled. "New friends, new beginnings."

Mrs. Verte laughed. "I'll drink to that, as well as Mr. Keyes's first visit to Chicago, and his first nightclub."

"Um, right. To new friends and new beginnings," Alan said.

"Yes, new friends, and a night of firsts," I added.

We raised our glasses and finished our drinks as the band played a foxtrot. When the waiter had returned and poured the champagne, we toasted once more, and this time I did the honors.

"To our charming hosts, the lovely Mrs. Verte, and the engaging and dapper Mr. Bennett."

We all raised our glasses. "Thank you for that, Mr. Barrington," Mr. Bennett said.

"Oh, George. They're playing a lovely waltz, 'The Blue Danube.' Dance with me. I know you can waltz, it's just one-two-three, one-two-three."

Mr. Bennett downed his champagne and set his glass on the table. "A waltz I can definitely handle, and with you I'll be floating." He stood up and escorted her to the dance floor. While they were gliding about the floor, I looked across at Alan and smiled.

"Having a good time?"

"Well, sure, Heath. It's swell."

"But?"

He leaned in across the table. "I wish I could dance with you."

"Me too, I really do. We will when we get back to the room tonight, okay?"

"Deal, Detective." Then he glanced toward the bandstand once more. "Gee, that Miss Eye is really something, isn't she?"

She was indeed a vision with a lovely voice. "Yes, she is. I suspect she may be going places."

"She should be in Hollywood."

"She just may end up there. We'll have to wait and see."

The waltz ended and Mr. Bennett and Mrs. Verte returned to the table, but then Mrs. Verte led me to the floor for a two-step. When that was over, we finally convinced her to sit one out, and we drank more champagne. I was beginning to feel slightly giddy. The band was playing "Victory Polka," a holdover from the war.

"What are your plans for tomorrow, Mr. Bennett, Mrs. Verte?" I asked in between sips.

"A little sightseeing and some more shopping for me, I'm sure, and lunch with my uncle," Mrs. Verte said.

"Tomorrow is supposed to be my day off, but I have a staff meeting tomorrow morning and then a few hours free in the afternoon before I have to work on scheduling. Perhaps during my free period I could escort you, Vivian."

"That would be lovely, George. I want to see Lake Michigan. I'm going to walk down to the pier in the morning after breakfast."

"Haven't you seen that old lake before, Vivian? You grew up here."

"Actually, Lake Michigan is more of an inland sea, Mr. Bennett. It's quite large," I said.

"There, you see, George? Old lake, indeed. I love Lake Michigan. The smell of it always takes me back to my childhood."

"The weather is supposed to be better tomorrow," Alan said.

"I certainly hope so. These last few days haven't been the nicest, and tomorrow is Father's Day," Mr. Bennett said.

I slapped my forehead. "Father's Day. Alan, I forgot the tie."

"What tie?"

"The one I bought for my dad."

"Golly, you're right, Heath. Blount never gave it to us. It wasn't in the bag with everything else."

I looked at Mr. Bennett and Mrs. Verte. "I bought a tie yesterday from Blount's—totally forgot to pick it up this afternoon when we got my other items. I can't believe he didn't give it to us, and he's closed tomorrow."

"And Monday," Mr. Bennett reminded us.

I pulled my wallet out and glanced at the receipt Blount had written out. "He charged me for it, too, but he never put it in the bag."

"I'm sure it wasn't deliberate, Mr. Barrington," Mrs. Verte said.

"I'm sure it was," Mr. Bennett said.

"Regardless, I wonder if he's still there," I said.

George glanced at his watch. "It's quarter after nine already. He closed shop at seven, so I'm sure he's gone home."

"Damn it." I glanced at Mrs. Verte. "My apologies, madam."

"Certainly."

I set my glass down. "Alan, I'm going to run down to his shop and just see if he happens to still be around. I remember him saying it would be a late night for him. Anyway, it won't hurt to check."

"Oh, really, Mr. Barrington, why interrupt a lovely evening just to go in search of a tie?" Mrs. Verte stated.

"It was a gift for my dad for Father's Day, as I said. I planned to give it to him Monday night when we get back, and I can't show up empty-handed."

"I could give you one of my ties, Mr. Barrington. I have a couple new ones I haven't worn yet. I would hate to see you in the doghouse with your dad," Mr. Bennett said.

"That's incredibly generous of you, Mr. Bennett, and I may take you up on it, but let me just check on Blount first. If he's not around, I can go to plan B."

"Have it your way, then. We're going to have another round of cocktails. The champagne's just about gone." Mr. Bennett signaled for the waiter.

"Want me to come with you, Heath?"

"No, thanks. I shouldn't be more than a few minutes. Besides, I think Mrs. Verte wants to do the Balboa." I winked at him.

"Oh, Mr. Barrington, I don't think I'm even up for that," she said.

"Well, they'll play a waltz again soon. Perhaps Alan and I can find partners and we can all dance."

"That would be nice," Alan said, looking at me with those puppy-dog eyes.

"I'll hurry back."

CHAPTER NINE

I tried Blount's door, even though the lights were off. It was, as I expected, locked. I did notice a light coming from under the curtain to the back room, though, so I rapped on the glass door and waited. Nothing. I rapped again, louder this time, attracting the attention of a young couple strolling by who gave me a curious look.

After a few minutes, I turned toward the lobby, almost running into Mrs. Gittings again, still in the same dark green dress, green velvet hat, and soiled gloves she had on yesterday.

"I beg your pardon, Mrs. Gittings. We really must stop meeting like this." I smiled at her, but her stare was cold and blank.

Finally the cloud lifted and she shook her head. "You're Mr. Barrington, from Milwaukee, bruck, bruck. I remember you now."

"Yes, that's right. You're out late, Mrs. Gittings, it's after nine."

"I was, bruck bruck, here. Had something to do." She clutched her pocketbook defensively, as if I might try and snatch it away.

"Is everything all right? Is there something I may be able to help you with?"

"Bruck, my hatpin, missing. My husband gave it to me. I left it somewhere."

"And you came back to look for it?"

"Bruck bruck."

"Well, if I see it I'll be sure and let you know. Have you asked at the desk?"

Her eyes were glazed as she stared at me. "Had something to do here, Mr. Barrington."

"Yes, you told me. I hope you find it."

"Evil must be destroyed—it's God's will."

"Uh, certainly," I said, puzzled. "Anyway, I'm looking for something, too—a package I left in Mr. Blount's shop. Have you seen him?"

"Evil. Eeevil, bruck, bruck."

A strong smell of alcohol emanated from her breath.

"Yes, so you've mentioned."

"Bruck, bruck. Blood on the hands. Blood stains. Stains the soul. I saw him."

I looked at her, somewhat alarmed now, and tried to determine if she was merely rambling or if there was really something to be concerned about. Blount *had* told us that she had threatened him.

"Who did you see? Mr. Blount? He had blood on him?"

"Bruck, bruck—up." She pointed a bony finger toward the elevators. "An angel, all in white—in God's hands now. God will judge thy actions."

"I don't think the elevators go all the way to heaven, Mrs. Gittings."

"God knows, Mr. Barrington, bruck bruck. Only God can wash away the blood."

"Ah yes, I suppose so. That and a good detergent."

She shook her head again and looked me up and down. "All dressed up, looking fancy."

"Yes, my friend and I are having cocktails upstairs in the Sky Star Ballroom."

"Bruck, bruck, Sky Star Ballroom. I remember that place."

"You're welcome to join us, of course."

She stared at me again, making me a bit uncomfortable. "I must get home. Stanley will be waiting, bruck, bruck, bruck."

"Your husband?"

"You know him?" she asked, cocking her head. Her hat slipped down a bit over her left eye.

"Ah no, but you mentioned him at lunch."

"Stanley. Poor Stanley. Bruck, bruck, must be going," she said, pushing her hat back into place.

"Right. Well, nice running into you, so to speak, Mrs. Gittings. Be careful going home. It's very late."

But before I even finished speaking she had tottered off, still clucking softly to herself and clutching her handbag to her chest.

I sighed and shook my head, then I headed in the opposite direction, toward the lobby and out the front doors onto the street.

"Cab, sir?" The doorman looked at me inquiringly.

"No thank you, just getting some air," I replied, not sure of what else to say. Michigan Avenue was still bustling with people hurrying here and there, carrying packages, waiting on busses and cabs, and milling about. The temperature had dropped about ten degrees, and the wind had picked up. I went around the corner and down Superior Street to the alley where I felt certain I would find the back door of Blount's shop.

The alley was dark, murky, and poorly lit, as alleys generally are. I got a momentary chill as I stared into the darkness and the shadows, wondering if I should proceed. But I shook off my fears and took a few steps in, glancing about, my senses on high alert. There was a loading dock just off the street, and a landing with a door on it marked *Stairs* in white paint, but no one was about. The wind rushed down the alley, blowing abandoned newspapers and other bits of assorted trash around as I moved slowly along, holding my tuxedo jacket closed against my chest.

A large rat passed in front of me, and I jumped as I watched it scurry behind a trash can on the opposite wall, probably more afraid of me than I was of it, but not by much. I wondered where all the alley cats were when you needed one. About a third of the way down from Superior, roughly where the back of Blount's shop would be, I noticed a sliver of light coming from a door standing slightly ajar. A small industrial light fixture shined above it. Curious.

My mind and body went into police mode as I remembered Mrs. Gittings's words of death and blood, and I drew my gun, glad I had brought it. Perhaps I was being overly cautious, but my training had taught me to always be prepared. I approached as quietly as I could in my dress shoes, trying to avoid the many puddles of black water I came across. I hoped there were no more rats about.

I braced myself flat against the brick wall of the hotel where I could peer in the open door unobtrusively. I saw nothing unusual at first, just his back room, lights blazing. No one was around, or at least I didn't hear any sounds from within. All I could hear was the continuous wind whistling through the alley. I pushed cautiously on the door, which swung open with an audible creak. I flattened myself on the outside wall once more, but no one and nothing came forth, so I swung into the doorway in a crouching position, my gun in both hands in front of me.

I saw Blount lying on the floor to the right of the door, amidst a large pile of thread spools from the overturned rack. He was partly on his left side, his eyes open. His white dress shirt and tie were soaked with blood, and a single line of red came from his nose. A shudder went down my spine as I got to my feet and scanned the back room to make sure no one else was about. Then I knelt beside him to check his pulse, but no luck. He was dead, all right, his skin cold.

With my gun still drawn, I got to my feet and checked the dressing room and small bathroom, the only places anyone could hide, but there was no one. I found the charred remains of something that had been burned in the bathroom sink, but nothing else. I went to the phone on Blount's desk and dialed, using my handkerchief lest I disturb any fingerprints. I kept my eye on the curtain to the front of the shop as I waited, watching for any sign of movement.

"Operator," a young female voice said.

"Get me the police, quick."

"One moment."

There was a click and a buzz, and then a man's voice. "Twelfth precinct, Sergeant Zutell."

"This is Detective Barrington of the Milwaukee police, I'm on vacation here in Chicago. There's been a murder at Blount's clothing store in the Edmonton Hotel, back room, off the alley. I just found the body, it's Mr. Blount."

"Roger that, don't touch anything. I'll get a squad over pronto."

"Right." I hung up and dialed the hotel operator.

"Operator."

"This is Detective Barrington. Find Mike Masterson and send him to the back door of Blount's right away, off the alley, it's urgent."

"I'm not sure where Mr. Masterson is at the moment, sir."

"Well, find him. This is important police business, understand?"

"Yes, sir. I'll see what I can do."

"Good. Also, send a message to Alan Keyes in the Sky Star Ballroom, with Mr. Bennett's party. Tell him he's needed by me at the back door of Blount's also. Got it?"

"Yes, sir. I'll have the front desk send a boy right away."

"Hurry." I hung up once more. My gun still drawn, I moved quietly toward the curtain separating the front of the store from the back room. There was a row of light switches on the wall, and I hit them all in succession, watching through the curtain as the front of the store lit up bank by bank. Nothing moved. I entered cautiously through the curtain, sweeping side to side, noting no one behind the counter. From there, I moved to the racks of clothes and displays, but after a few minutes, I concluded the shop was empty. The killer must have exited out the alley door.

I returned to the back room, wondering where in the hell Masterson and Alan were as I holstered my gun. I walked over to the desk once more. I knew I shouldn't, but I pulled open the drawers. I didn't find the gun he'd talked about, but in the top right drawer there was a box of bullets, and a space where it most likely had been. I closed the drawer again and looked about the back room once more while I waited impatiently.

He must have overturned the rack of thread spools when he fell after being shot. Besides that, nothing else seemed to have been disturbed. Not much of a struggle, apparently. The safe under the work table was open, but I couldn't tell by looking if anything was missing.

Blount looked ghastly white. The blood from his nose had run into his thin mustache, turning it an odd color. He was grasping a spool of green thread from the rack in his right hand, a needle thrust into the top of the spool. Interesting. Was he holding it when he was shot, or did he grab it after he had fallen? And if so, why? I could read the name of the thread on the top of the spool: Jewel Green. I wondered if he was trying to send a message, but if he was, I didn't know how to read it. Just above the pool of blood, he had scrawled a capital "W" on the floor with his own blood. Another message, but I had no idea what it meant, either.

I heard a sound from the alley then, and I rose and spun on my heel, reaching for my gun once more. I was relieved to see Mike Masterson's face in the doorway, with Alan right behind him.

"Heath, what the hell?" Mike said.

"Blount's been murdered, looks like a gunshot." I put my gun away again.

"Did you call the police?"

"Yes, I called them first, then you two."

"Thanks," Mike said, "but Blount's store is a leased space in the hotel. Not my jurisdiction."

"I know, but I thought you'd want to know."

"Robbery, probably," Alan said. "Are you okay, Heath?"

"Yeah, I'm fine. Perhaps it was a robbery." We all looked toward the safe under the work table then, which as I noted earlier was standing open.

"Any sign of forced entry?" Mike asked.

"No, the door was ajar when I got here. I came by to see if he was still around, as I forgot to pick up a tie I had purchased earlier."

"Did you touch anything?"

"Come on, Mike, you know me better than that."

"Sorry, force of habit." He cocked his head, listening. "Sounds like the cops are on their way. That siren is getting closer."

We all listened until the sound was in the alley right outside and we could see the red light flashing through the still open doorway. Then the siren stopped abruptly and the slamming of car doors echoed off the building walls. Our eyes were on the door as two uniformed policemen entered with their guns drawn. The three of us instinctively put our hands up. Behind the police a sour-looking older man in a dark suit and fedora came in, followed by a tall, pale, younger fellow in a gray hat and suit. The first man glanced at the three of us, then at Blount, then back to us.

"Mike Masterson, what the hell are you doing here? And what the hell happened?"

I could tell Mike was relieved. "Glad to see you, Marty. Would you tell your boys to put their guns away?"

The man in the suit snapped at the cops. "It's all right, boys, holster 'em. So what happened?" he asked again. "And who are these two?" He motioned with his large chin toward us.

"I can vouch for them. This is Detective Barrington from Milwaukee, and a colleague of his, Officer Keyes, also of Milwaukee. Heath's the one that found the body and called you."

The man's eyebrows went up in an arch. "Heath Barrington?"

I looked at him, surprised. "Yes, that's right, do I know you?"

He shook his head. "No, but I've heard of you, your name's been in the *Tribune* lately, and my chief has mentioned you. Apparently you're quite a crack detective."

"Thanks. I've had some good breaks, and Mr. Keyes has been an enormous help with every case so far."

"Uh-huh, I see. Well, this is the big city. Things work differently here. Our cases are more brutal, more complex than you all get up north."

I bristled a bit but didn't argue. "I'm sure they are, sir." I felt Alan looking at me, but I kept my eyes on Marty.

"Anyone check the front of the store to see if anybody's hiding in there?" Marty asked.

Mike glanced toward the curtain. "I'm not sure, Marty. We came in the alley door."

"I checked it out. I'm the one who turned on the lights up front. It was all dark. I didn't find anyone. I also checked the dressing room and bathroom back here."

"You shouldn't be nosing about like that, Barrington. This isn't your city, not your jurisdiction. You could get yourself killed. The criminals in Chicago are a little tougher than in Milwaukee."

I bristled again but said nothing.

"Let's have a look for ourselves. You might have missed something," Marty said, drawing his gun. He motioned for the two uniformed officers to follow him. "DeCook, check the bathroom and dressing room again, too." After he and the two in blue had gone up front, Alan turned to me.

"Geez, Heath. He's acting like you're a child."

"It's fine, Alan, and he's right. This isn't our city, not our jurisdiction."

"Yeah, but still…"

I shrugged, knowing DeCook could probably hear us.

Shortly the detective and the two police officers returned. "Nothin' out there. Anything back here, DeCook?"

"Somebody set fire to something in the bathroom sink, but otherwise no," the tall redhead replied.

Marty scratched his chin. "Somebody burned something, eh? Interesting. Investigate that, DeCook. But no sign of anyone hiding back here?"

"No, sir."

"No one out there, either, like I said, and the front of the shop is locked tight. The killer must have gone out the alley door," the detective said.

"I know," I said. I couldn't help myself.

It was Marty's turn to bristle as he turned toward me. "And you two are here why and how?"

I gave him the details as best I could, but his eyes were not on me as I spoke. He looked about the room furiously, taking in every detail.

"Uh-huh. So, he was dead when you got here."

I nodded. "That's right. I checked for vital signs, then called the police."

"Anyone ID him positively?"

"I did. It's Victor Blount, the owner of this store," I said. "Mr. Keyes and I met him yesterday right here in his shop."

Marty pushed his hat back on his head, exposing a pale, wrinkled brow and a jagged scar above his right eye. "Jesus, Mike. How did you get involved in this?"

Mike shrugged. "Heath's a friend of mine, old school chum. When he found Blount's body, he figured he should call me since I'm the hotel dick."

"Not your jurisdiction in the leased shops, Masterson."

"I know that, but Heath didn't."

"I did know it, but I didn't stop to think. I'm sorry I called you, Mike." I shouldn't have involved him.

Mike looked at me and then back at Marty. "It's okay, Heath. Marty and I go back a long way, too, don't we, Marty?"

Marty grumbled. "Yeah, we've known each other a long time. I guess a friend of Mike's is a friend of mine, and fellow cops, even if you are from up north."

"Nice to meet you," I replied, then regretted it, realizing it sounded pretty stupid considering the circumstances. "I uh, didn't catch your full name."

He glanced at me sideways. "Detective Martin Wilchinski, homicide, eighteen-year veteran on the streets of Chicago. I've seen it all." He looked grizzled, hardened. Eighteen years in this business would do that, I suppose. I wondered if that would happen to me. He turned to the other man in the gray hat and snapped sharply, "DeCook, I want this place dusted for fingerprints, every inch. I want to know who's been in this place recently. Get the boys from the lab down here pronto and call the coroner."

"Yes, sir." DeCook left to radio for the lab crew, then returned. I was thankful I had used my handkerchief to dial the phone and open the desk drawer earlier.

Wilchinski continued barking orders. "Ask the doorman if he noticed anything, check with folks on the street, find out who was the last to see him alive. Find out if he had any enemies. You know the routine, DeCook. I suspect it's a robbery gone bad, but we have to go through the motions nonetheless."

"Yes, sir."

"From what I've heard, Mr. Blount wasn't well liked by several people," I said.

"I'll want your statement in writing," Marty said, still staring at me sideways. Then he turned to Mike again. "Jesus Christ. Another twenty minutes, and I would have been off duty, Masterson."

Mike shrugged. "Sorry, Marty."

The detective sighed. "It's all right. Death never did punch a clock, I guess." Then he took out a cigarette, lit it, and blew out a cloud of smoke, his face relaxing a bit. He turned to the two uniformed police officers still standing by. "You two, Baril and…"

"McNulty, sir," the brunette said.

"Right. Cordon off the alley. I want no one in and no one out without my authorization, especially the press. Where the hell is the coroner?"

I wondered to myself what exactly Wilchinski was going to do himself, but then everyone had their own way of doing things, I supposed. It was fascinating to observe someone else in action as I stood on the sidelines. Wilchinski kneeled down by Blount's body and examined the chest wound, then the spool of thread still grasped tightly in the dead man's hand.

"Looks like he wrote this 'W' on the floor with his blood before he died. Find out if he knew anyone that had the initial 'W,' DeCook. Specifically, anyone who was in here tonight."

"Yes, sir." DeCook vanished into the night again to start on his long list of orders, while Wilchinski got to his feet and made some notes in his notebook. He returned it to his breast pocket before kneeling again and moving Blount's left hand.

"The watch is smashed, probably when he hit the concrete floor. Looks like the hands are stopped at two minutes after eight. Make a note of that, Barrington," he said to me, since DeCook had already left.

"Ah, right. Alan, you have your notebook?" I said, glancing over at him.

"No, I left it in the room."

"Never mind, I'll do it myself," Marty grumbled as he took out his notebook again and made his notation, his cigarette dangling from his lips. "Probable time of death, 8:02 p.m."

"Expensive-looking watch," he added.

"Blount told me it was a Longines."

"Did he now?" Wilchinski looked up at me.

"We were just making conversation yesterday while we were shopping."

"Did he say anything else?"

"Not that I can recall, nothing of importance. Can you think of anything, Alan?"

"Nope. Just shop talk, small talk, that's all."

"Right. Well, I'm finished with you three for now. I'll want written statements, of course. DeCook can take them, then you're free to go. But be sure we know where to find you."

"Sure thing, Detective. Alan and I are staying here at the hotel until Monday morning, room 804."

Marty made a note of that. "What brought you to the big city, Barrington?"

"Just an outing, a weekend away, see the sights. You know how it is."

"Uh-huh. Seeing the sights, just the two of you. Not married?"

"No, we're both single, so far anyway."

"Uh-huh. Maybe you came down to find a couple of pretty girls."

"Chicago's full of them, I hear," I said.

"Full enough, and not enough fellows to go around since the war. Of course, I'm married. Nine years now, two kids."

"Congratulations," I said.

"Uh-huh. Well, Detective, enjoy the city but don't leave without checking in with me. And if you think of anything you forgot to tell me, don't hesitate to call. Here's my card." He handed me a business card, which I put in my wallet next to the one Blount had given me yesterday.

"Thanks. I'll keep you informed if I turn anything up."

"Don't go turning anything up, Barrington, not in my city, not on my beat. Just keep me posted if you remember something you hadn't before, got it?"

"Got it."

"Good. Make your statements to DeCook, he's probably out on the sidewalk, then get the hell out of here."

The three of us left him standing over Blount's body, the coroner and lab crew just arriving. We made our way past the police barricade, where curious onlookers and a few reporters, some with cameras, tried to catch our attention.

"Sorry, boys, we have nothing to say. The detective on the case will be out shortly," I said, holding up my hand as a few flashbulbs went off.

We exited the north end of the alley and went around to the front of the hotel, where the doorman gave us a curious look. "Have you seen a tall, redheaded fellow in a gray fedora and dark coat, Henry?" Mike asked.

"Yes, sir, Mr. Masterson. He asked me all kinds of questions, said he was the police. What's going on?"

"Police business. Where is he?"

"He went inside to talk to the bell captain and the desk clerks."

"Right, thanks."

"Everything okay, Mr. Masterson?"

"Blount's been murdered, shot, but keep it to yourself. I don't want the guests to get wind of it just yet," Mike said quietly.

"I understand, sir."

"Good." Mike went into the lobby and we followed, glad to be out of the cold, damp night air.

"Was that wise, Mike, telling him what happened?" I asked.

"Henry's worked here twenty-eight years. He has secrets he'll take to his grave, Heath. He can be trusted."

"Good to know."

"Besides, word will be out soon enough. You can't keep a murder under wraps for long."

"I suppose not," I said. "There's DeCook over there."

We walked up to him as he was furiously scribbling notes into his notebook. He glanced up at us, somewhat surprised, his hat pushed back on his head, revealing a shock of red hair.

"Detective Wilchinski said to give you our statements."

He looked annoyed. "Oh good. One more thing for me to do." He sighed and turned back to the clerk behind the counter. "That's all for now."

"Yes, sir."

Then DeCook turned to us. "All right, one by one. I'll start with you, Mr. Masterson. You two wait over there."

The process was brief, probably briefer than it should have been, but DeCook looked stressed and tired.

When all three of us had given separate statements, Mike said good night. "I still have to finish my shift, boys. You going back to your party?"

I took out my pocket watch. "Coming midnight, I think I'm done in. How about you, Alan?"

"Call me Cinderella."

I laughed. "Careful, I just might."

"I'll send a note up to Mrs. Verte and Mr. Bennett explaining that something came up and we're off to bed," I said to Mike. "See you tomorrow?"

"Yeah, sometime. I'm here until two in the morning, then back at nine, remember."

"Right. Sorry again about dragging you into this."

"S'okay. I needed a little excitement, it's been a long dry spell around here. Nothing but noise complaints and drunks."

I smiled. "Well then, glad I could perk things up for you. Did you know Blount very well?"

"Not very. Like I said yesterday in my office, I said hello to him when I saw him, and I bought a few things in his store, some ties, handkerchiefs, and whatnot. He gave me a nice discount since I work in the hotel."

"Considerate of him," I said.

"Yeah, though I must say he always kind of gave me the creeps."

"Why's that?"

"I don't know. Just something about him, like I said before. I hate to speak ill of the dead but he was an odd duck, the way he'd look at you, talk."

"Did he ever mention some dark, secluded rendezvous? In dark, secluded rooms? Beautiful women, handsome men? Entertainment to be had, discreet, private?" I asked.

Mike looked at me strangely. "Uh, no. I think I'd remember that, why?"

"Just curious. He mentioned it to us when we were in his shop yesterday afternoon. He said he could set us up with an experience we would not forget, for a small fee, of course."

"Interesting. Sounds to me like he was definitely involved in something shady."

I nodded. "Yeah, that occurred to me as well."

"Did you mention any of this in your statement?"

"No, I just remembered it."

"Better let Marty know, could be important."

"Right. I'll call him in the morning," I said.

"Do that."

"I will. Good night, Mike."

"Night, Heath, Alan."

When he walked away, I went over to a desk near the front window and wrote out a quick note on hotel stationery to Mr. Bennett and Mrs. Verte, which I then slipped in an envelope.

"What did you say?" Alan asked.

"Just that something came up and we will explain tomorrow." I flagged down a nearby bellboy. "Take this to the Sky Star Ballroom and give it to Mrs. Verte. They're at a window table, and she's in a white dress with a blue sapphire necklace. Blond, very attractive."

"Yes, sir," he replied, pocketing the dime I gave him.

"Well, this has been an interesting turn of events," I said to Alan.

"My thoughts exactly. Let's get some sleep, eh? I think I'm danced out for tonight."

"Me, too."

Without another word we walked over to the elevators and headed up to our room.

CHAPTER TEN

I woke up slowly, though I hadn't really slept well all night. I opened one eye, then the other, and found I was nose to nose with Alan, who still had his eyes closed. Even asleep, mouth slightly agape, snoring softly, he was so damned attractive. I turned over and looked at the clock on the nightstand, which we had moved off to the side. Alan stirred and yawned as I moved.

"You up?" I asked quietly, looking back at him over my shoulder.

"Ugh, not really. What time is it?" he asked groggily.

"Seven twenty."

"Too early. Wake me at eight."

"Right. I didn't mean to disturb you." I crawled quietly out from under the covers and sank my feet into the lush carpeting. I might have to invest in some of that for the hardwood floors in my apartment. I sat on the edge of the bed for a while wiggling my toes back and forth in the warm softness before finally getting up, stretching, and peeking out the window. The fog had lifted, the skies were clearing, and it looked to be a beautiful day. I rubbed my eyes and scratched myself.

"Heath, what the hell are you doing? It's too early, come back to bed," Alan grumbled from behind me.

"Sorry, I can't sleep. Too much on my mind. Go back to bed, I'll try and be quiet."

"What's the weather like?"

"Clear, sunny, and much improved, it appears." I looked back at him, looking so adorable, stretched out on the bed, his head snuggled into the pillow. "Get some more sleep, I'll wake you at eight."

He sat up, his bare chest glistening with just a touch of sweat. "Too late. I'm awake now." He stifled a yawn.

"I'm sorry, Alan. I didn't sleep much at all last night. The elevator was rumbling more than usual."

He looked at me. "Funny, I didn't notice more noise from the elevator last night than the night before. If you ask me, I'd say you didn't sleep last night because you had something on your mind."

I grinned at him. "Guilty as charged. I *was* thinking about something."

Alan smiled back at me. "And I think I can guess what you were thinking about."

"You, of course." I laughed.

Alan laughed, too. "Nice try. But I know you better than that. You were thinking about Blount's murder, weren't you? You thought about it all night, probably."

I nodded sheepishly. "You know me so well already."

He yawned again and threw back the covers. "You have a one-track mind sometimes, and I know this particular track all too well. I might as well get up, too, since I'm awake. Open the window, it's a bit warm in here."

He stood up and stretched before padding to the bathroom as I pulled the curtains open, flooding the room with morning light, and opened the window. A soft breeze billowed the drapes. Feeling hungry, I walked over to the phone and ordered room service for Sunday's breakfast. Alan reappeared just as I was hanging up.

"Who was that?"

"Room service. I ordered us breakfast."

"Room service? That's expensive. Why don't we just go down to the coffee shop again?"

I shrugged. "I don't feel like getting dressed yet."

"Because you want more time to think about the case." Alan rubbed his eyes and walked over to the window to peer outside.

"Just so many odd things about it, that's all."

He turned back to me. "We're on vacation, remember? Let that Detective Wilchinski fellow handle this one. He doesn't want you butting in anyway."

I rolled my eyes. "I know, but it's curious. No sign of forced entry, nothing obviously missing, the clutched spool of green thread, the 'W' written in blood."

Alan sighed. "Did you order me a glass of orange juice?"

"I did."

"And you know me so well already. We'd better get the room back in order before it arrives."

"Right, that." Once more we pulled the two twin beds apart, moved the nightstand back into position, and tidied up.

Alan glanced around. "I think everything's back to normal. So what do you think it all means?"

"What do I think what all means?"

"The spool of thread, the bloody 'W,' all that."

"Oh, so now you're interested, are you?"

Alan smiled. "Maybe a little. And I know you are, so I am, too."

"Good. And I don't know yet what any of it means. I *have* been thinking about it all night, as you guessed. It seems to me Blount was trying to send a message, possibly a clue, as to who shot him."

"Cryptic."

"Yes. So I think he must have known his killer. If it *was* a random burglary by some unknown burglar, Blount wouldn't have known who it was and wouldn't have left a clue."

"If he *did* leave a clue," Alan chimed in. "Maybe it wasn't a clue at all, Heath. Maybe as he was dying he thought of a lost love, possibly named Wesley or Wilma, and with his last dying breath, he wrote out the initial."

"Romantic," I said sarcastically.

"I'm just saying a guy like Blount would be bound to have regrets as he was dying, maybe about someone he left back in France. It doesn't necessarily have to mean the initial of his killer. It could mean anything, really."

"Good point. Keep thinking, but I'm working on the theory at the moment that the green thread and the 'W' are clues. I don't think Blount would let a random stranger in the back door of his shop, not late at night like that."

"That's true enough. But maybe someone knocked on the door, Blount opened it, perhaps expecting someone he knew, only instead it's a burglar with a gun. He forces his way in, makes Blount open the safe, and then shoots him and flees. As Blount lies dying, he writes the 'W' in blood for his lost love Wesley."

"What happened to Wilma?"

"I think it had to be Wesley. You weren't the one getting felt up by Blount as he fitted my pants."

I laughed. "I noticed he *was* rather attentive."

"Very attentive. So I think the 'W' was for Wesley, or maybe Wolfgang."

"Wolfgang?" I said, arching my brow.

"Hey, it worked for Mozart. Besides, Mr. Blount was a bit on the exotic side."

"I see your imagination is in full swing this morning. What about the green thread?"

"Hmm, that one is trickier. Of course, he might have been holding it when he got shot."

"Not if he had to open the safe."

"True. Maybe the safe was already open when the burglar knocked."

"Perhaps. And maybe he just happened to grab the thread as he fell, no hidden meaning."

"Exactly. Or maybe Wolfgang was a fellow tailor back in France, and green was his favorite color."

I laughed again. "Maybe so. But I'm still going with the theory that Blount knew his killer. After all, he certainly had a lot of enemies. Mr. Bennett, Gloria Eye, Walter Gillingham, and Mrs. Gittings among them."

Alan nodded and stretched again. He could be very distracting. "It's true none of them cared for Mr. Blount, but people just don't go around murdering folks they don't care for. If they did, you'd be a very busy man."

"Point taken," I said, admiring his form in his soft white boxer shorts but still trying to concentrate, "but those four seemed to almost despise him. George Bennett, Gloria Eye, Walter Gillingham, and Mrs. Gittings. Say, did you notice what they all have in common?"

"Besides Blount, you mean?"

"Yes, they all have a 'G' in their name. George Bennett, Gloria Eye, Walter Gillingham, and Mrs. Gittings."

"So what?"

"The spool of green thread. Maybe Blount grasped it while he was dying because it was green, which starts with 'G.'"

"Now you're grasping, Heath. That's a stretch."

"But Wolfgang being a fellow tailor back in France whose favorite color was green isn't?"

Now it was Alan's turn to laugh. "You have me there. But if you're right, who was he trying to point to if *all* the suspects have a 'G' in their name?"

I scratched my unshaven chin. "Hmm. Well, the bloody 'W' could be for Walter? The bloody 'W' for Walter, the green thread, 'G' for Gillingham."

"Walter Gillingham, the trumpet player?"

"Why not? He so much as told us he didn't like Blount and wanted to teach him a lesson."

"Why wouldn't Blount just write out 'WG,' then? Why write just the 'W' and then be all cryptic with the green thread?"

"Good question."

"And all good questions need answers," Alan said.

"Exactly. Maybe he was going to write 'WG' but died after he finished the 'W.'"

"Possible, I suppose."

"Besides, writing in your own blood as you lie dying on the floor must be difficult. I imagine he could only manage an initial or two at best."

"So you think he wrote the 'W' and intended to write the 'G' but couldn't manage it or died before he could?"

I shrugged. "Maybe. Supposedly Blount was murdered at 8:02, which would leave Mr. Bennett out, as we ran into him in the hallway upstairs about 7:40 as we were waiting to go up with Mrs. Verte, and we didn't part again until I came downstairs to look for my dad's tie around 9:00. Which, I just recalled, I still don't have. Remind me to ask Mr. Bennett about buying one of his ties to give to my dad."

"Mr. Bennett said he'd give it to you with his compliments."

"Yes, but I'd feel better paying for it. I'd feel even better if I could somehow get the one from Blount's, since I already paid for that, but I doubt that will happen."

"Not likely."

"Right. So anyway, if Mr. Bennett is in the clear, that leaves Miss Eye, Mr. Gillingham, and Mrs. Gittings, and certainly Miss Eye and Mr. Gillingham could have been in it together. Maybe that's what Blount was getting at. 'W' for Walter, 'G' for Gloria."

"I think you're overthinking this, Heath. It still could have been a random burglar or somebody we don't even know."

I shrugged. "Maybe so. Say, I'd better phone my dad before the day gets away from me. Today is Father's Day."

"Long distance?"

"It's Sunday, so weekend rates apply. I'll bill it to the room."

"Okay, big spender."

I laughed as I picked up the phone on the desk and dialed for the hotel operator.

A moment later a young woman's voice answered. "Operator."

"Yes, I need an outside line, long distance to Milwaukee, Wisconsin, please, Juniper Lake 5-2327. Bill it to room 804, Heath Barrington."

"Yes, sir. One moment, please."

A click and a buzz, then another female voice, this one a bit older. "Long distance."

"Yes, long distance to Milwaukee, Wisconsin, please, Juniper Lake 5-2327."

"Just a moment while I connect you."

Soon I heard it ringing, once, twice, three times, and then my mother's voice.

"Hello?"

"Oh, hi, Mom, it's Heath."

"Heath. What a nice surprise. We're just heading out to church."

"Oh, okay, I won't keep you. I was just calling to wish Dad a Happy Father's Day."

"I'll let you talk to him, but why don't you join us for church? You don't go at all anymore, and it would make us so happy."

"Gee, Mom, that *would* be fun, but I'm in Chicago this weekend, remember? A little getaway?"

"Oh. That's right." She paused. "With that friend of yours."

"Yes, Alan. Alan Keyes. We're having a nice time. It's been, uh, interesting."

"I don't understand why you had to go down there on Father's Day weekend, Heath. You hardly see your father at all anymore. It's like he doesn't even have a son."

I sighed. "I'll be over for dinner tomorrow night, Mom, when I get back into town, remember? We talked about this Thursday night."

"Yes, I remember. Monday is meatloaf night. I'll set an extra place for you. We eat at six, in case you've forgotten."

"I know, so you and Dad can listen to *The Bell Telephone Hour* at seven."

"That's right. I ran into Rosemary Adams the other day at Schuster's. She works in the millinery department there, you know."

"Yes, I ran into her myself a while ago."

"She mentioned that. She's seeing Henry Applegate now, from over on Sixth Street."

"That's nice, Mom. Rosemary's a nice girl."

She made that clicking noise with her teeth again. "She *is* a nice girl, and you're a much better catch than Henry Applegate. She said you never called her."

"I've been busy, Mother."

More of the clicking noise. "Well, Adele Swanson is still available. I'll see her mother at church today, most likely. I'll ask her if Adele can come to dinner tomorrow night."

"Who's Adele Swanson?" I asked, though I knew I shouldn't have.

"Marjorie Swanson's daughter, little Adele, only she's not so little anymore. Her husband was killed in the war, poor thing. Oh, she's a lovely girl, Heath, and she's a Methodist."

"Of course she is."

"Well, it's short notice, but hopefully she can come. Are you going to church today, Heath? They do have churches in Chicago, you know."

"So I've been told."

"People talk when you don't go to church, son."

I sighed. "If I may quote President Truman, Mother, he said, 'I've always believed religion is something to live by and not to talk about.'"

"What's that supposed to mean?" The teeth clicking had gotten louder.

"Nothing to you, apparently. Look, Mom, I'm calling long distance, so if Dad's handy…"

"Long distance, oh my goodness, yes, I suppose you are, all the way from Chicago. Frank. Heath's on the phone, long distance from Chicago, hurry up."

I heard shuffling and scratching noises, then my father picked up the receiver.

"Hello, son."

"Hi, Dad. Happy Father's Day."

"Thanks. How's Chicago?"

"Oh, fine, the weather hasn't been too nice."

"Same here. Better today, though."

"Yes, same here, Dad."

"That's good. Did I hear you're coming for dinner tomorrow?"

"Yes, that's right."

"Fine. Meatloaf, you know."

"Yes, I know."

"Fine. See you tomorrow, then."

"Right, Pop. Good-bye."

"Bye, son."

I hung up the phone and glanced at Alan. "Meatloaf tomorrow."

He laughed. "Meatloaf Monday, could be worse."

I grinned. "Yeah, I suppose so. Mother says they have churches here in Chicago now."

"Do tell?"

"Yes, and she's going to try and fix me up with someone named Adele Swanson tomorrow night."

"Is she a Methodist?"

"It's like you know her."

"I know you, and that's all I need to know."

"Good. Let's forget about my mother. Now, where was I in regard to this whole Blount thing?"

"You were saying Mr. Bennett was in the clear because he was with us at the time of the murder. But don't forget, he did use the bathroom just before eight, and he was gone a fair amount of time."

"Good point. But was it enough time for him to take the elevator downstairs, run around to the alley, shoot Blount, and get back upstairs?"

"It depends, I suppose. I think he was gone about ten minutes."

"Yes. Still it doesn't seem likely, though. He would have been winded and frazzled. But when he returned to the table, he was calm and put together, not a hair out of place. In fact, he was more calm and put together then when we first ran into him getting off the elevator."

"Because he'd been out hunting for purple passion or whatever it was."

"Lavender Lilacs."

"Right."

"But Miss Eye and Mr. Gillingham, both of whom were supposed to be onstage at eight p.m., didn't show up until nearly eight twenty, both looking definitely frazzled. Very curious."

"I agree with you on that, Heath."

"And I think Mrs. Gittings is still a suspect, too. I ran into her downstairs when I went to find Blount last night. She was out very late and acted quite odd."

"Acting odd is normal for her, Heath, I think."

"I know, but she was saying something about blood on the hands. Blood stains the soul, and something about in God's hands now and a white angel. And remember, Blount did tell us she had threatened him. She clearly despised him, she said he was evil. I think she knew more about him than she let on."

"But gee, Heath, she's a character and all, but she looks like such a nice lady."

"Looks can be deceiving, and all kinds of people are capable of doing all kinds of things. I also noticed she clutched her handbag more tightly than normal. As if she had something in it she didn't want me to find out about."

"Like a gun? You think she shot him?"

"Perhaps. Blount's gun is missing, by the way. I checked his desk before the police arrived."

Alan shook his head. "You're going to get in trouble doing stuff like that."

"Don't worry, I didn't leave any fingerprints. But if I recall correctly, when Blount mentioned having a gun in his desk, Mr. Bennett and Mrs. Verte were with us."

"Yes, that's right. It was Friday night when we were having cocktails in the lobby."

"Right. So Mr. Bennett would have known the gun was there, and he bought a suit yesterday afternoon and tried it on. He would have been alone in the back room and could have easily taken the gun."

"Yes, he could have."

"And certainly Mrs. Gittings would have known about the gun, since she had worked for him in that very back room. Remember she was back there alone yesterday, too."

"Talking to the headless dress form," Alan said with a grin.

"Yes. But she also could have easily taken the gun before Blount came back and found her."

"Maybe, but I just can't believe it."

"You're a sucker for the sweet, batty old ladies."

He laughed. "I guess so. She reminds me of my grandmother on my dad's side."

"Did she drink too much?"

"No, but she was an odd old lady. And sweet."

"Sweet old ladies can still be killers. Remember *Arsenic and Old Lace* with Cary Grant?"

He sighed. "I guess you're right. She certainly didn't care for Mr. Blount."

"That's putting it mildly."

"So, she's a suspect."

"Yes, I'm sorry, Alan, but she is. She had motive and opportunity. And then there's Miss Eye and Mr. Gillingham. I wonder if they knew about the gun in the back room, too."

"They both knew about it. I told them at breakfast yesterday morning, remember? We were in the coffee shop, and Mr. Gillingham was talking about teaching Blount a lesson."

I sighed. "That's right, I'd forgotten about that. So everyone knew."

"I'm sorry, Heath."

"It's all right, it was just a comment. Under normal circumstances, no harm would have been done at all, and it still may be nothing."

"But still…"

"Don't give it another thought, Alan, please."

"And Miss Eye was in the back room alone yesterday when we were picking up my tux."

"Yes, and she insisted on trying on the dress, even though it had only been steamed and pressed."

"You think she used that as an excuse to get back there and pocket the gun?"

"Possibly. Perhaps she came in close to closing, hoping to find him alone. She'd slip in the back on the pretense of trying on her gown, find the gun, and shoot him, possibly through the curtain, then flee out the back into the alley."

"Only we were there when she came and fouled up her plan, so she had to come back later. Maybe using the excuse she left something behind in her haste."

"A definite possibility. And Gillingham may have been an accomplice. Maybe she unlocked the back door when she was trying on the gown, and he was waiting in the alley."

"And he slipped in, maybe hiding in the dressing room, until Blount closed up. Then he stepped out, shot him, and fled out the back."

"Yes, except that Blount was shot just after eight. Do you think Gillingham could have hidden back there for an hour?"

"Maybe. Or maybe he confronted Blount and they talked, argued, that sort of thing, Blount hoping to convince Gillingham not to shoot. It all took some time."

"There's the burned ashes in the bathroom, too."

"Right. What do you think that was?"

"Evidence of some kind. Whatever it was, maybe Mr. Gillingham forced Blount to hand it over. Maybe it was in the safe. I suppose that all would take some time. And if Gillingham shot him just after eight, that would explain him and Miss Eye being late to take the stage upstairs."

"That's true."

"And that spool of thread. The name of it was Jewel Green, and Miss Eye was wearing a large emerald that night. And the spool had a needle stuck in it."

"So?"

"So, needles have eyes. Blount could have been pointing the finger to Miss Eye by grasping the thread, and Walter Gillingham with the bloody 'W'. Maybe they were both there."

"Jeepers. So it looks like Miss Eye and Mr. Gillingham are the prime suspects, huh?"

"Suspects, yes, but not exactly prime. This is all very circumstantial. Remember, Mr. Bennett, Miss Eye, and Mrs. Gittings were all at one point in the back room alone yesterday. Any of them could have pocketed Blount's gun with the intention of coming back later."

"True, since they all knew it was there. But the idea of Miss Eye unlocking the back door and letting her fiancé in to hide seems so logical."

"But crime and passion don't always follow logic. We must keep an open mind to all possibilities until they are ruled out."

"Including it being a robbery gone bad, like Detective Wilchinski said?"

I shrugged my shoulders. "Maybe. I can't rule it out yet. But of all the scenarios, of all the suspects, that one to me seems the least likely."

"How come?"

"Maybe because it's the most obvious, the easiest, but why the green thread? Why the 'W' in blood? Why wasn't anything missing?"

"Nothing we *noticed* was missing. He might have had cash the robber took. And possibly the robber got scared and fled before taking anything."

"But there was no forced entry. As I said before, why would Blount let someone he didn't know into the store after hours? And as I recall, there's a peephole in that back alley door. He wouldn't just open it up to some stranger without looking out the peephole first, would he?"

"As you're fond of saying, Heath, all good questions."

"Indeed."

Chapter Eleven

We both jumped at the knock on the door. I threw on my dress shirt, letting it hang open, and padded over to the door in my boxers as Alan fled to the bathroom again, also in his boxers. It was the bell boy with the room service cart.

"Just set it up over there by the window," I said.

"Yes, sir. Good morning. Supposed to be a beautiful day."

"Good morning," I replied. "Yes, supposed to be warmer today."

"I brought your newspaper in too, mister. I'll set it on the desk for you. Anything else I can get ya?" he asked as he walked back to the door.

"No, thanks." I signed for the tray and gave him a quarter.

"Thanks. Did you hear about the murder last night? Right here in the hotel."

"Uh, yes, I did. Mr. Blount of Blount's clothing."

"Yes, sir. Somebody shot him, I hear, five times. Blew his head nearly clean off. There was blood everywhere, I hear."

I shook my head. "Not quite. He was only shot once from what I could see, and it was in the chest. His head was completely intact, and there really wasn't all that much blood."

"You were there?" His eyes widened.

"I found the body. I'm a police detective."

"Wow, a real live dick, just like in the movies."

"Something like that."

"Golly, that sure is something."

"I'm afraid detectives in real life aren't as exciting as in the movies," I said.

"But still, a real live dick, wow. I've never seen one in person. You're the first one I've met."

"I'm honored."

"Say, Mr. Blount was having a terrible argument with a fella in his store yesterday afternoon, you know."

"Oh?"

"Sure, we could practically hear it in the lobby."

I looked at the bellboy, so sharp in his dark green uniform. "So, you were in the lobby near the shop yesterday afternoon?"

"Yes, sir, that's right. I was going to deliver a message to Mr. Blount."

"And you heard Mr. Blount arguing with someone?"

"As soon as I got off the elevator and near the glass door to the shop. They were quite vocal."

"What were they saying?"

The bellboy looked quite excited, and I could tell he relished telling his news to a police detective. "Well, one fella was yelling about not taking it anymore, or something like that, and the other was telling him to shut up. Not that I was listening or anything. As I said, you could hear them from the elevator, practically."

"Interesting. About what time was that?"

"Just before two, I think."

"Okay. So eventually you went in."

"Oh, yes. I had a message for Mr. Blount, like I said. The minute I entered, it got real silent in there. The gentleman at the counter never turned around. Mr. Blount motioned for him to go in back, which seemed odd."

"Do you recall what he looked like? What he was wearing? The man with his back to you, I mean."

"I didn't get a good look at him, it was as if he didn't want me to see him. I supposed he was embarrassed, figuring I'd heard them arguing."

"Naturally. Anything distinctive about him? How was he dressed?"

"Oh, golly, I don't really remember. He was wearing a dark suit, I know that. But I didn't see anything unusual about him."

"Very nondescript."

"Very what?" the bellboy asked, a puzzled look on his young, fresh face.

"Nondescript. It means basic, ordinary."

"Oh. Right. Nondescript he was. Anyway, Mr. Blount asked me what I wanted, snapped at me really. I walked over and gave him his message, and then I left. He didn't even tip me like he usually does."

"Did you hear anything else once you were back in the lobby?"

"No, sir, but I didn't stick around. I had to get back to the desk. You think that guy killed him?"

"I have no idea at this point."

"I bet he did. I bet he came back later and shot him, bang."

I raised my brow. "Perhaps. Do you know what the message was that you delivered?"

The bellboy shook his head. "No, but I know it was from Miss Eye. She's a singer in the Sky Star Ballroom, a real looker."

"Yes, I'm familiar with Miss Eye. Probably the message she mentioned saying she would be late picking up her dress. Anything else?"

"Not that I can think of, but if I remember something else, I'll be sure and let you know."

"Thanks, kid, and thanks for the information. Here's another quarter."

He beamed at me. "Thank you, sir."

He left, and I shut the door behind him, not realizing how hungry I was and how good the food smelled.

Alan came out of the bathroom freshly shaved, and he looked over at the tray on the cart, filled with silver domes covering the plates.

"What all did you order, Heath?"

"Scrambled eggs, toast, two orange juices, black coffee, a whole pot of it, and two bananas."

"How much did that set you back?"

"Two dollars and thirty cents plus tip, but don't worry about it. I can afford it."

"We could have eaten in the coffee shop for half that."

"But I couldn't go to the coffee shop in my boxers, and I would have had to shave first."

"I've already shaved, and you're going to have to do that anyway if we're going to go to the conservatory."

"I know, but I'm feeling lazy this morning. It's Sunday."

Alan poured the coffee and handed me a cup. "It's your money, mister." Alan glanced about the room. "There's only the one desk chair. How are we going to manage this?"

"You take the chair, I'll sit on the edge of the bed."

"Fair enough, since this was your idea," Alan replied, picking up the newspaper from the desk.

He pulled the chair over and sat down as I made myself fairly comfortable on the bed.

"Want part of the newspaper?" Alan said.

"Sure. Give me the front page. You'll want to read your horoscope."

"Ha, very funny. It's horoscope, and you know it."

I smiled and glanced at the headlines, which I read aloud. "'Truman names board to probe air safety.' Hmph. You wouldn't catch me in one of those flying tin cans."

"It's the wave of the future, Heath, don't be left behind."

"Your horoscope tell you that?"

"No, I'm just saying it's a changing world."

I sighed. "Yes, I know. Everyone keeps telling me. That, unfortunately, doesn't change."

"Anything on Blount's murder?"

"Not that I've found so far. Not front-page news in a city this size, I suppose."

"I suppose not."

"The bellboy knew all about it, though. News travels fast."

"Golly, what did he say?"

"He told me Blount was having a heated argument with some fellow in his shop yesterday afternoon. Something about the guy not taking it anymore, and the other, presumably Blount, telling him to shut up."

"Who do you suppose the fellow was?"

"No idea, but it could have been Mr. Bennett or Mr. Gillingham," I replied.

"Wowzer."

"Wowzer, indeed."

"My money's on Gillingham."

"With Miss Eye as his accomplice," I said.

"That's right."

"You may be right, Alan. You may be right."

We ate the rest of the meal in relative silence, each of us reading something of interest to the other from the various parts of the newspaper. It wasn't great food, but it was passable, and it filled us up.

Finally, we put the newspaper aside and drained our coffee cups.

"Say, Heath, I was just thinking about the bloody 'W' some more. Do you think it could be a French word? What's a French word that starts with 'W'?"

I frowned. "There are dozens, probably hundreds."

"Hmm. It was just a thought."

"And a good thought. Not to be discarded just yet. More logical than Wolfgang, I think."

Alan laughed. "Maybe so, but I still think somewhere in Blount's past is a Wolfgang with a broken heart."

"I do like the way you think."

"Thanks. Of course, this is all speculation, right? All this talk about suspects, and who did it? We are still on vacation, right?"

"Of course."

"And it is still that Wilchinski fellow's case, not yours. Not your jurisdiction, remember?"

"I remember. Don't worry."

"So we spend the day at the conservatory as planned, right? Not questioning suspects and chasing down clues?"

"Right."

"Good."

"All done with breakfast?" I asked.

"Just about, yeah. I should shower and get dressed, it's already ten to nine. What time does the conservatory open?"

"I'm not sure. We can ask at the desk when we go down. Go ahead and shower, then, I'll shave."

"Sounds like an excellent use of time, Detective."

We both squeezed into the tiny bathroom, Alan climbing into the shower while I lathered up my face. The room soon filled with steam, and I had to wipe the mirror constantly to see myself. Finally I gave up, wiped off the rest of the soap, and traded places with Alan as he finished. Soon we were both showered, shaved, dressed, and ready to face the day.

I strapped on my shoulder harness once more and put on my suit coat as Alan slung his camera over his shoulder. "All set?" I asked.

"If you're waiting for me, you're wasting your time."

"To the conservatory we go."

CHAPTER TWELVE

I opened the door to our room and almost slipped on a *Chicago Tribune* laid in front of the door.

"That's odd. We already got the newspaper," Alan said as I bent down to pick it up.

"Yes, I know. Even odder, this is yesterday's newspaper."

"Why would they leave yesterday's newspaper at our door?" Alan asked, peering over my shoulder as I perused it, still standing in the hall.

"Hmm, interesting. Let's go back inside for a moment."

"What's interesting?" Alan asked, following me back in and closing the door.

"This newspaper. Someone is trying to tell us something. What do you see?"

Alan looked again at the paper and read aloud off the front page. "'Threatens two Congressmen. Reps. Thomas, Rankin tell of death letter.' That's the headline, anyway. What about it?"

"Not the headline. Someone's folded over the corner at the top. Look at that page," I said, handing the paper to him.

"'Search reveals Britain is low on seismographs.' Somebody circled the word 'search.'"

"So I've noticed."

He turned a few more pages, scanning each section. "Hey, look on page twelve at the ad for ladies' hankies, fifteen cents. The fifteen is circled, followed by the number twenty-seven in the ad for screen wire, twenty-seven cents a square foot at Montgomery Ward.

And in the ad for Douglas, Michigan, weekend getaways, the word 'Michigan' has been circled."

"Search 1527 Michigan," I said.

"I don't get it."

"If I'm not mistaken, that's the street address for Blount's Menswear and Furnishings." I took the newspaper back from him and finished looking it over myself. "Look here, on page fourteen under *Complete Radio Programs and Highlights for Today*, someone circled the word 'Murder' under 8:30: WGN, *Murder at Midnight.*"

"What do you think it means, Heath?"

"It seems pretty obvious to me someone wants us to search Mr. Blount's shop."

"That seems like a pretty complicated way to send a message. Why not just write it on note paper?"

I shrugged. "Somebody being theatrical, perhaps. Someone who's seen too many movies and listened to too many *Murder at Midnight* programs on the radio. Or just someone who doesn't want their handwriting to be recognized."

"Who?"

"I don't know. All of the prime suspects know we're staying here—Bennett, Miss Eye, Gillingham, Mrs. Gittings. Anyone of them could have left it."

"Why leave it here? Why us? Why not contact Detective Wilchinski?"

"My thinking is that it was one of those four who left it. None of them know Detective Wilchinski, but they know us, and they want us to find something out."

"What do they want you to find out?"

"That remains to be seen," I said, "or found."

"I see," Alan said, frowning. "I think you should call Detective Wilchinski and tell him about this. You were going to call him to tell him about Blount's mysterious offer to us the other day anyway, remember?"

"Yes, that's right." I sat back down on the edge of the bed and flipped through the rest of yesterday's newspaper again in case I missed anything.

"We're going to be late for the conservatory, Heath. Give Wilchinski a call and let's get going. This is his business, remember?"

I sighed. "You're right, of course. But still, so very curious. Okay, I'll call him right now and then we can go. I promised you the conservatory, mister, and you shall have it."

Alan smiled. "Thanks. We're on vacation, don't forget. You're not getting paid to solve mysteries."

I smiled back. "Very true, Officer. The only mystery I plan on solving the remainder of this weekend is finding out what you're wearing under that suit."

He laughed. "That, Detective, is no mystery. You watched me get dressed."

"Still, I think it shall require some investigating later."

"You always get your man, Detective."

I smiled. "One way or another. All right, I'll call and then we can be on our way. The sooner we go, the sooner we get back here and I can start my investigation of you."

Alan grinned. "I like the sound of that."

As I sat down at the desk and reached for my wallet with Wilchinski's card in it, a sharp rap came at the door. I glanced over at Keyes, who walked over and opened it. Another smart-looking bellboy in a green uniform was standing there, this one with an envelope on a silver tray.

"Message for Mr. Barrington, sir."

"I can take it," Alan said. He took the envelope off the tray, dug in his trousers pocket, fished out a dime, and handed it to him. This tipping thing was getting expensive for both of us. "Thanks."

"Thank you, sir."

"Where did this come from, by the way?" Alan asked.

"I was told someone brought it in and left it at the desk, sir."

"Know anything about yesterday's newspaper being left at our door this morning?"

He scratched his head. "Yesterday's? Must have been a mistake. I will see to it you get today's."

"No, that's all right, we got today's already, too. Someone left us yesterday's *and* today's."

The bellboy looked puzzled. "Gee, that's strange."

"Yes, it is. Well, thanks again." Alan closed the door and turned back to me.

"A message for me?"

"Yes, addressed to H. Barington, missing an 'r.'"

"Curious."

"Very. Rather shaky handwriting, too," Alan said as he handed it to me.

I slid open the envelope and pulled out a single piece of faded pink stationery, lightly perfumed:

Dear sir, please come see me immediately—
Aimsley Arms, 132 East Erie Street, Apt. 212.
Utmost importance.
Mrs. Gittings

"Mrs. Gittings? Well, I would never have guessed that," Alan said.

"Nor I."

"What do you suppose she wants?"

"I'm not sure, but she was here in the hotel the night of the murder. She may have seen or heard something and might be in danger. She's also still a suspect. I think we have to see her right away."

"As in right now?"

"I'm sorry, Alan. The conservatory will have to wait."

"What about Detective Wilchinski? Aren't you going to call him?"

"I will, but not right now." I slipped Wilchinski's card back in my wallet. "I want to see what Mrs. Gittings has to say first."

"Maybe he could talk to her."

"She trusts us. I don't think she'd talk to Wilchinski."

Alan sighed. "Somehow I almost knew something like this would happen. It's okay. Let's go."

I stood up and put my hand on his shoulder. "Thanks, I'll make it up to you, I promise."

"I understand. At least we're together."

"Always."

He set his camera on the desk as we headed out the door, down the elevator, and out onto Michigan Avenue.

The doorman tipped his hat. "Good morning, may I get you gentlemen a cab?"

"I don't think so. Do you know the Aimsley Arms apartments on Erie Street?"

He furrowed his brow. "I'm not familiar with that building, but Erie Street is just south of here."

"Thanks. Lovely day for a walk, isn't it?"

"Yes, sir." He tipped his hat again and we were off, heading south from the hotel.

It was a short walk to the Aimsley Arms Apartments, and we found it easily enough. It was a narrow, dark brick building just off Michigan Avenue, set back from the street a good distance, with a small courtyard in front. A lanky, older doorman was dozing on a stool just outside, basking in the morning sun as we approached. His legs were sprawled out across the entrance, and we couldn't pass without disturbing him.

I nonchalantly kicked the leg of his stool, causing him to come crashing down, a rude but effective awakening. He jumped to his feet, looking abashed.

"I was just resting a bit."

"So I noticed, Jenkins," I said, reading his name off the gold engraved badge on his uniform. "I'm Heath Barrington, and this is Alan Keyes. Mrs. Gittings is expecting us."

He looked the two of us up and down. "Mrs. Gittings doesn't get many visitors, but she told me to send the two of you up. She's in 212, toward the back."

"Thanks." We stepped inside and climbed the stairs to the second floor, a musty odor hitting our nostrils.

"This place needs some airing out," Keyes said.

"Indeed it does. It must be down this way."

We found it and knocked, but no response.

"Maybe she's gone out," Alan said.

"The doorman didn't mention it, and I don't think Mrs. Gittings could have high-hurdled over him. Besides, he said she was expecting us."

"True."

I checked my pocket watch. "It's twelve after ten, still early." I knocked again, louder this time. A door across the hall opened, and a nice-looking, barrel-chested fellow with a mustache looked us up and down. I turned to him.

"Good afternoon. We're friends of Mrs. Gittings, do you know if she's in?"

"She got home about an hour ago. She was over at the Edmonton again, I believe. I haven't heard her go back out."

I glanced at Keyes, then back at the mustached fellow. "I see. Was she alone?"

"She's always alone, mister. I've never known her to have visitors or friends."

"Well, you know two of them now. I'm Heath Barrington, and this is Alan Keyes. We're friends of hers."

"Oh ya are, are ya?"

"Yes. Are you a friend of hers, too?"

"I'm her neighbor, I live across the hall."

"Good neighbors make good friends, Mr..."

"Laska. I've got to get back to my work. I'm an artist, you know."

"I did not know that. A pleasure meeting you, Mr. Laska."

"Yup. Likewise." He nodded, then closed the door on us.

"Now what, Heath?"

"Jenkins must have a passkey. Go see if he will let us in. Tell him we're worried about her because she doesn't answer the door."

"Right. Back in a minute."

It was more like five or six minutes. As I paced, the door to 214 opened, and an older gentleman stepped out. "Who's there?" he asked.

I stopped abruptly and stared at him, realizing at once that he was blind.

"I'm sorry, I hope I didn't disturb you. I'm Heath Barrington, here to see Mrs. Gittings."

"She lives in 212," he said.

"Yes, I know. She doesn't answer her door."

"She can be a bit hard of hearing. I should know, I live right next door to her. I'm Joe."

"Pleasure to meet you, Joe. Did you hear anything out of the ordinary coming from her apartment this morning?"

He shook his head. "No, actually real quiet in there so far today, not even the radio. I'm from Nashville originally."

"How nice," I said, unsure of what else to say as I glanced down the hall impatiently.

"Where are you from?"

"Milwaukee."

"Ah, a Yankee."

"Yes, I suppose so."

"Want to come in for a cup of tea? I just put the kettle on."

"Thanks, but I'm waiting on my friend and Mr. Jenkins."

"Oh, okay." He looked disappointed, and I got the impression he was a bit lonely. He seemed a kind man.

"Perhaps another time. Here they come now." I saw Alan striding quickly down the hallway with Jenkins's lanky frame in tow, brandishing a key ring.

"Right. Another time, then. Have a good day, Mr. Barrington."

"You too, Joe." He closed the door as I turned toward Alan and Jenkins and walked back to the door of the apartment.

"Thanks for coming up, Mr. Jenkins. We're concerned about Mrs. Gittings. She doesn't answer the door."

"That's what this fellow said," he replied. He rapped on the door with the back end of his flashlight, the noise echoing up and down the hall. Somewhere toward the front of the building, another door opened and a young woman peered out at us, then stepped back into her apartment again and closed the door.

"She doesn't answer, all right," Jenkins said.

"I noticed," I said sarcastically.

He gave me a look, then inserted his passkey. The lock turned easily enough, but the door opened just a couple of inches before stopping abruptly.

"She's got the chain on," he said.

Keyes looked at me. "Then she's definitely in there."

"It would seem so. These apartments only have one entrance, don't they, Jenkins?"

"Yes, that's right, and the fire escape out the window, of course."

"I can't picture Mrs. Gittings climbing down the fire escape," Alan said.

"That would be a sight, all right," Jenkins said.

"Stand back, I'm going to see if I can force the chain," I said.

"Hey there, now, we should call the police before we go doing that," Jenkins said.

"Actually, we *are* police officers." I flashed him my badge, intentionally neglecting to tell him we were Milwaukee Police officers.

"The hell you say."

"The hell I do say. Stand back."

I heaved my body against the door to no avail, except for a sharp pain in my shoulder.

"Son of a bitch. That chain must be anchored in cement," I said, rubbing my shoulder.

"Let me try." Keyes braced himself against the opposite door, then lunged forward, wood from the door frame splintering everywhere as he literally fell into Mrs. Gittings's apartment.

Jenkins and I stepped in after him, and I helped him to his feet. "You okay?"

"Yeah, I'm fine. That's one solid chain. Or was," Alan said, brushing himself off.

"I'll say. Good job. And most of the door is even still intact."

Keyes laughed nervously. "What a way to make an entrance." The three of us then perused the living room and tiny adjoining kitchen, but Mrs. Gittings was nowhere in sight. "She doesn't appear to be here."

"Strange." I walked over to the living room windows that led to the fire escape to see if they were locked. They were. "Doesn't look like anyone would have been in here that wasn't still here, including Mrs. Gittings." I felt instinctively for my gun but left it holstered for the time being.

From behind me I heard Jenkins say, "Maybe she's in the bedroom." He moved surprisingly quickly down a small hall off the entrance. Almost at once, I heard him call out loudly, "Mrs. Gittings. Mrs. Gittings."

A shudder went down my spine, and I knew something was wrong as I hurried toward him, Alan right behind me. We literally ran into Jenkins as he stepped out of the bedroom looking ashen. "She's dead, gentlemen. Poor old soul."

I glanced over his shoulder at the lifeless, tiny figure lying on the bed. "Dead? Good God. Jenkins, call the police."

"I thought you were the police."

"Different district. Just call the police, now."

"Mrs. Gittings doesn't have a phone. She always has me call if she needs a taxi or something."

"Then call from your office, or wherever it is you call from."

"Right, right." He looked confused and upset, but he hurried out the main door and down the hall, where I noticed other neighbors had gathered, including Joe and Mr. Laska, all of them chattering and asking questions.

"Keyes, get out in the hall, and do your best crowd control until the cops get here."

"Yes, sir."

He strode out into the hall, leaving the shattered door open, flashing his badge as he attempted to keep the nosy occupants of the second floor at bay.

I knew I should go in the bedroom and get a close look at Mrs. Gittings before the police arrived, but I shuddered at the thought. I didn't want to see that quirky, strange, delightful woman dead, to have that be the last vision I had of her. I had a few minutes to spare, and I looked around her living room. It was where she spent most of her time when she wasn't at the Edmonton, I suspected, yet it was sparsely decorated, old, dark, and rather depressing. It smelled of must and rosewater. The wallpaper of faded green vines was peeling in places, and the threadbare carpet was stained. All of the corners of the apartment had cobwebs, and pale jade-colored drapes hung lifelessly at the windows.

A small brown easy chair, its upholstery dirty and worn, sat on the side of the console radio, a plain wooden rocker on the other. Next to the easy chair, on a little table, were stacks of newspapers and magazines. Against the far wall stood two chairs next to a small table with dirty dishes on the top, alongside what appeared to be an empty whisky bottle. Through the door to the kitchen I saw more bottles, some empty, some full, some half full, and still more dirty dishes.

A yellowed, faded Christmas card sat on the radio. I walked over and picked it up. *Christmas greetings!* adorned the outside, above a wintery scene of a boy sledding down a hill. Inside, *Merry Christmas and a joyous New Year.* Below the printed script, neat handwriting: *Wishing you the best of holidays, Aunt Violet. I'm sorry we won't be able to see you this Christmas, but hopefully next year. All the best, Mike and Julie, December 8th, 1946.*

I set the card back in its place, my heart suddenly even more heavy.

At last I decided to head to the bedroom to have a look, but as I did, I noticed something moving down the hall. It was a tiny figure, all in gauzy white, with long, gray, wispy hair flowing down the back. Mrs. Gittings was alive. I was overjoyed at first as I watched her marching barefoot to the front door, her arms stretched out before her. But she would soon catch me in her apartment with the door broken. I panicked. There was nowhere to hide. She shuffled to the door and pushed it closed, the lock clicking tightly in spite of the broken frame. She seemed not to notice the chain dangling down or the splintered wood around it.

As I knew she would, she saw me, a shocked expression on her face as I stood there in the middle of her living room. She screamed and started yelling in that raspy voice. "What are you doing in my apartment? Who are you? I'm going to kill you! Get out! I have a gun, you know." She went to a small table by the front door, opened the drawer, and pulled out a revolver, which she aimed rather shakily at me.

My hand went to my own gun, but I kept it holstered for the time being. I knew the light from the windows was behind me, and she couldn't see me clearly.

I could hear Keyes pounding on the door. "Heath! Heath! What's going on? Why did you close the door?"

I kept my voice calm, but spoke loudly. "Mrs. Gittings, it's Heath Barrington. Mr. Keyes is out in the hall. We were worried about you, so Jenkins let us in. You sent me a note, asking me to come here." I stared at her and she stared back, her hand shaking, the gun wobbling back and forth, until finally a look of recognition crossed her face. The clucking started abruptly, and she dropped the gun. She walked unsteadily to the easy chair and collapsed into it, crying.

I went to her, kneeling by her side, and cradled her in my arms as the smell of whiskey and body odor hit my nostrils. It emanated from every pore of her body. "It's all right, it's okay, you're okay. I'm here, Mr. Keyes is here. I'm just going to go let him in, all right?"

She continued to cry inconsolably, so I slowly got to my feet and went to the door, opening it to a very bewildered Alan and several nosy neighbors. "She's alive. Jenkins was mistaken. I think she was just in a deep, drunken stupor. Go tell Jenkins to call off the police."

"Yes, sir," Alan replied, obviously relieved.

I closed the door again and picked up the revolver from the floor. It was an older model but in good condition. I shuddered again as I checked the chamber and found three bullets. I couldn't tell if it had been recently fired or not. I returned the gun to the drawer, wondering if it was the one missing from Blount's desk. Then I went back to the small, gray figure in white, still sobbing and clucking into the worn brown upholstery of the chair. I knelt beside her once more.

"Mrs. Gittings? Please don't cry. I came to see you because you sent me a note. You asked me to come see you, but you didn't answer the door when we knocked and we became concerned. You're safe, no one will harm you. You had something to tell me, remember?"

The sobbing abated, and she turned her head to me. Her eyes were red and puffy, and she stared at me as if from in a cloud. "Bruck, bruck, bruck, bruck." More clucking.

I took out my handkerchief and handed it to her.

"Thank you," she said softly, wiping her eyes and blowing her nose.

"Mrs. Gittings? What did you want to tell me?"

Still more clucking as she waddled her small little head back and forth. "I saw him, I did. I saw him."

"Who did you see, Mrs. Gittings?"

"Him. Through the looking glass behind the mirror, the cyclops sits in wait. Through the door they enter, and unknowingly seal their fate, bruck, bruck, bruck."

"What do you mean? You saw a cyclops? Someone with one eye?" I thought immediately of Walter Gillingham.

Her eyes were red and swollen as she gazed up at me, and I wasn't sure she could even see me. She dabbed at them once more with my handkerchief, which I got the feeling I wasn't going to get back.

"It was dark, so dark. Then an angel came out of the light, all in white. I went toward the light, and I could smell smoke, something burning. It was the devil, I'm sure. But the angel must have won."

"An angel?"

"Yes. I went toward the light, and I saw him. There was blood on him. I knew it was blood, it stood out so on the white, and the smoke of the devil hung in the air. Something was burning."

"Mrs. Gittings, I don't understand what you're saying. You saw Mr. Blount after he'd been shot?"

"Bruck, bruck, bruck, I need a drink."

I sighed. "All right, just a moment."

I got back to my feet and went into the kitchen. The glasses I found in a cupboard were dusty and dirty. I rinsed one off as best I could and filled it with cold water from the tap.

Returning to the easy chair, I held it out to her, but her hand

trembled so fiercely she couldn't hold the glass. "Let me help you."
I held it to her lips as she took a sip and then made a sour face.

"Whiskey." Then more clucking.

I sighed and returned with the glass to the kitchen, where I
poured most of the water into the sink and added whiskey from one
of the many bottles to the glass. Once more I brought it to her and
held it to her lips. One sip, then two, then three. The clucking grew
softer. Two more sips, and she sounded more contented, like a baby
after its bottle.

I set the glass on top of the radio next to the old Christmas card.
"Mrs. Gittings, what did you want to tell me? What did you send the
note for? Did you do something? Did you *see* something?"

She looked up at me, then over to the glass, still half full of
whiskey, and pointed a shaky hand to it. I gave her some more.

Her eyes looked glazed, still red and puffy. She finished the
whiskey and brucked contentedly, clutching my handkerchief in one
hand, the empty glass in the other as a child would a teddy bear.
"Mr. Barrington, I saw him. There was blood all over. Bruck, bruck,
bruck."

I sighed, growing impatient in spite of myself. "You saw Mr.
Blount after he'd been shot, Mrs. Gittings? Is that what you mean?"

"Bruck, bruck. Dead, blood. Good and dead. And I saw an
angel, come to take him away, I imagine, bruck, bruck. The devil
had been there. I could smell him, but the angel must have won."

"Mrs. Gittings, we ran into each other at the hotel last night,
remember? You said something then about all this. Why did you
send for me now?"

"Bruck, bruck, you're a detective, aren't you? I thought about it
all night, didn't know what to do. Bruck, bruck, bruck."

"About what you saw? Or about what you did? Where did you
get that gun? The one in the drawer by the door."

She looked at me, a bit of drool from the side of her lips. "Gun?"

"The gun in the drawer, the one you just had. Where did you
get it?"

"He gave it to me."

"Who gave it to you?"

"My husband. Do you know him? Have you met him?"

I shook my head. "No, Mrs. Gittings, I've never met him, but I'm sure he's a fine fellow. He gave you the gun?"

"Shot him dead. Evil. Bruck, bruck, bruck." Her voice trailed off.

"Who shot him dead, Mrs. Gittings? Who did it? Do you know who shot him? Did you shoot him?" But I couldn't get anything more out of her at that point as she closed her eyes again, and her breathing became shallow and soft. She had fallen asleep, or more likely, passed out again.

I pried the empty glass from her hand and returned it to the kitchen, where I washed it and put it away. Then, as gently as I could, I picked her up, noting how incredibly light she was, how I could feel her bones, and I carried her to the bedroom, where I tucked her softly back into bed, her left hand still clutching my handkerchief.

I returned to the living room once more, and on a hunch glanced at the stack of newspapers next to the easy chair. Sunday was on top, and below that was Friday's. Saturday's was missing.

I went quietly out, though I'm not sure why, as it would take the building falling down to rouse her again. I closed the door behind me, making sure it locked. The neighbors, I noticed, had all grown tired or bored and had returned to their respective apartments.

Downstairs I ran into Keyes, chatting with Jenkins. "Were you able to stop the police?"

"Yes, sir. They've been here a few times before for Mrs. Gittings, so they understood," Jenkins said.

"Oh? What happened before?"

"She tends to play her radio too loudly, and we get a lot of noise complaints. Sometimes she wanders the halls incoherently, making that clucking noise. Once she came home from the Edmonton, could barely walk, clucking like all get-out. She went up to the third floor, took off all her clothes down to her underthings, and started banging on the door of apartment 312, trying to get in."

"She was on the wrong floor," Alan said.

"Yes, poor thing. Though I still don't understand why she

took all her clothes off. Police had to come and get her back to her place."

"Doesn't she have any family? Any friends?" I asked.

"There's a niece out in Philly, but no one else I know of. She's gotten worse over the years. Kind of sad."

"Very sad," Alan said.

"I've worked here eleven years. She's been here nine, I think. Moved in after her husband died. From what I understand, he left her with a small pension from the gas company and not much more. He was a gambler, I hear. Some of her neighbors watch out for her, Mr. Laska and the blind guy, but she keeps to herself most of the time."

"She definitely doesn't seem to have much," I said.

"Nope. Pretty much wears the same outfit every day. The pension is enough to pay her rent and expenses each month, but that's about it, I think."

"Will she be charged for the damage to her door? To repair the chain?" Alan asked.

"It won't be much, but the building manager will send her a bill."

I took a card out of my wallet. "Here's my address up in Milwaukee. Have the manager send the bill to me."

"Sure thing, Mr. Barrington. Mighty nice of you," Jenkins said.

"It was my fault to begin with. And if anything does happen to her, try and let me know, okay?"

Jenkins nodded. "All right. What for?"

"Because she's a nice lady, because she's a human being all alone." *And hopefully not a murderer*, I added to myself. "Did Mrs. Gittings go out this morning, by the way?"

Jenkins cocked his head. "Yes, she did. She was up early for her. She left around seven thirty or so, I'd say."

"Anything unusual about her?"

"Unusual? Gee, I don't think so. Although come to think of it, she was carrying the newspaper under her arm. Never saw her do that before. I didn't even think the newspapers had been delivered yet."

"Right. Well, thanks, Jenkins. We'll be on our way."

"Very good, Mr. Barrington, Mr. Keyes. Have a nice Father's Day."

"Thanks, likewise."

Alan and I walked back to Michigan Avenue and turned toward the hotel, and I recounted to him what had occurred in the apartment and what Mrs. Gittings had said. He whistled.

"Jeepers, Heath, do you think that gun is the missing one? Do you think she shot him?"

"I think it's entirely possible, unfortunately. I imagine the gun can be traced and tested to see if it is the murder weapon."

"And if it's not, she's in the clear?"

"Not quite. It could still be her gun, and she still may have stolen Blount's and disposed of it."

Alan nodded. "I suppose so, but she sure doesn't seem like a killer to me."

"Alan…"

"I know, I know. All kinds of people do all kinds of things, and people are not always what they appear."

"Exactly."

"What about that newspaper?"

"It seems likely to me she had it delivered to us. Yesterday's paper is missing from the stack in her apartment, and that doorman saw her leaving this morning carrying a newspaper, which he said was unusual for her. I suspect she got up early this morning, took yesterday's paper since today's hadn't come yet, circled the key words, then carried it to the hotel and gave it to a bellboy to deliver to our room. Then she toddled back here, picked up today's newspaper from the hall, undressed, and took a nap, perhaps after a cocktail or two."

"Why would she leave that newspaper at our door and send a note for us to come see her? Why do both?"

"I'm not sure, Alan. Perhaps she wrote out the note and sent it along with a neighborhood boy, then forgot about it and decided to send the newspaper. Or perhaps she sent the newspaper but felt we might not pick up on the clues and decided to tell us in person instead. She may even have had the note in her purse when she dropped off the newspaper and gave the note to one bellboy, the newspaper to another. We may never know; it's difficult to have a clear conversation with her."

"I gathered that."

"One small consolation for you. If she did kill him, the courts would probably find her not guilty by reason of insanity. I doubt she'd serve time."

"So you do think she did it?"

I shrugged. "I really don't know. From what she said, it sounds like she saw Blount dead, anyway, but whether she stumbled upon the open door in the alley and saw him after the fact or if she actually did the crime remains to be seen."

"So why do you think she wants us to search Blount's store?"

"Maybe to find her hatpin, maybe no reason at all, other than she didn't like him and still feels he has something to hide, or maybe there is something there."

"She said she saw an angel," Alan said.

"Yes, all in white, come to carry him away."

"I wonder."

"What?" I asked.

"If she saw a ghost, maybe his ghost."

"You and your spirits, Alan."

"It could have been."

"I suppose so, but I'm not counting on it."

"All right, Mr. Skeptical, so what are we going to do next?"

"I've been thinking about that. I suppose, Alan, it's time to phone Detective Wilchinski."

CHAPTER THIRTEEN

We returned to room 804 and made ourselves comfortable, noting the maid had already been in to make up the room. "I could get used to maid service, Heath."

I laughed, "Me too, but not on our salaries."

"No, guess not. Are you going to make the call?"

"Yeah, I have his card here." I walked over to the desk and picked up the phone, asking the operator to connect me to the number listed on the card Detective Wilchinski had given me last night.

It rang three times, then I heard his voice, still gravelly.

"Detective Wilchinski, homicide."

"Good morning, this is Heath Barrington, from Milwaukee, we met at the Edmonton last evening."

"Oh right, the Blount case."

"Yes, that's right. I was wondering if you could meet me in his shop this afternoon. I'd like to have a look around."

"It's not a tourist attraction, Mr. Barrington, go visit a museum."

He had a way of getting under my skin, but I let it go. "I have reason to believe there may be something in his store or back room that would have significance to his death, Detective."

"Like what?"

"I'm not sure, but I want to investigate."

"I thought I made it clear the other night—not your city, not your case."

"I'm just trying to help, Detective."

"Help me by telling me what you know, not playing games."

"I *am* telling you what I know—I have reason to believe there may be something in his shop we didn't see the other night, but I won't know until I look. Someone sent me a newspaper here at the hotel this morning telling me to search Blount's store. They had circled key words in it."

"Who sent you that?"

"I don't know, it showed up in front of my hotel room door this morning." It wasn't a total lie, as I didn't know with certainty Mrs. Gittings was behind it.

"Why would anyone send you something like that instead of reporting it to the police?"

"Again, I don't know, Detective. Maybe one of my fans."

"Funny guy. You've had your name in the papers too often, your head's getting big."

I bristled again. "Do you want my help or not?"

"Fine. I guess I can spare you a few minutes. Meet me in an hour in the alley behind the hotel. The locks have been changed, but I have a key to that entrance. Bring that newspaper along, I want to see it, and try not to disturb any fingerprints."

"I'll do my best. See you in an hour. It's 11:57 now. Let's say 1:00 p.m."

"Let's." He rung up the phone rather abruptly, and I did the same.

"How did it go?" Alan asked.

"About as well as I expected. We're to meet him in the alley at one p.m. He also wants to see that newspaper that was left at our door this morning, too. What can I put it in so I don't disturb any more fingerprints?"

"Hmm. I don't know. Could you fold it up inside a towel?"

"Maybe, but I'm afraid the ink would come off on the towel. I'll just take it as is and he can deal with it," I said, picking it up off the desk. "Let's hit the coffee shop for a quick bite first."

"Good idea, I'm hungry."

"Same here."

"Ready?"

"After you, Officer."

We grabbed our hats, left the room, and hit the down elevator button, waiting beside a younger man and woman who were holding hands. I envied them that. Soon the elevator came and the four of us got in, riding in silence to the lobby, where we said good day to them and then headed to the coffee shop behind the marble staircase. It was just after noon and quite busy, but we managed to get a table for two toward the back, across from a portly man chain-smoking cigarettes in between bites of his sandwich. We put our hats on the wall hooks and I put the newspaper gently on the rack above them where I felt it would be safe and out of harm's way. That done, we settled in across from each other at the table as the waitress brought over menus and two glasses of water.

"Coffee?" she asked.

"Absolutely. Two, black."

"Right." She walked away as we picked up the menus.

"What looks good?" I asked Alan.

"It all looks good, Heath. I'm hungry."

"Good, get what you want. I'm buying."

"Let's go Dutch, if anything."

"Don't argue, Officer, I outrank you."

"But you've spent so much on me all ready this weekend."

"Because I want to. Now order what you want."

"If you insist. But *I'm* buying dinner tonight."

"We'll see."

The waitress reappeared with the coffee, and we ordered, Alan getting the country ham omelet, hash browns, and toast, and I got the corned beef hash with a poached egg.

She jotted it down on her pad, returned the pencil to behind her ear, and walked away without a word.

"Friendly sort, isn't she?" I said.

"Probably having a tough day. Waiting tables is hard work. My cousin does that at a place in Racine."

"Every job dealing with the public can be challenging, I imagine. Including ours."

"No arguments there."

The waitress dropped off a check at the portly cigarette-smoking man's table. He clambered rather awkwardly to his feet and left, replaced shortly by two priests, one older, one younger. Alan and I nodded to them politely as the waitress handed them their menus and water and then returned to our table and poured more coffee. In less than five minutes, she was back again with our food.

"Anything else, gentlemen?"

I looked at Alan, but he shook his head. "No thank you, miss."

She left us to it as she took the priests' order.

As we ate, I noticed Alan was unusually quiet. "Everything okay? How's the omelet?"

"Hmm? Oh, needs salt."

I picked up the shaker and handed it to him and he took it without a word, shook some on his food, and set it back on the table.

"What else?"

"What do you mean?"

"I mean you're not usually this quiet."

He looked up at me, his blue eyes penetrating. "Sorry. It's fine. I was just thinking, that's all."

"I figured you were, and I can guess what about. Look, I'm sorry we got involved in another murder case, Alan. Once we meet with Detective Wilchinski, we can tell him everything we know and then let him take over and we can enjoy the rest of our last full day here."

Alan swallowed a bite of his omelet and then shook his head. "No. You wouldn't be happy doing that. We're in the middle of this case, like it or not. After all, you found the body, and that newspaper was delivered to you, not Wilchinski. And Mrs. Gittings...well, she talked to you, not him."

I nodded. "That's true. But I want you to be happy, too, Alan."

He smiled. "Thanks. I know that. And I am happy, more than you could know. We had a wonderful Friday and a great Saturday together. Well, up until the murder and all, anyway. And I'm with you, doing what you love. I'm a part of that, so how could I not be happy?" He smiled at me, and I could tell he was sincere.

"That means a lot to me, Alan, it really does." I wished at that instant I could reach over the table and kiss him or at least put my hand on his, but we were in public, so the best I could do was smile back at him. Both of the priests at the next table, I noticed, were leaning in our direction, doing their best to listen to our conversation. The older priest was staring at us.

"I know how you feel," Alan said softly, the edges of our hands just touching on the table top. From the other table, I heard the older priest cluck disapprovingly.

I turned from Alan and looked over at the priests directly. "Sorry, not confession time." The older one shot me an indignant look, the younger one looked embarrassed, and both of them looked away, busying themselves with their silverware.

I turned back to Alan. "Sorry about that. So, why so quiet if you're happy?"

He shrugged. "I'm just thinking about Blount, the suspects, the clues, Mrs. Gittings."

"You really like that dotty old woman, don't you?"

"I do. I know it's crazy, I know *she's* crazy, but I like her, and I feel kind of sorry for her."

"I feel the same way. But we can't let that get in the way of the fact that she's still a suspect and may be a murderer."

"But she said Blount was evil."

I set my coffee cup down and looked at him hard. "Alan, she could have said he was the devil himself, but that doesn't make it so, nor does it justify killing him, even if it was so."

He sighed. "You're right, of course, but I really hope she didn't do it."

"Me too, Alan. Me too. Did the salt help?"

"Oh, yeah. Not the best omelet I've had, but it filled me up enough, anyway. I think I'm done. How about you?"

"Yes, I'm through. They certainly don't skimp on their portions here. The hash would have been more than enough on its own, but the poached egg was a treat. I should order that more often."

"I can poach an egg—I'll make you one sometime."

I grinned. "For breakfast after a long, hard night."

He grinned back. "You're on. You bring the orange juice."

"Deal. We'd better get moving." I signaled for the waitress, who brought over the check. Once we had gathered our hats and the newspaper, I turned once more to the two priests.

"Enjoy your lunch, gentlemen."

The younger one smiled, but the older one just scowled. "We weren't eavesdropping, sir, but you were talking about murder, bodies, and uh, other unnatural things."

"Unnatural for you, perhaps." Then I looked over at the young priest, who was blushing again. "Or perhaps not. Good day."

I left a tip on our table, paid the bill at the register, and together Alan and I headed out the door.

"Those two seemed to be listening to everything we said."

"Oh, they were, from the time they sat down. Old busybody, that's all. I probably shouldn't have confronted them, but then again, why not?"

Chapter Fourteen

We went out onto Michigan Avenue and around to the alley, which was deserted. Not even a rat was in sight at this time of day. The police barricades at either end of the alley had been removed, and no one was in sight. The lock on the back door of Blount's had obviously been changed, as Wilchinski had said, but other than that everything seemed just as it was yesterday, except now it was broad daylight. I tried the door, but it didn't give, so I knocked, not really expecting anyone to answer. No one did.

"What time is it now, Heath?"

I checked my watch again. "Twelve fifty-eight."

About fifteen minutes later, I began to pace and fidget, mulling over things, thinking about what Mrs. Gittings had said. The alley was now flooded with sunlight, and I was glad for my wide-brimmed fedora.

"Do you think he forgot, Heath?"

I stopped and looked at him, leaning against the wall of the hotel, his hat pulled low. "No, I think he's making us wait. Childish." I paced some more, aimlessly kicking an empty can of soup about, bouncing it off trash cans and walls.

Finally, a maroon Pontiac Torpedo pulled into the alley off Superior and came to a stop about five feet from where we stood. Wilchinski got out of the driver's side, apparently alone.

"I was beginning to think you weren't coming, Detective. We did say one o'clock, didn't we? It's one thirty now."

"Chicago's not like Milwaukee, Barrington, and this isn't my only case. You're lucky I showed up at all. I have things to do, places to be, and this seems like a big waste of my time."

"Why?"

"Because I've already been in there, and so have my boys. We took fingerprints and photographs, and checked for evidence. What do you think you're going to find that we haven't already?"

"I don't know. I won't know until I get in there. Maybe nothing, maybe something, but I won't know if we don't at least look."

"Fine, but let's make it quick. DeCook's off today, so I'm running solo." He scowled in Alan's direction. "Who are you again?"

"Alan Keyes, also from Milwaukee. A police officer and a friend of Mr. Barrington's."

Wilchinski looked him up and down. "I see. So, Mr. Keyes, what are you, Barrington's assistant?"

Alan looked somewhat embarrassed. "Yes, I guess you could say that."

"I wouldn't say that," I said.

Wilchinski and Alan both looked at me, and Alan seemed surprised. "No?" he asked.

I shook my head. "No. I'd say we're partners, in a manner of speaking."

"Partners in fighting crime, eh?" Wilchinski grumbled.

"Yes, exactly." I smiled at Alan, who beamed back at me.

"Whatever works for you two, I guess."

"It works. Here's the newspaper you wanted. You can see the folded-over page, and the circled words in the ads and articles." I held out the paper for him.

Wilchinski took it and glanced at it, turning the pages, squinting to read in the bright sunlight.

"You said someone left this at your door at the hotel?"

"That's right, this morning. I don't know who for certain."

"Interesting. Somebody's playing games." He glanced at it once more and walked over and tossed it on the seat of his car. So much for handling it carefully. He slammed the door shut again and grunted in my direction. "Let's get inside and get this over with. Don't go touching anything in there."

"Why?" I asked. "You said your lab guys have already been over the place."

He nodded. "Yeah, they have, they're a pretty thorough bunch."

"Then what does it matter if I touch anything?"

Wilchinski scowled again. "Because this is my case, and you do as I say, got it?"

"I got it, but I'm not going to be able to have a very thorough look around if I can't handle things," I said.

"Fine, but be sure and put things back the way they were. Everything's been photographed."

"I understand, Wilchinski. Did your guys find anything?"

He shook his head. "There were dozens of sets of prints in there, on everything. More like Union Station than the back room of a store."

"Well, he did use it as a changing room for his clients, and apparently he did photography back there as well. I imagine there would be quite a few prints."

"Right. Too many to make any sense out of."

"Okay."

"Look, Barrington, I'm pretty confident this was just a random murder, a robbery gone bad, but I'm willing to explore possible suspects, motives, and opportunities and look at any clues you happen to find, *if* you find any. And if you do find anything, you turn it over to me, understand?"

"Yes, sir."

"Good, but I don't think you *will* turn anything up."

"Because you've already looked?" I asked.

"That's right."

"Sounds like you have it all under control, then, so this won't take me long at all. Open the door."

He unlocked the door and the three of us went in, Alan flipping the overhead light switch next to the door. I pushed my hat back on my head and surveyed the room. Everything was as it had been last night, except for the chalk outline where Blount's body had been. The bloody "W" was now more of a dark brown stain. A faint smell of death hung in the air, an odor I had smelled too often before.

"So, what are you supposed to be searching for, Barrington?" Wilchinski asked.

"I told you, I don't know."

"Right, you don't know. Like I said, big waste of time."

I ignored him and began walking slowly around the room, circling the headless dress form that still stood in the center. Something protruding from it caught my eye, and I leaned in for a closer look.

"What?" Wilchinski asked.

"It looks like a hatpin," I said. "Where have we seen that before, Alan?"

Alan came over and examined it. "That's Mrs. Gittings's."

"That's what I thought, too. She said she was missing it."

"How did it get stuck in the dress form?" Alan asked.

"Who's Mrs. Gittings?" Wilchinski asked, and I felt I had to tell him.

"Just an old lady who used to work for Blount, that's all. She misplaced her hatpin and asked me to keep an eye out for it. If I had to guess, she probably stuck it in there yesterday without even realizing it."

"Seems like an odd thing to do," Wilchinski said.

"Mrs. Gittings is rather odd. She has a bit of a drinking problem."

"Oh, one of those," he said.

"I'll leave it here for the time being, if you want, but I know she wants it back."

He took out his notebook. "I'll make a note of it and see it gets returned to her when we wrap things up."

"Thanks. She lives at the Aimsley Arms Apartments, but you could leave it at the desk for her. She comes in regularly," I said.

"Duly noted. Is that what you were supposed to be searching for?" Wilchinski said.

I didn't reply at once, wondering to myself if all Mrs. Gittings wanted was for me to find her hatpin. But there had to be something more. She had been so cryptic and so adamant. "I don't know yet, Detective. Give me a few more minutes."

"The clock is ticking, Barrington, and you can't turn back time, or stop it. I have things to do this afternoon."

"Right." I didn't bother reminding him that he was almost a half hour late getting here. I walked over to Blount's desk, turned on the desk lamp, and looked around the top of the desk. Apparently Blount had been working on the books when he was fatally interrupted. His sales ledger was open to this week, and I quickly scanned it. Every sale had been neatly recorded in Blount's tidy script. Most were routine: two shirts on Tuesday, June tenth, to a Mr. A. Winberry for a total of $8.02, cash, and a box of handkerchiefs to a B. Cadbury, on account. On Wednesday, a suit, shirt, and tie to a Mr. Pazdan for a total of $31.41, on account, and a pair of socks to a M. Bloom for fifty-two cents. Thursday, June twelfth, was apparently the start of last-minute Father's Day shopping, as I noted seven ties, three pairs of socks, and a pair of leather gloves sold, all gift boxed. There was also a sale to Mr. Bennett that day for two dress shirts and two silk ties, for a total of $54.41. *Wow, pricey shirts and ties, especially compared to the other sales that week*, I thought. Then on Friday the thirteenth, I found my name, one black tux, $30.00, one tux shirt, $4.98, a stud set, $9.49, and one silk tie, $2.49, gift boxed. Above that was an entry for a fedora and a pair of socks to a Mr. Maynard Henning for $38.00, and four dress shirts for Miss Gloria Eye, $58.50. I whistled softly to myself.

"What did you find, Heath?" Alan asked.

I pointed to one of the entries in the book and Alan glanced at it. "A sale of a fedora and a pair of socks to a Mr. Maynard Henning for $38.00. Jeepers, that's an expensive hat and socks."

"I agree," I said.

"I know that name, Maynard Henning, but I can't place it," Alan said.

"I know it, too. It was on the banner in the Sky Star. He's the pianist."

Alan grinned. "You're right, good job. Only from back where we were sitting, I thought it said, *Heming.*"

"Easy mistake," I replied. "And look here. There's also an entry in Blount's sales log for two shirts and two ties to Mr. Bennett for $54.41, and four dress shirts to Miss Gloria Eye for $58.50."

"Wowzer, that's a lot of money, too."

"Even top-of-the-line dress shirts shouldn't have cost more than $5.00 apiece, tops. No wonder she was upset. I'm sure Wieboldt's on State does have much better pricing, as she said, so why shop here? And why are hers, Mr. Henning's, and Mr. Bennett's purchases so much higher than anyone else's?"

"What are you trying to prove, Barrington? That Blount's store was expensive? So what? I don't think people go around murdering people because they charge too much," Wilchinski said.

I looked up at him but didn't say anything before returning my attention to the sales book. Yesterday's entries for Saturday the fifteenth saw even more tie sales, along with socks, shirts, a pair of pajamas, and handkerchiefs, mostly gift boxed. It looked like the dads of Chicago were going to have a fine Father's Day. There was the sale of Mr. Bennett's latest $34.00 suit, too.

I knew I shouldn't, but I flipped through the sales register and went through it quickly, week by week. For the most part it was some days with no sales, some with a few, some good days, some bad. But in amongst the suits, the shirts, the underwear, and the tie sales were ones for very large amounts for relatively inexpensive goods. There was Bennett's name again a few months back, and Gloria Eye's, along with the names of several other men, including Mr. Henning's, some repeated over and over again, some just a one or two-time occurrence.

"Find anything else interesting?" Alan asked, pushing his hat back on his head.

"I think so," I said. "Blount seemed to have several repeat customers, all men, except for Miss Eye, who paid two, three, even four or five times the going rates for his product. Very curious indeed. And besides the two sales I mentioned before, Mr. Bennett and Miss Eye both have multiple entries of large amounts for small purchases."

"What do you mean?"

"I mean, for example, that the tie I bought he would have sold to those two for four to five times as much as he sold it to me. There are listings for other repeat and some one-time customers with the same thing, large amounts of money for relatively inexpensive purchases."

"Interesting," Alan said.

"Very." I replied.

"What's so interesting about that, Barrington?" Wilchinski asked. "So he knew who had money and who didn't and he charged accordingly. Sounds like a good businessman to me. Like I said, no one murdered him because they were overcharged."

"Charging one person more for the same goods than someone else is illegal, Detective," I said.

"Ah, so what?" he said.

"So I can't help but wondering if that's really what he was doing."

"What do you mean, Heath?"

"Yeah, Barrington, you just said yourself that's what he was doing."

I nodded. "The books certainly make it seem that way. But why would these customers keep coming back to him, over and over? Surely they couldn't all have been so stupid as to not eventually realize they were being grossly overcharged."

"Maybe they didn't care," Wilchinski said. "Folks with money will pay anything. The Depression's over."

"*Maybe* they didn't care. Or maybe they were getting something else for their money besides clothes."

"Like what?" Alan asked.

"That's a good question," I said, scratching my chin. "What could he provide these men that they'd be willing to pay large amounts of money for? And something Blount wanted to hide in the books by making it seem like they were just buying merchandise?"

Wilchinski laughed. "Girls comes to my mind, since Prohibition's over."

I glanced over at him. "That was my thought, too, Detective."

"I was joking, Barrington."

"But I'm not. Blount could have been running some kind of prostitution ring. Men would come in and buy small goods, he'd charge them a large amount, maybe give them a sales check with a code on it that told them where to find the girl," I replied. "Or if the men were staying at the hotel, he'd send the girl to their room."

Wilchinski shook his head as he lit up a cigarette. "Not likely, Barrington. Not on Michigan Avenue, not in the Edmonton. Mike Masterson would have sniffed that out in a heartbeat."

He was beginning to annoy me a lot. This would be so much simpler if I could just get rid of him. But he did have a point. Mike wasn't one to let unaccompanied girls go wandering the halls without question.

"Well, maybe he arranged for the girls to meet the men somewhere else. He certainly had a good front for it, a respectable clothing store in a top-notch hotel. He gets a lot of older businessmen, probably fairly well off, alone in the big city."

"And some private, discreet entertainment would be very enticing," Alan added.

"Exactly. The entries for a one or two-time overcharge were probably out-of-town businessmen, and the multiple occurrences were for businessmen who come to Chicago regularly or locals," I said.

"Like Mr. Bennett," Alan said.

I nodded. "My thoughts exactly."

"You two are dreaming. Besides, even if Blount was mixed up in some prostitution ring, so what? Why would someone murder him for that?"

"Maybe someone got double-crossed or wasn't happy with services provided for what they paid. I'm not sure, but that's my theory at the moment, Detective. What's yours?"

Wilchinski pushed his hat back too and scowled at me as he took a long drag on his cigarette. He blew the smoke in my direction.

"My theory, Barrington? My theory is that Blount closed up his shop last night and was working on the books. He'd had a good day because of Father's Day, and any bum crook on the street would know that and know that most of his sales were cash transactions. Blount steps out in the alley, maybe to have a cigarette. He wouldn't smoke back here in his shop."

"How come?" Alan asked.

"Because of all the clothes and fabrics. A man like Blount wouldn't risk a fire, and he wouldn't want all these fancy silks and what not smelling like smoke."

I had to admit Wilchinski was probably right about that, and as I glanced at the desk top again, I noticed there was no ashtray. "And yet you just lit up a cigarette like you did in here last night."

Wilchinski looked embarrassed, then irritated. He walked over to the alley door and flicked the cigarette out, then closed the door again. "Like I said, he went out in the alley for a smoke."

"All right, Detective, so he goes out to the alley for a smoke, then what?" I asked.

"Some bum crook who was waiting for him to come out pulls a gun on him and forces him back inside. The crook takes the money, shoots Blount, and flees."

"I admit that is possible, Wilchinski, but why the bloody 'W' on the floor, and the spool of green thread?"

"Ah, geez, you watch too many movies, Barrington. Not everything is some mysterious clue. When Blount was lying there dying his mind probably went to some lost love of his, that's all."

Life Wolfgang, I thought. Score one for Alan. "Well, Detective, that is indeed one theory."

"Makes a lot more sense than yours," Wilchinski sneered, pointing a finger at me.

"What about whatever was burned in the bathroom sink?" I asked.

"Burned beyond recognition. Nothing to examine. Besides, you said all those people that were being overcharged were men except for Miss Eye. How do you explain her? She paying for some hot little number, too? Some hootchy-kootchy?"

"I thought about that also, Wilchinski. Maybe she was one of those hootchy-kootchy girls for a while, and now Blount's blackmailing her, or was."

"If that's true, she'd be a prime suspect all right," Alan said.

"Yes, indeed."

"So who is this Miss Eye, Barrington?" Wilchinski asked.

"Gloria Eye. She's a singer in the band that played the Sky Star Ballroom last night."

"And you think she may have been a call girl for Blount and now he's blackmailing her?"

"I'm saying it's a possibility," I said.

"You're overanalyzing this, Barrington. Typical rookie, and a small town cop mistake. This was just a case of a robbery gone bad, clean and simple. There's no real clues here. You look at a sales ledger and see some people were overcharged and all of a sudden you've got Blount running some prostitution ring." Wilchinski laughed. "You need to get out of Milwaukee more and experience the real world. Now wrap it up and let's get out of here, the clock is ticking."

I bristled again but didn't say anything. "Right, Wilchinski, I'm almost finished. But still…"

"But still what?" he said, clearly impatient.

"There *has* to be something more." I flipped open Blount's black leather telephone directory and scanned the contents. Most numbers were ordinary: a Chinese take-out, a market, the bank, a florist, and what appeared to be clients of the store. But one stood out. I read the name aloud. "David Greene, editor, *Girls Aplenty Magazine*. Ever hear of it, Wilchinski?"

He looked slightly embarrassed. "Yeah, sure I've heard of it. So what? It's a sleazy pin-up magazine, nudies, that kind of thing."

"It doesn't sound like something Mr. Blount would read," I said.

Wilchinski laughed. "He was a man, wasn't he?"

I looked at him. "Yeah, but he didn't strike me as the type to read girlie magazines."

"Because he was a buttoned-up businessman? Guys like Blount can surprise you, Barrington."

"Maybe, but even if he did read it, why would he have the editor's phone number in his directory?"

"Beats me," Wilchinski said. "Maybe Greene's a client of the store. Makes sense he would keep the numbers of regular clients so he could inform them if he was having a sale or something."

I sighed. "I suppose so. Maybe I am imagining clues that don't exist," I said, feeling somewhat defeated.

"First sensible thing you've said all day. Now let's get the hell out of here."

"Right, right." I closed the telephone directory and put it back in its place, unsure of what else to do or look for.

"I guess Mrs. Gittings and all her talk of mirrors and cyclops was just the alcohol taking."

"Hmm? Cyclops, yes." I looked over at Alan. "I'd nearly forgotten about that. What was it she said again?"

"What the hell are you two talking about?" Wilchinski said, clearly confused.

I ignored him for the moment.

"She was talking about a cyclops. Through the looking glass, remember?"

I nodded. "Yes. A cyclops. Who or what has one eye?"

"Walter Gillingham, of course," Alan answered.

"Exactly. Perhaps that is who she meant. Maybe she saw him leaving the shop that night"

"That would make sense."

"Who's Walter Gillingham?" Wilchinski asked, looking from me to Alan and back to me again.

"A trumpet player and the fiancé of Miss Eye," I said. I closed my eyes, trying to remember her exact words. "Through the looking glass behind the mirror, the cyclops sits in wait. Through the door they enter and unknowingly seal their fate."

"What the hell does that mean?" Wilchinski growled.

I glanced at Wilchinski but didn't answer him.

"Something behind a mirror," Alan said.

"Right. You enter through a door, into a room presumably, and seal your fate while the cyclops sits and waits."

"You two been drinking, Barrington?"

"She also said what evil lurks in our reflections, and something about looking into a mirror hard enough that you can sometimes see the evil within," Alan said.

"She sounds daft," Wilchinski scoffed.

"She was trying to tell us something, but what? She wanted us to find something," I said, more to myself than either of them.

"Maybe she was trying to tell us that Mr. Gillingham was waiting for Blount back here," Alan suggested.

I looked at Alan thoughtfully. "That's an idea, but how would she have known that? She said through a door, into a room, behind a mirror. Do you think she meant a mirror here in the store?"

"That would make sense. There's a mirror in the bathroom."

"I thought we were going," Wilchinski said, annoyed. "Now all of a sudden you're both talking nonsense."

"There's also a big mirror in the dressing room," Alan said.

"You're right, good call." I turned off the lamp on the desk and walked over to the dressing room door. "You enter through a door and seal your fate." I pulled it open, gazing at myself once more in the large mirror opposite. "Interesting."

"Admiring yourself, Barrington?" Wilchinski said. In the reflection I could see both him and Alan behind me in the doorway. I ignored him again, knowing that if I didn't find anything this time I would be utterly defeated.

I stepped farther into the dressing room and looked into the mirror, cupping my hands to block the light. "I can't be certain, but I think there's something behind this." I ran my hands along the edges of the mirror until I felt something near the top on the right edge. I pressed what felt like a tiny button and I heard a slight click, then I pulled on the mirror and it swung silently open, revealing a small chamber behind.

"Holy cow," Alan said.

"What the hell?" Wilchinski added.

Staring back at me from the chamber was the cyclops, a camera mounted to a stand. I turned and looked at Wilchinski and Alan. "It appears, gentlemen, that Mr. Blount was taking pictures or movies of people in the dressing room via a two-way mirror, unbeknownst to them."

"Jeepers. I used that dressing room," Alan said.

"I know," I replied, turning back to examine the camera and the chamber.

"Hey, wait a minute," Wilchinski said from behind me, though I could no longer see him with the mirror swung open. "This is a men's clothing store. Blount was a guy, and he was filming men changing clothes?"

"Brilliant detective work, Marty," I said.

"Well I'll be, he was a perverted pansy," Wilchinski said.

I flinched. "I hate the word 'pansy.' And don't make assumptions," I said.

"What's the matter? Did I touch a nerve, Barrington?"

"I don't want you touching any part of me, Wilchinski, including my nerves."

Wilchinski laughed. "Don't worry."

"How did he control the camera? Surely he couldn't fit in there with it," Alan said.

"If I had to guess, I'd say this camera was rigged to a switch. When you went to change, Blount fiddled with something out front under the counter, and he did the same thing when you came back. A client goes in back to change clothes, Blount turns on the camera. He comes back out, Blount turns it off."

Alan's face flushed red. "Good thing I at least kept my underwear on."

"And a damned good thing I never bought anything in this place," Wilchinski added. "You about finished now?"

I shook my head. "No, there's something else in here, too." I reached in and pulled out a large, black leather file case and carried it out to Blount's desk.

"What's that?" Wilchinski asked, following me to the desk.

"Let's find out," Alan said.

"It's locked."

Wilchinski pulled out a pocket knife and expertly picked the lock. "Not anymore."

"That's illegal," I said.

"So call a cop, Barrington. Just open the damned thing."

I glanced over at Alan, undid the clasp, and opened it. Inside were small movie reels, each labeled in neat script with a man's name and a date. There were also manila folders containing files with black-and-white photographs that looked like they were made from the films, all of men in various stages of undress, taken inside the dressing room. I took them out and set them on the desk.

"Yup, big, blooming pansy all right." Wilchinski laughed, glancing at them.

"You're hysterical," I said dryly, pocketing a small reel that said *Alan Keyes* on it and hoping Wilchinski didn't notice.

"What else does the pervert have in there? Or don't I want to know?" Wilchinski asked.

"More folders, all arranged alphabetically by last name, apparently, with files in each," I replied, taking a few folders out, "but these are different." I removed the rest of them and set them on the other side of the desk.

Wilchinski picked up one and whistled. "Well, I'll be damned. Now I'm totally confused."

"What's in those files, Heath?"

"Color photographs of posed young women, many scantily clad or nude, and it looks like they were taken right back here in his makeshift studio, in front of those red velvet drapes."

"Golly," Alan said, blushing a bit.

"I don't get it, Barrington, why would a pansy also take girlie pictures?" Wilchinski asked.

I ignored him once more for the moment and started going through the files. "This folder's empty, curious. Between Ginger Doud and Alice Dove there's just an empty folder with no file in it." I continued scanning the contents until I came to one file in particular with a name on it I recognized. "This one is labeled 'Gloria Eye, Sept. 10, 1943.'" I flipped it open, and I must say I blushed a bit myself. "The photos of her are revealing, to say the least, taken four years ago. She was a brunette back then." I set it back down on the desk and Wilchinski quickly picked it up.

He whistled again. He really was annoying. "Well, what do you know?"

"As you said earlier, Wilchinski, guys like Mr. Blount can surprise you," I said.

"No kidding," Alan said.

"Still think it was a random burglar, Wilchinski?" I asked, looking at him.

He scowled. "So you proved he was a pervert. That still doesn't mean he was murdered because he took some hidden pictures and movies."

"Maybe someone found out what he was doing, and they killed him," Alan suggested.

"I know I would have," Wilchinski replied.

I glanced over at the detective. "Nice."

"But I still don't get the girlie pics," Wilchinski added. "Even pansies can go the other direction sometimes, I guess."

"Actually, I'd say the hidden pictures and movies of men were indeed for his own entertainment, but the photographs of scantily clad young women I bet he took to sell to David Greene. Look, there's a copy of the magazine here."

I picked up a thin tabloid magazine in the file case, the cover emblazoned with a redheaded girl on a bearskin rug.

"Let me see that," Wilchinski said, grabbing it out of my hands. He flipped through the pages attentively.

"Do you want to take that home for further study, Detective, or do you already have that issue?" I asked.

"Ha, ha, funny guy." He handed it back to me, and I scanned the pages, stopping halfway through. "Look at the girls on these two pages. Doesn't that backdrop look just like the one over there?" I asked, showing both Wilchinski and Alan the photos in the magazine.

"It does, Heath. Those pictures were taken right here."

Wilchinski squinted. "Eh, that's a black-and-white photo, and the backdrop is just curtains, could have been taken anywhere."

I shook my head. "But the curtain on the left has a dark spot on it, and so does the one hanging back there." Both of them looked at the red drapes hanging behind the platform.

"You're right."

"So what?" Wilchinski said.

I set the magazine on the desk next to the files I had removed and examined the case more closely now that it was empty. "There's a false bottom in this file case, I think." Using my fingertips, I lifted it out carefully. Inside the false bottom were more folders and small movie reels.

"Wow, there's more?" Alan said.

I removed them and glanced at a few. I felt myself blush.

"What's the matter, Barrington? More nude girls?"

"Not quite. Rather graphic, candid photographs of men."

"We saw those already," Wilchinski said. "The first ones you took out of the case."

I shook my head. "No, these are different. They weren't taken in a dressing room, that's for sure. The men in these photos all appear to be engaging in various sexual activities with other men and women, all of them undressed. Each folder is labeled with a man's name, address, and a date." I handed a few of them to Wilchinski and Alan.

Wilchinski glanced at one and then threw it down on the pile in disgust. "Vile."

"Jeepers, where were these taken?"

I glanced over at Alan, who was staring at some of the photos wide-eyed. "My guess would be a cheap hotel or rooming house. It looks kind of seedy. The men, I imagine, are or were clients of Mr. Blount's. Look here. This movie reel has the name G. Bennett on it. There's a folder of pictures of him, too."

"Mr. Bennett? Golly, you think he knew about that?"

"Yes, but not at the time it was being taken. I suspect this and the photographs were taken through a two-way mirror, similar to the set-up he had back here in the dressing room."

"Who's this Bennett fellow?" Wilchinski asked.

"A man we met the other night and a client of Blount's. He's an assistant manager here at the hotel. I can imagine something like this would be ruinous for him were it to get out."

"Interesting. This Blount was more than a pervert and a pansy. He was a real son of a bitch," Wilchinski said, making no attempt to hide his disapproval.

"He was certainly crafty and cunning," I replied. "He may have taken the initial pictures for his personal pleasure, like the dressing room ones, but then discovered he could make money by blackmailing some of these men. The wealthy, married, or influential ones, anyway."

"Like Mr. Bennett," Alan said.

"Yes."

Wilchinski looked skeptical. "What makes you say he was blackmailing them?"

"Diversification. Mr. Blount had expensive tastes, more than he could afford from just his earnings at his little shop, I would say. He drove a fancy new car, lived in an expensive neighborhood in a ritzy apartment building, had a pricey watch and a gold lighter and cigarette case, among other things. So he sold pictures of girls to pin-up magazines and offered the girls' services to lonely businessmen."

"Still doesn't mean he was blackmailing people, Barrington. Maybe he made enough money off the girlie pics and he took all those other pictures and movies for his personal sick pleasure."

"Maybe, but I doubt it, Wilchinski. The hidden camera in his dressing room was most likely just for his own pleasure. But then he realized his store wasn't making enough money and he needed to earn some extra cash. With his interest in photography, he decides to set up a makeshift studio back here and he maybe puts an ad in the paper offering his photography services for a small fee. Pretty young girls answer, hoping to break into show business, get their pictures taken. Step one, a new side business is born."

"Okay, then what?" he asked, wiping the back of his neck with his handkerchief.

"Then he finds some of the girls are willing to pose scantily dressed, and he connects with the girlie magazine editor, who probably was a client of the shop, like you said earlier, Wilchinski."

"So step two, he sells the girlie pictures to the editor, maybe giving the girls a small percentage," Alan said.

I nodded. "Very good, Alan. And a second side business comes into being."

"Is there a step three?" Wilchinski asked, putting his handkerchief back into his pocket.

I nodded. "Indeed. He realizes he gets a lot of lonely businessmen in his store. He approaches a couple of the girls and asks if they want to make some fast cash, and boom."

"Yeah, yeah, all of a sudden he's got a third side business."

"Exactly. And he's suddenly making some money, using his shop as cover. But then he figures out that some of these lonely businessmen have a lot of money. He has their names and home addresses from checks and bills of sale, and he figures if he takes hidden pictures of these men in the act with these young women, he can blackmail them for some tidy sums. His final side business, and probably his most profitable."

"You seem to be reading an awful lot into a few photographs and movie reels, Barrington."

"Not just the photographs, Wilchinski. I've also noticed in my interactions with him and people who know him that certain people didn't care for him much, and I'd say they had good reason if he was blackmailing them."

"Reason enough to kill him?" Alan asked.

"It could be reason enough for some people."

"Who are these certain people?" Wilchinski asked. "This G. Bennett fellow?"

"George Bennett. That's definitely one, yes."

"That's the one whose name was on one of these movie reels," Wilchinski said.

"Correct. Also Miss Gloria Eye, the same one of the photographs, and her fiancé Walter Gillingham, the trumpet player I mentioned earlier. And then there's Mrs. Gittings, whom I also mentioned before. She used to work for him and felt he was an evil man."

Wilchinski had taken out his notebook and was jotting down the information as I gave it to him. "I'd say she was right." He picked up Gloria's folder and glanced at it again, whistling. "I think I should have a personal word with this Miss Eye, in private."

I shook my head. "You'll find you're up against a tiger if you do. She's not the same, innocent, cow-eyed girl in those pictures. She's tough as nails."

"Well, maybe I'm a hammer," he said.

"Don't flatter yourself, Wilchinski," I said.

He dropped the folder back onto the desk. "Eh, there's no point in talking to any of them anyway."

"Why not?" I asked.

"This Blount guy was a pervert and a pansy, and he's dead. Case closed."

I bristled once again. "So because he was a pervert and a pansy, as you say, you don't care who killed him?"

"I know who killed him."

"Who?" Alan asked.

"An unknown street thug."

I rolled my eyes. "Seriously? That's your final word on it?"

He glanced at his watch. "I have bigger cases to work on, so yeah, that's my final word on it."

"What about all this?" I asked, motioning to the pile of folders and movie reels. "And the bloody 'W'? The spool of thread? The burned remains in the bathroom sink?"

He laughed. "You have a wild imagination, I'll give you that. You find some overcharged customers, a hidden camera, some pictures and movie reels, and suddenly you've got this pervert running prostitution rings, selling nudie pics, and blackmailing people. Maybe that bloody 'W' was for 'weirdo,' which is what this guy obviously was."

I sighed. "Before you knew he was a pansy, as you call him, you were open to suspects, motives, and clues, all of which I have since provided. Now because you find out he's queer, you're writing up his murder to an unknown street thug?"

"Fine, Barrington. Pack up all your so-called evidence back into that case and give it to me. I'll take it all downtown and have it logged and documented."

I started tossing the material back into the case angrily. "Logged and documented? Really? More likely you're going to take this downtown and lock yourself in the men's room with it, aren't you? You don't care about this case."

"Shut the hell up, Barrington. I told you before this isn't your case, not your jurisdiction. You got it?"

I closed the case and slid it over to him. "I got it. Loud and clear."

"Good. Because there's no point in questioning the suspects you mentioned. Why waste the taxpayers' money? From the looks of what we found here today, Blount was a pervert, like I said, and a real sick one, so no loss to the community."

"Blount certainly was not without his faults, Wilchinski, to put it mildly. I think he was a Peeping Tom, a blackmailer, an extortionist, a pimp, and God knows what else, but he was also a human being."

Wilchinski shrugged. "Maybe so, but a lousy human being. I'm a father of two girls, Barrington. I wouldn't want a creep like that on the loose, and I can't say I'm not glad he's gone. Just goes to show you, even the normal-seeming ones working in stores, selling you shirts and underwear, can be perverts."

"Even cops, I imagine," I said.

"What's that supposed to mean?" he growled.

"Just that no one really knows what's beneath the surface of anyone. People are like icebergs, Wilchinski. They can be all cool and seemingly harmless on the surface, but beneath the water, there is a whole lot more, and sometimes that whole lot more is dangerous. We just never know, and it applies to everyone, fathers, mothers, sons and daughters, cops, shopkeepers, priests, innkeepers, everyone."

"No cop I know is a pervert or a pansy, Barrington, unless

you're trying to tell me something about yourself or your friend here."

"You're missing the point, Wilchinski. No cop you're aware of, but that's not to say they aren't."

"You go to hell."

"Have it your way. Live your life with blinders on. I'm finished here, I can see that."

"Good. Some of us have real police work to do."

"You're right about that, some of us do," I said.

"Screw you, Barrington, and your buddy, too. Don't leave town without checking in." He picked up the case and walked to the alley door without another word, flicking off the lights as he yanked it open. We followed behind, stepping out into the alley. When we were out, Wilchinski turned and locked it up once more. "You can waste your vacation chasing phantom suspects if you want, but I say this case is closed." He stopped just long enough to set the case down and light a cigarette, then he picked the case up once more and threw it in the back seat of his car.

He opened the driver's side door and looked back at me and Alan still standing by the shop door, our hats now pulled back down. "Take my advice, Barrington. Forget about Blount and his little perversions. Go find some of those nice Chicago girls and have a good time. Then go back to Milwaukee and play cop on your own time on your own turf." He climbed in behind the wheel, slammed the door, started the engine, and roared past us down the alley, leaving us in a cloud of dust.

"Jeepers, he sure turned out to be a jerk."

"I'd say he has issues of his own. Possibly the whole subscription."

"He's not even going to bother questioning anybody."

I shook my head. "It doesn't sound like it. I'm sure he'll file a report for his chief that it was a robbery gone bad, and that will be the end of it."

"Wowzer."

"Indeed." I turned and looked at him. "*You* don't think I'm reading too much into all this, do you?"

He paused a moment before replying, and I held my breath, wondering what he was going to say. Finally, he said, "I trust your instincts, Heath. I think your idea of what Mr. Blount was up to is right, and I think the bloody 'W' and spool of thread have to mean something. So, no, I don't think you're reading too much into it at all."

I released my breath. "Thanks. I wonder myself if I'm getting carried away sometimes, you know?"

"You're on the right track, I can feel it. So now what?"

"Regardless of his advice, I think we should play cop right here in Chicago and see what we can find out on our own about our four suspects."

"But we don't have any authority to question anybody."

"No one says we can't have a friendly conversation or two. Let's go see if Mr. Bennett is around."

"All right, Heath. You're the boss."

I grinned and slapped him on the shoulder. "Partner, remember?"

Chapter Fifteen

Together we walked back around to the main entrance of the hotel on Michigan Avenue and into the lobby. "What do you plan on asking him, Heath?"

"I've been thinking about that. For starters, I'd like to find out if it was him the bellboy was talking about having an argument in Blount's shop yesterday afternoon."

"You think it was?"

"Not sure. It was either him or Gillingham, I'm willing to bet."

"And you think whoever was having that argument is the killer?"

"It's a possibility, but there are other factors to consider as well. I'd say it's just one possible piece of the puzzle."

"Okay, what about that film reel and the pictures?"

"I might bring those up. Let's wait and see what he has to say first."

"I'll follow your lead, partner," Alan said with a grin.

A middle-aged man stood at the front desk talking to a man and woman I assumed were hotel guests. When he had finished with them, I approached.

"Good afternoon. I'm Heath Barrington. I was wondering if Mr. Bennett was available. We'd like to see him."

He looked surprised. "Mr. Bennett? Our junior assistant manager?"

"Yes, that's right."

"Mr. Bennett is off today, but he does happen to be here. He came in for a staff meeting this morning, then stepped out for a bit. He returned a short time ago, and I believe he's in his office."

"Which is where?"

"On the mezzanine level, just there." He pointed up and over my left shoulder. "Shall I ask him to come down?"

"No thanks, we'll go up."

"All right. I'll just ring him and let him know to expect you, Mr. Barrington."

We took the marble staircase up to the mezzanine level and quickly found the door marked *G. Bennett, Junior Assistant Hotel Manager.* We knocked and presently heard him call out, "Come in."

His office was small, but larger than Mike Masterson's, and it had a window. In the air was the faint scent of cigars. As we entered, he got up from his seat at the desk.

"Mr. Barrington, Mr. Keyes, this is a surprise."

"We weren't sure you'd be here, Mr. Bennett."

"I just got in. I'm actually off today, but I had a staff meeting this morning and now I'm working on scheduling."

"I'm sorry to interrupt. We were hoping to chat with you."

He was in his shirtsleeves and slacks, his tie loosened. "No bother at all. How may I help you? We got your note last night that something had come up. Vivian and I were wondering."

"Yes, I'm sorry about that. I assume you've heard about Mr. Blount?" I asked.

"I'm afraid everyone's talking about it. Dreadful, really."

"Of course. When I went downstairs last night to look for Blount about the tie I bought, I found him dead."

Mr. Bennett motioned for us to sit as he settled back into his chair. "Yes, I wondered if you were the one to find the body. How awful for you."

We took seats opposite him. "Being a police detective, I'm afraid I've seen my share of dead bodies, though I can't say I'm used to it yet. In a way, I hope I never get used to it."

"I understand, Mr. Barrington. Can I offer either of you a drink or a cigar?"

"Not for me, thanks."

Alan shook his head. "No thank you, sir."

"Very well. I didn't like him much, as you know, so I can't say I'm too heartbroken to hear of his death."

"I would imagine not," Alan said.

"Still, it was a shock. Mrs. Verte is quite upset by the news, but then she was one of the few people that actually cared for him, it seems. Or at least didn't hate him," Mr. Bennett said, leaning back in his chair and clasping his hands. "And how sad is that, I must say."

"Very sad, Mr. Bennett. When did you last see him, by the way?" I asked.

"Blount? It was yesterday afternoon when Vivian and I were in his shop. I bought that suit, which I'll probably never get now, and Vivian left her dress to be hemmed. Why?"

"Just wondering. Being a police detective, I'm naturally curious."

"Curious about what?" he asked.

"Someone told me you were also in Blount's shop early yesterday afternoon, having an argument."

He looked surprised. "Whoever told you that is mistaken, Mr. Barrington. I didn't go to his store until later in the afternoon, and we didn't argue."

"You didn't argue with Blount yesterday afternoon in his shop around two p.m.?" I pressed.

"I most certainly did not."

"We have a witness that says someone did. A messenger says it was a man, and that he was having a rather heated argument."

"Did he say what the man looked like?"

"No. How do you know it was a he?" I asked.

"I don't, I didn't, but you said it was a messenger, and generally they're men, aren't they?"

"Not always, Mr. Bennett," Alan stated.

"I was just using 'he' in the general sense. During the war we used a few girls as pages and bellboys, but generally they're all men now."

"I see. What were you doing yesterday afternoon?" I continued.

"I was here, working most of the day. I had lunch, then I went out for a bit. I took in a movie."

"In the middle of the afternoon?" Alan asked.

He nodded his head. "I do that sometimes. I work long hours and many days, so sometimes I treat myself to a matinee."

"Anything good playing?" I asked.

"*The Egg and I*, at the RKO Grand on Clark and Randolph."

"Did anyone see you?"

"No. I mean, yes, of course people saw me. Other people on the street, shop clerks, the usherette and ticket taker at the theater, and whatnot, but I'm sure they wouldn't remember me."

"You were alone?"

"Yes." He had crossed his arms and looked flustered, annoyed.

"Ticket stub from the show?" Alan asked.

"I threw it away. What is all this, you two? Why are you giving me the third degree over some argument I supposedly had with Blount, which I didn't?"

"I'm sorry, Mr. Bennett. I'm just trying to make certain things clear, that's all," I said.

"What things? What's this all about it?"

"You know Blount was murdered," I said, watching his face.

Bennett nodded. "Yes, someone said he was shot, multiple times. Apparently the whole back room is covered in blood, and it even seeped out into the alley under the door."

I sighed and rolled my eyes. "That would be a gross exaggeration. You know, I saw *The Egg and I* myself in Milwaukee last week, but I got called away. How does it end?"

"Happily, I imagine. It was a silly farce. I left before it was over."

What time was the movie?"

"Quarter past two. I got back here to the hotel around five. I happened to see Mrs. Verte going into Blount's shop."

"I see. So you went in, too?" I continued, still watching him.

"Yes, about quarter after five or so, I'd say. She wanted a dress she'd bought hemmed, and I bought a new suit. Vivian asked me to join her in the Sky Star, so she went upstairs to her room and I went back to my apartment to start getting ready for the evening. Then around quarter of seven I returned to pick her up as she had asked. When I knocked on her door, she told me she had broken her perfume bottle and she sent me out in search of a replacement."

"Which took you almost an hour," Alan said.

"Lavender Lilacs is a difficult thing to find at that hour on a Saturday, Mr. Keyes."

"Yet it was for sale right here in the hotel boutique," I said.

"I told you I didn't think to look there." He was scowling now, his arms crossed.

"There's a display of it in their window," Alan said.

"I'm not a window shopper, and I certainly don't pay attention to displays of perfume."

"I suppose not," I said. "Well, we won't keep you any longer, Mr. Bennett. But I wonder if you know where I might find Miss Eye and Mr. Gillingham?"

He raised his eyebrows. "I believe they're up in the ballroom right now, running through some numbers. My security fellow rang me before my staff meeting earlier to ask if they could be allowed access."

"I see. Perhaps you and Mrs. Verte, if she's available, would be so kind as to join us up there, in say, half an hour?"

"What on earth for? There's no show tonight."

"Nothing planned, but there might just be a show. Would you join us, please?"

He shrugged. "I'll see if Mrs. Verte is available. You certainly have my curiosity aroused."

"Perfect. And thank you, Mr. Bennett. Good day," I said, as Alan and I got to our feet.

"Good day to you," Mr. Bennett said. I noticed he had started sweating.

Alan and I left his office and walked back to the marble staircase where we stopped, looking down at the lobby below.

"So what gives?" Alan asked me. "Why do you want those two up in the ballroom?"

"Just a gathering of the suspects. I want Mrs. Gittings there, too. I find it easier to sort through my thoughts if I can talk to everybody together."

"Wilchinski's not going to like it."

"Ask me how much I care. I wonder if Bennett's telling the truth about the perfume."

"You think he really did buy it here in the hotel?"

"If he did, it would be easy enough to check. We could ask the salesgirl who was working last night. I would imagine she'd know him or at least remember him, and they can't possibly sell that many bottles of Lavender Lilacs."

"True. But why would he lie about it in the first place?"

"To give himself an alibi. He could have used that hour to buy the perfume in the hotel boutique, then go around and shoot Blount, destroy the evidence, and get back upstairs, where he ran into us."

"Which would explain why he was winded and not put together."

"Exactly."

"Except he didn't destroy his own evidence. It was all still there," Alan said, looking confused.

"Maybe there was more than one film reel, more than one set of pictures. Perhaps Bennett thought he was destroying all of it."

"Wowzer."

"Of course, he could have actually not known the perfume was for sale in the boutique, and he may have been traipsing up and down Michigan Avenue in the wind looking for it like he said, and he isn't the murderer."

"But if he *did* shoot Blount, the timing is all wrong. Remember, Blount was shot at a little after eight."

"Yes, I've been pondering that, too."

"What do you mean?"

"I mean, what do we have to go by to determine the time of Blount's death?"

"His smashed watch," Alan said.

"Yes, exactly. Remember when we were in the back room and

Wilchinski said, 'The clock is ticking and you can't turn back time, or stop it'?"

"Yeah, so?"

"You can't move time forward, either. Or can you?"

"What do you mean?"

"What if Blount was actually murdered earlier, but someone set his watch ahead?"

"Why would someone do that?"

"To give themselves an alibi, of course. Let's assume for the moment Mr. Bennett did it. He shoots Blount at quarter after seven. Mrs. Verte and probably the doorman know he's out and about. So Bennett changes Blount's watch to just after eight and smashes it, stopping time and making it look like Blount was shot then. That gives Bennett time to get back upstairs with the perfume to Mrs. Verte's room."

"And at just after eight when the murder appeared to have happened, he was with us in the Star Sky Ballroom."

"Yes, indeed. A perfect alibi."

"Wowzer."

"This is all just theory, though. It's still possible Blount was murdered just after eight and the time on his watch wasn't altered."

"But the *possibility* of changing the time on his watch makes Mr. Bennett a suspect for sure."

I nodded. "Yes. So really we're still back to Mr. Bennett, Miss Eye, Mr. Gillingham, and Mrs. Gittings, and I'm a tad curious about Maynard Henning."

"The piano player?"

"Yes. He was clearly a client of Mr. Blount's, and not just for clothing, though we didn't see any photos or movie reels of him, so Blount probably figured he wasn't worth enough to blackmail."

"Then why do you think he may be involved?"

"He may have become aware of what was happening with Miss Eye and decided to act on her behalf. And I keep coming back to that bloody 'W.'"

"What about it?"

"Maybe it wasn't a 'W' at all, maybe it was an 'M.'"

"You mean he wrote it upside down?"

"Or he wrote out an 'M' for Maynard and then rolled over, making it appear he wrote a 'W.'"

"Jeepers, this is all getting confusing."

"I know, and I still can't figure out the green thread."

"Huh."

"My thoughts exactly. I should very much like to talk to Miss Eye and Mr. Gillingham, as well as Mr. Henning, but first let's send a message to Mrs. Gittings."

We went down the staircase to the lobby and crossed over to the desk once again, where I wrote out a message to Mrs. Gittings, put it in an envelope, and addressed it before handing it to the little man behind the counter. "Would you see this gets delivered right away? Send a boy, please."

"Yes, sir." The little man rang a bell and handed the envelope to a messenger boy as we walked over to a bank of pay phones next to the elevators.

"Now what, Heath?"

"Now I need to borrow a nickel."

Alan reached in his trousers pocket, pulled out a small leather coin purse, and handed me a nickel from it.

"Thanks. I think I'll invite Wilchinski to this party, too. After all, the clock is ticking." I picked up the receiver, dropped the nickel in the slot, and dialed "O" as I took out Wilchinski's card from my wallet.

"Operator."

"Yes, King's Lock 5-2825, please."

"One moment." I heard a click, then three rings before he picked up.

"Wilchinski."

"Good afternoon, Detective. This is Heath Barrington."

Silence. Then, "What's good about it?" His voice was raspy.

"There's a show in the Sky Star Ballroom in about half an hour, and I was wondering if you'd be interested in attending."

"You're hilarious, Barrington. Quit wasting my time."

"I didn't know I was wasting your time, Wilchinski. Is the Blount case still open?"

"So far. I haven't filed my official report yet. Why?"

"I have new evidence that will prove it wasn't a random burglar."

"Something someone left at your door again?"

"Now you're the funny one. No, but I may have your suspect and the evidence on hand if you stop by the ballroom this afternoon just after four."

Silence again. "I was just on my way out. I can swing by there, but I'm warning you, no guessing games, no smoke and mirrors. If you got something on someone, I want to know about it. Otherwise I'm filing my report."

"I understand. Just be there." I hung up without another word.

"Is he coming?"

"I think so. Let's head upstairs."

We took the elevator to the Sky Star, which opened onto the reception corridor. The double doors to the ballroom were closed and a sign said *Open at 7:00 p.m.* I strode over to them and pushed, but they were unlocked and swung open effortlessly.

The ballroom looked completely different in the afternoon sun, light flooding in from every direction through the many windows. The chairs were all turned upside down on the tables, which had been stripped of their tablecloths and candles. Stains on the floor that were invisible at night now appeared, and the glittering walls now looked drab. The twinkling lights in the ceiling had been turned off, and somehow the wonderful mystery was gone. It was as if we had peeked behind the curtain at the county fair magic show. At the far end of the room, on the stage, I could see a man sitting at the piano. Miss Eye, in an emerald green dress, her hair swept back into a ponytail, was standing nearby, looking over some sheet music. The man turned as we entered.

"Sorry, fellas, we're closed. This is a private rehearsal."

"I'm Heath Barrington, this is Alan Keyes. We were wondering if we could have a brief word with Miss Eye," I said as Alan and I walked closer.

"It's all right, Manny, I know these two. My friends from the coffee shop and Blount's store, correct?"

I looked up at her on the stage and smiled. "That's right. I'm surprised to find you here on a Sunday."

She smiled back, utterly charming. "I'm not the church-going type. Sundays and Mondays are our days off, but I had an idea to change a couple of my numbers, and Manny here was nice enough to come in and help me out before I run the changes by Mr. Storm. This is Maynard Henning, the band pianist."

I nodded at the little man in brown trousers and rolled-up shirt sleeves. He held the stub of a cigar between his thick, ruddy lips.

"How do you do, Mr. Henning," Alan said. "I'm sorry, I saw your name on the banner last night and I thought it said Mr. Heming. I guess from where I sat the two 'N's looked like an 'M.'"

Mr. Henning laughed. "It's okay, mister, I've been called worse." The cigar stub never left his mouth.

"Guess I should get my eyesight checked," Alan said.

Mr. Henning glanced up at the banner across the top of the stage." "It's bad script, I can see where it would look like Heming."

Alan grinned. "Thanks, I appreciate that. You play very well, by the way."

"Practice, practice, practice. But the singer gets all the glory," he said, the cigar stub bobbing up and down.

Miss Eye laughed.

"You're a customer of Mr. Blount's, I understand," I said to Mr. Henning.

"I was. He got a bit too expensive for me, so I quit going to him a couple weeks ago."

"I see. Mr. Blount appeared to be rather expensive for a lot of his clients."

"Uh, yeah, so I understand. I heard he got popped last night in the back room of his shop."

"Yes, he was shot in cold blood."

"Couldn't have happened to a nicer guy." He was chewing the cigar stub now, and bits of tobacco flew out as he spoke.

"That seems to be the general consensus."

"Give us a few, okay, Manny?" Miss Eye said.

"Sure thing, Gloria. I could use a break anyway." Manny got up from the piano bench, glanced in our direction, and then strode backstage, dropping the cigar stub in a bin as he left.

"So, what can I do for you two gentlemen? An autograph?"

I smiled. "I'd like that, actually. Or rather, my mother would."

"Oh? Is she a fan?"

"I doubt she's heard of you, but you might make it big. And if I tell her I met you personally, Gloria Eye, the Eye of the Storm, she'll be impressed. I may even buy one of your records for her."

Gloria smiled. "I'd be delighted. What's your mother's name?"

"Ramona. Ramona Barrington."

I watched her as she picked up a program left over from last night and signed the back of it.

"To Ramona Barrington, with love from Gloria Eye. That okay?"

"That's swell, Miss Eye, thank you."

"You'll have to come get it, Mr. Barrington."

"Uh, sure, sure." I climbed up the side stairs onto the stage, looking back down at Alan, who stood there with his hat in his hand.

"Here you go." She handed me the program, and I put it in my inside jacket pocket.

"Where is Mr. Gillingham?" I asked, removing my hat as well.

"Backstage. As I said, I wanted to run through some ideas for a new number with Manny, and Walter decided to tag along. He doesn't like sitting home alone."

"I can understand that. I live alone," I said.

"Pity."

"I make do. Alan and I enjoyed your performance last night very much."

"How kind of you to say."

"Your voice is melodious, soothing, rhythmic. I really think you could go places."

"That's my intention, Mr. Barrington. I hope others agree with you."

"I know I do," Alan said.

She looked down at him. "Would you like an autograph, too, Mr. Keyes?"

Alan beamed. "Gee, that would be swell."

"All right, handsome, come get it. I think I have another program here. For your mother?"

"No, ma'am, my mother's dead," he said as he climbed onto the stage with us.

"Oh. I'm sorry."

"It's all right. You didn't know. If you could just make it to Alan Keyes, that would be great."

She signed another program and handed it to him. "I'm glad you liked the show last night. We're not on again until Tuesday."

"Gee, we'll be gone back to Milwaukee by then."

"Well, you never know. We might play Milwaukee some time. I'm from Shiocton, Wisconsin, originally. Anyway, I'm glad you came last night. I'm sorry we got a late start."

"Yes, I noticed you and Mr. Gillingham were rather late getting onstage last night," I said.

She smiled and then laughed. "Entertainers are notoriously late, Mr. Barrington. You don't get out much, do you?"

"I get out enough. The bandleader seemed rather annoyed."

"Mr. Storm? He gets annoyed easily. Walter and I had an argument, that's all. He felt my dress was too low cut."

"The one you had Mr. Blount steam and press for you yesterday afternoon."

"That's right. Walter felt it was too revealing. He can be overprotective sometimes. You know how men are, no offense. Anyway, I got angry and went out."

"Out?"

"That's right. I took the service elevator downstairs and went out the back door to the alley by the loading dock."

"Curious."

"Not really. I wanted to be alone. I didn't want to be disturbed. Unlike Walter, I don't mind being alone. I've been alone most of my life, at least until I met him. Anyway, I had a cigarette or two, then I came back upstairs."

"And what time was that?"

"I'm not sure. It was about eight fifteen when I got back upstairs, so I suppose I got down there around eight. Why?"

"Just wondering. And you didn't see anyone else in the alley?"

She laughed. "At that time of night? No, I didn't. I stayed up on the landing, though, near the door. You never know who you might meet in a dark alley, and it's almost always going to be someone you don't want to."

"Makes sense. What about Mr. Gillingham?"

"What about him?"

"What did he do? He was late getting to the bandstand, too."

"He did the stairs."

"I beg your pardon?" I said.

"He does the stairs when he's upset or angry, to help him blow off steam. He goes down several flights of stairs, then runs back up, then goes down again until he's cooled down."

"Interesting." I glanced about the stage, taking it all in from this perspective.

"Never been onstage before?" Miss Eye asked.

"Not since fourth grade when we did a play about the pilgrims. I was a turkey."

She laughed, and I thought I heard Alan chuckle. "It's not so different on this side as it is down there."

"I beg to differ, Miss Eye. Up here you're all alone in the spotlight, aren't you? And everyone's judging you. Down there, we're the anonymous ones in the dark doing the judging."

"Well, that's certainly an interesting way of putting it, Mr. Barrington."

"Heath's an interesting fellow, Miss Eye. We've never talked to a singer before, at least I haven't," Alan said.

"You talked to me yesterday, in the coffee shop, Mr. Keyes," she said softly, a smile on her lips.

"Yes, I know. But now you're here onstage, and I know you as a performer. It's different somehow."

"A bit starstruck, Mr. Keyes? You don't seem the type."

Alan smiled back at her. "Maybe I am, a little. You really are quite lovely, and after hearing you sing last night, well, perhaps I'm seeing you differently."

"Perhaps you're *seeing* me differently, but I'm not different, not really."

"Gee, you're not like anyone I know, Miss Eye. I know plenty of wives, mothers, teachers, secretaries, clerks, nurses, all kinds of women, but no one who looks or sings like you do," Alan said, his cheeks rosy.

She smiled. "Those wives, mothers, teachers, secretaries, nurses, and clerks you know? Actresses and singers are just like them. We're all women, no different, no better, no worse. Some people put actresses and singers on pedestals, others put us in the gutter."

"I suppose that's true, Miss Eye," I said.

"It is true, Mr. Barrington. Aren't we all alike in our most basic form? Don't we all have the same wants, needs, and desires?"

"Of course."

"Men, women, rich, poor, laborer, or housewife, all of us."

"Very true, Miss Eye. You're pretty smart," Alan said.

She laughed again. "You sound surprised. Because I'm pretty and can sing I'm not supposed to be smart?"

"That sounds pretty stupid, I suppose."

"It certainly does. No offense."

"None taken, ma'am."

"How did you hear about Mr. Blount?" I said. "About his death, I mean."

She turned her attention to me. "One of the maids told me. Manny heard it from the janitor. Yes, it's pretty dreadful. He was a nasty little man, but still…"

"It was pretty obvious you and Mr. Gillingham didn't care for him."

"I made no attempt to hide it. Why should I?"

I shrugged. "I don't know."

She fiddled with her ponytail, taking out the yellow ribbon and shaking her hair, letting it fall upon her shoulders before speaking again. "Rumor says it was a robbery. Someone from the alley. Like I said before, you never know who you're going to meet in a dark alley, and it's almost always someone you don't want to."

"Indeed, Miss Eye, indeed. Speaking of rumors, I heard Mr. Gillingham was in Blount's shop yesterday afternoon, having a rather heated argument with him."

She bristled, wrapping the yellow ribbon between her fingers. "Rumors. Yes, Walter was there. I told him not to go, that we would talk to him together, but he is rather headstrong at times. He told me he and Mr. Blount exchanged words."

"What about?"

"Nothing that concerns you, Mr. Barrington. Walter and I weren't happy with Blount's terms of sale any longer, that's all. Like Manny, we were tired of his high prices."

"I see. Well, we shan't keep you from your rehearsal any longer," I said.

"A pleasure, gentlemen. What time is it, anyway?"

I took out my pocket watch. "A couple minutes after four."

"Right. No rest for the wicked, they say."

"Are you wicked, Miss Eye?"

She gave me a sly grin. "Aren't we all?"

I shrugged my shoulders. "Perhaps so. By the way, I asked Mr. Bennett and Mrs. Verte to join us here shortly, along with Mrs. Gittings. I hope you don't mind."

She cocked her head. "Do I know them? More fans?"

"Mr. Bennett is the junior assistant manager here at the hotel, Mrs. Verte is a guest in from New York, and Mrs. Gittings lives nearby."

"How interesting. Are we having a party? I'm sorry, but I do have to rehearse more."

"I don't think it will take long. I wonder if we could sit at a table, though. Would you mind asking Mr. Gillingham to join us?"

"I'm afraid I would, Mr. Barrington. As I said, I have work to do. As much as I enjoy socializing, I have to earn a living. To do that, I need to rehearse."

"Of course, but this is about Mr. Blount's murder. As a police detective, I really must insist. Oh and by the way, a Chicago police detective by the name of Wilchinski will be joining us as well."

"All right, I'll give you fifteen minutes. I'll go get Walter and tell Manny to relax." She walked backstage as Alan and I went back down the steps and started turning chairs back down around an eight top after setting our hats on top of a nearby table.

"Gee, Heath, she admitted being down in the alley right about the time of the murder," Alan said quietly.

"Yes, she did."

"So, you think she did it?"

"Possibly. Or maybe she was covering for Walter. If he did do it, she gave him an alibi by saying she was on the landing in the alley and saw no one."

"True."

"And that bit about doing the stairs makes for a perfect alibi since no one would have seen him, and it explains why he was rather disheveled and out of breath when he finally reached the ballroom."

"I was thinking that same thing. So now what?"

"I honestly don't know. My head is swimming, but if things don't start coming together fast, I am going to have to deal with one angry detective."

"So, who do you think did it?"

"I have an idea, but I'm still not sure. I can't place the pieces in the right spots. I'm hoping once I have everyone together, things will start to click. What's your opinion?"

Alan turned the last chair down and leaned against the back of it. "Like you said, all four of them had motive and opportunity. It's possible, I suppose, that they all did it together."

"That's becoming your standby theory."

"I know, but I don't really believe it this time. I mean, Mr. Bennett and Mrs. Verte didn't even know Miss Eye and Mr. Gillingham, and none of them knew Mrs. Gittings."

"So we were led to believe."

Alan looked surprised. "You mean you think they *did* know each other before?"

I grinned. "No, sorry. Just pulling your leg. But also a caution to not ever assume anything."

"Right. Good point."

"So, if you don't believe they all did it, what is your theory?"

"I just can't believe it was Mrs. Gittings," he said. "I'm sorry, but I just can't."

"Okay, so then who?"

"My money's still on Miss Eye and Mr. Gillingham, much as I hate to think that. I mean, she's so pretty and talented and nice and all."

"None of that means she couldn't be a murderer."

"I know, I know. That's why I'm saying I think if any of the four did it, it was them. They had a motive and opportunity, especially working together, with her unlocking the door and him slipping inside from the alley. And they were both late getting onstage."

I nodded. "Very well thought out, Alan. I'm impressed."

He scratched his chin and looked at me with his big puppy-dog eyes. "Say, maybe it was that piano player, Maynard Henning and Mr. Gillingham. Maybe Gloria is innocent."

I smiled. "You really are kind of starstruck by her, aren't you?"

"Maybe a little," he said, blushing. "She's the closest I've ever gotten to a big star. I hope she didn't think I was being foolish. I just stood there staring at her."

"With a blank, stunned look on your face, just like Blount had the other night when we were talking with Mrs. Verte and Mr. Bennett. I couldn't tell what you were thinking."

"I don't think my face looked as bad as his. He looked shocked, almost."

"He did. You just looked starstruck. But don't worry about it. I'm sure she didn't give it another thought."

"I hope not."

"And if she did, well, *c'est la vie*."

"You and your French. What does that mean?"

"Such is life, more or less."

"That's a pretty good saying, I guess."

"Yes, it comes in handy for a lot of things. If you like, I could certainly teach you the French I know, though I am pretty rusty. We could maybe take a class together sometime, if you want."

"Sure, or *oui*," Alan said. "How's that?"

I laughed. "Good start. *Oui, non, une, deux, trois, rouge, blanc*...hmm."

"What? Your head still swimming?"

"Drowning, but I think you just tossed me a life preserver," I said.

"What do you mean?"

"I mean, Mr. Henning, the pianist, blank, stunned looks, Wilchinski, and French. The pieces, I think, just fit, and just in time."

CHAPTER SIXTEEN

It was 4:17 p.m.

Finally, with the late arrival of Wilchinski, we were all present in the ballroom, with the exception of Mrs. Gittings.

"Thank you for joining us, Mr. Bennett and Mrs. Verte. You know Miss Eye and Mr. Gillingham?"

"Only professionally. We've never met," Mr. Bennett said.

"My apologies, then. Mr. Bennett, Mrs. Verte, I'd like you to meet Miss Gloria Eye and Mr. Walter Gillingham."

"How do you do?" Mr. Bennett and Mrs. Verte said, almost at once.

"Very well, thank you," Miss Eye responded. Walter only nodded.

"And this is Detective Wilchinski of the Chicago police." He stood next to me, his big arms folded across his chest, a scowl on his face. Wilchinski tipped his hat but didn't remove it.

"So what's this all about, Mr. Barrington?" Miss Eye asked.

"Exactly what I'd like to know," Wilchinski growled.

"I wanted to speak with the four of you and Mrs. Gittings about Mr. Blount's murder. Detective Wilchinski is the investigator on the case."

"Then why isn't he doing the talking? How are you involved?" Mrs. Verte asked.

"I found the body, and in talking with each of you earlier, I think I may have uncovered some interesting information. Clues, if you will."

Miss Eye was still fiddling with her hair ribbon, twisting it about her fingers. "His death was shocking, certainly. But why talk to us? It's my understanding it was a robbery, as I mentioned before."

"It was a robbery," Wilchinski said flatly. "But Barrington here likes to play cop and waste people's time."

I shot him a look. "Robbery is one theory, Detective. I have others. I was hoping to get everyone's cooperation in helping me clear a few things up. Why don't we all be seated?" I motioned to the chairs and table.

"Fine by me," Walter Gillingham said, adjusting his eye patch and taking a chair.

Miss Eye sat next to him, and eventually everyone was seated. To my left sat Wilchinski, and next to him was Mrs. Verte, followed by Mr. Bennett, then Walter Gillingham, Miss Eye, and Alan, leaving one chair empty to my right for Mrs. Gittings.

"Now then, all of you knew Mr. Blount and were aware of his business practices. So, I'd like to go over various points about each of your whereabouts last night, for starters," I said.

"I thought we already went over that," Gloria said, sounding somewhat irritated.

"Yes, but perhaps one of you may know or may have seen something. As Detective Wilchinski alluded to, I'm not acting officially, but I was hoping I could clear some things up. Does anyone object to that?"

"How long is this going to take?" Gloria said. "As I said before, I have work to do, and Manny is waiting."

"I'll try to be as quick as possible, Miss Eye."

Mr. Bennett shrugged. "I suppose I don't have any objection to a few questions. Would that be all right with you, Vivian?"

"I've nothing to hide, but what about this Mrs. Gittings woman? Where is she?"

"I am hoping she will be along shortly. In the meantime, in the interest of keeping this brief, why don't we get started? I'll get right to the point. I have reason to believe that one of you, or Mrs. Gittings, murdered Mr. Blount."

They all glanced at one another, and then back at me. "Don't be absurd," Miss Eye said at last.

"I have evidence to support my theory, Miss Eye."

"What evidence?" Mrs. Verte asked.

"Yes, Barrington," Wilchinski growled again. "You said you had facts. I warned you I didn't want to play your foolish games. If you have something to say, say it."

I stood and moved behind my chair, putting my hands on the back of it. "As some of you may or may not be aware, Blount was found clutching a green spool of thread. That had me puzzled. Was it green for 'G'? There was also a bloody 'W' on the floor next to his body that Mr. Blount apparently wrote before he died. I was puzzled by that, too. Was the 'W' for Walter, as in Walter Gillingham? And was the green thread for Gillingham?"

"Hey, what are you getting at?" Walter said, getting to his feet also and almost knocking over his chair.

I took a step back. "Calm yourself, Mr. Gillingham. I'm hopefully getting at the truth, eventually. You're engaged to Miss Eye, yes?"

"That's right. That's an easy truth, and you know it."

"Yes, that's a happy thing. But there's some darkness, too. You were being blackmailed by Blount, weren't you? Or rather, Miss Eye was, and you, Mr. Gillingham, were aware of it."

"How dare you," Miss Eye said, uncrossing her legs and sitting bolt upright, the ribbon now held tightly in her fist.

"What do you mean, mister?" Walter asked, taking a step behind Miss Eye and closer to me.

"Miss Eye, you're a fairly successful singer, aren't you?" I continued.

"Somewhat. I've done okay with the band, and I've cut a few records with them. Why?" She was eyeing me warily.

"You have the talent, looks, and personality to make it big. But a couple years ago when you first came to Chicago from…where was it?"

"Shiocton, Wisconsin."

"Ah yes, that's right. You found yourself in Chicago, young, broke, all alone, and eager, I'm guessing. You answered one of Blount's ads, didn't you?"

"You shut up." Walter fairly shouted, his fists clenched.

She looked up at him. "It's all right, Walter. I can handle myself. Yes, Mr. Barrington, I answered one of his ads for modeling."

"Yes, and you posed for some photographs, including some nudes. And from there, it was fairly simple for Blount to convince you to entertain some of his clients in their rooms, wasn't it?"

"Watch your mouth," Gillingham snarled, glaring at me from his one good eye and moving closer still as if preparing to swing.

Alan stood up, blocking his path and putting his hand on Gillingham's arm. "Easy, Mr. Gillingham. Let's not add an assault charge."

"Sit down, Walter," Miss Eye said sternly. Wilchinski was watching with an amused expression, as if he hoped Walter would sock me.

Like a frustrated little boy, Walter returned to his seat but continued to pound his fist into the palm of his other hand and glare at me. Alan sat back down as well, keeping watch on Walter as I continued.

"But then, Miss Eye, you met the charming Mr. Gillingham here, home from overseas early because of his injury. He got you a tryout in the band he was in, and you fell in love. And now you both have respectable jobs, promising careers, even. But your past, Miss Eye, has come back to haunt you, hasn't it?"

"Who told you all this?" Mr. Gillingham growled, his face red. A bead of sweat had popped out on his brow.

"Some of it I found out on my own, with Alan's help and Detective Wilchinski, I must admit. You see, as I believe you all know, Mr. Blount diversified his business to include photography. But not just any photography. He offered to take photographs of young women who were new to the city, just starting out, trying to break into modeling or show business. They'd answer his advertisements and he'd take photos. Perhaps he'd offer them a few bucks if they were willing to pose nude or partially nude."

"That's disgusting," Mrs. Verte said.

"It certainly is, Mrs. Verte. Mr. Blount took advantage of their youth, their inexperience, their eagerness. He exploited them. Once he had the nude photos, he'd sell them to various underground publications. Occasionally, if a girl was very eager and willing, he'd give her the opportunity to make even more money, offering her services for the night to a lonely businessman in town for a meeting or two."

"So you're saying he took photos of this young lady here?" Mr. Bennett said, indicating Miss Eye.

"Yes, I'm afraid he did. And I suspect he exploited Miss Eye, continuing to blackmail her after she became a success. Isn't that right, Miss Eye?"

"Don't answer him, Gloria," Gillingham growled.

She shook her head. "It's all right, Walter. He already knows."

"Yes, I'm afraid I do. We found some of his photos, including some of you, and some of those magazines and advertisements in the back room of his shop, hidden away for safekeeping."

"So what now?" Miss Eye asked quietly, her head down, the ribbon now limp in her hands.

"Are you saying those two murdered Mr. Blount?" Mr. Bennett asked, his eyes wide.

I looked over at him. "I believe, Mr. Bennett, that they made their way to his shop last night with the intention of working him over—beating him up, as it were, teaching him a lesson. Isn't that correct, Miss Eye?"

"I didn't kill the louse, and neither did Walter."

"But I'm curious, Miss Eye. You made a point of getting to Blount's shop late last night, almost at closing. And you insisted on trying on your dress, even though it had only been pressed, not altered. That struck me as odd, and I felt you used it as an excuse to get into the back room alone, but why?"

"Yes. Why, Mr. Barrington? Please tell us why I did that," she said, now looking up at me. Her eyes were moist and red.

"Two possible reasons, Miss Eye. You either wanted to get the gun out of the drawer and shoot Blount, or you wanted to unlock the back door so you or Mr. Gillingham, or perhaps both, could come back later. But you hadn't counted on me and Mr. Keyes being in the shop when you arrived. I suspect you went in the back room, unbolted the back door, and left again. You may have searched for the gun but found it missing. Perhaps you wanted to make sure Blount didn't use it on the two of you after you learned of its existence. Then you met with Mr. Gillingham. You probably told him the gun was missing, and perhaps Blount had it on his person. You may have tried to talk Gillingham out of confronting him because of that, but Gillingham is headstrong and I doubt he could be persuaded to abandon his plan. So, the two of you went down the fire stairs to the loading dock in the alley, and then into Blount's shop through the unlocked alley door about 7:40 or so, later than originally planned, because of you trying to persuade Walter to change his mind. Isn't that correct?"

"There's an awful lot of *probablys* and *possiblys* in your story there, mister," Miss Eye said.

"But still quite accurate, I'd say."

"We didn't kill him. He was already dead when we got there," Walter blurted out.

"Walter," Gloria exclaimed.

"It's all right, Miss Eye. I had already surmised that," I said.

"What's that mean?" Walter asked, his face still red, his one good eye bulging.

"It means, Mr. Gillingham, that I had already figured out you hadn't killed him, that he was already dead by the time you got there."

"What are you on about, Mr. Barrington? Is this some sort of game?" Mrs. Verte asked.

"Not a very good one. I must admit I suspected Miss Eye and Mr. Gillingham may have been planning on killing Blount, or at least roughing him up and scaring him into stopping the blackmail."

"Planning on it, but they didn't?" Mr. Bennett asked.

"No, because a random burglar had already shot him," Wilchinski said, his arms folded across his chest once more as he leaned back in his chair.

I glanced over at Wilchinski but didn't reply. Instead I turned my attention back to Miss Eye. "When you found him shot to death it must have been quite a shock, yes?"

"I suppose so," Miss Eye responded.

"I would say so. What to do next? Call the police? But how to explain why you were there? Do nothing? But what if someone saw you? Finally, you decided to do nothing and take your chances. You fled back to the Sky Star Ballroom, getting onstage late. Of course I'm speculating on most of that, but I would say that later, after your performance, you came up with the excuse of having the argument over your dress, and then Mr. Gillingham running the stairs to explain why he was disheveled and out of breath when he got to the stage."

"How do you know they didn't do it? Maybe she did take the gun and they did shoot him, together," Mrs. Verte said.

"Vivian," Mr. Bennett said. "Clearly, Mr. Barrington, Blount was a cad, a lowlife who took advantage of young women, but why drag me and Mrs. Verte into this?"

I walked closer to Mr. Bennett. "It all comes back to the clues Blount himself left, Mr. Bennett, as I mentioned before. The photos we found, and the sales ledgers, all point to you, along with Miss Eye, Mr. Gillingham, and Mrs. Gittings as possible suspects."

"But you just said those two didn't do it. That means you think either I or this Mrs. Gittings killed him," he exclaimed, turning his head to look up at me.

"That is a theory, Mr. Bennett. You were a client of Mr. Blount's," I said.

"Of course. You know I was. I bought a few things from him. I've told you that before."

"But clearly you didn't care for him, and he didn't care for you."

"It's no secret we didn't like each other, Detective."

I looked at Vivian. "But you were quite fond of Mr. Blount, Mrs. Verte, is that right?"

She looked uncomfortable. "I found him exotic and interesting, and rather funny. He was amusing. I must say his death was a shock. Of course, I wasn't aware of all this nasty business."

I glanced back down at Mr. Bennett. "For not liking Mr. Blount, Mr. Bennett, you certainly bought a lot of clothes from Blount's store, expensive clothes. Very expensive clothes."

"I liked his merchandise, even if I didn't care for him. He had good taste. Good fashion is worth paying for."

"You seemed to be telling a very different story Friday night when we had cocktails. As I recall, you said his clothes were overpriced, and I would have to agree with you. Dress shirts for $20.00 apiece—you can get nearly the same thing at Sears, three for $2.75."

"Nearly the same thing and the same thing are two different things, Detective," he said.

"True. And he sold you ties for $15.00 each. Sears has them for seventy-nine cents."

"I don't shop at Sears, Mr. Barrington."

"Maybe you should. Mr. Blount sells those same ties in his shop for $1.99, yet you paid $15.00."

"Not the same, I assure you," Bennett replied. He had taken out a cigar from his pocket and was turning it over in his hands, end to end.

"You're probably right. Yours came with a guarantee of silence, can't get that at Sears."

"What's that supposed to mean?" Bennett snarled, his mustache twitching, the cigar spinning faster between his fingers.

"Blount was blackmailing you, wasn't he? And you paid him off by buying overpriced merchandise, over and over again."

"Don't be ridiculous." His face was red, almost the same shade as Gillingham's had been earlier.

"I try never to be ridiculous, Mr. Bennett. I don't always succeed, but I do try."

"I refuse to discuss this in front of Vivian and these people." The cigar was now clamped in his fist and he was slowly squeezing it to death.

"Oh, I think Miss Eye and Mr. Gillingham are very familiar with Mr. Blount's business tactics. As we've already discussed, Miss Eye was one of his victims also."

"Maybe so, but I don't want Mrs. Verte subjected to this. She didn't even really know Blount. If you want to discuss the matter, let's do it in private, in my office."

"We could, Mr. Bennett, but I think Mrs. Verte needs to hear what you have to say. I think we all do," I said, moving further around the table.

"You must be mad, Mr. Barrington," Mrs. Verte said.

"No, not mad, Mrs. Verte. Though certainly all of you were, and with good reason."

"What are you trying to say? That we all killed him?"

I smiled. "That, Mr. Bennett, is a possibility, and a frequent theory of Mr. Keyes, here. I believe Blount wasn't satisfied to make money from selling his nude pictures, or from his cut in the prostitution fees. He discovered that if he took secret photos of some of these lonely businessmen in the act, as it were, he could use those photos, and the threat of them going public, to blackmail those businessmen. Businessmen like you, Mr. Bennett."

"That's absurd and a disgusting allegation. You'll be hearing from the Edmonton's lawyers." A vein on his neck started to throb, his fists were clenched, the cigar in ruins, and he had started to sweat.

"I doubt you'll want those lawyers involved in this, sir. The photos were found, at least some of them, hidden in Blount's back room, as I said, along with a movie reel with your name on it. Not just of you, but others, too. He had quite a little racket going, didn't he? He would force you to buy overpriced merchandise in his store in exchange for his silence."

"Let's go, Vivian. I think we've heard enough of this nonsense." He started to get up but she just sat there, staring at him. The remains of the cigar were now in a pile on the tabletop.

I put out my hand and Bennett sank back down. "Not yet, please. Blount's account book shows consistent, fairly large deposits, increasingly so over the past few months. If I had to guess, and I do, I'd say Blount was putting increasing pressure on you for more money and you wanted to be rid of him. The police have the photos and the film reel in their possession, Mr. Bennett. Isn't that right, Wilchinski?"

Wilchinski nodded. "Quite a stash of perverted stuff. We took it all downtown."

Bennett's face fell and he knew he was defeated. "Please, those photos, that movie, it can't see the light of day. Please." His voice fairly squeaked.

"How did this all happen, Mr. Bennett?"

He glanced at Mrs. Verte, his face now almost purple, eyes moist and red. A vein in his neck was throbbing. "Vivian, you must understand…"

She stared at him, her face a mixture of shock and disgust. "I don't believe this, George. Is this true?"

He turned back to me. "Those pictures are horrible."

"Why don't you tell me how it happened in the first place?" I asked as gently as I could.

He dropped his head and stared at the remains of his cigar. He shook his head slowly. "How did it happen? I ask myself that every day. It was just a year ago. I stopped into his shop after work one Saturday night. I needed a sweater. Blount was there, of course. He was amicable, chatty, and a good listener. He knew I was a bachelor, and he asked if I ever got lonely."

"And you said?"

He stared down at the table top again, avoiding Mrs. Verte's glare. "I told him that of course I get lonely. I'm not what most women would call handsome, you know. I don't get the chance to meet many girls, and the ones I do meet usually have no interest in me."

"Go on."

"Well, Blount told me he could fix me up with a nice massage by a pretty girl. I said no at first and thought that was the end of it. But I ran into him again in the hotel bar the next night. He bought me a couple drinks, we started talking again, and what he had to say sounded like just what I needed, so I said yes. A girl came to my flat that night. He insisted it would be completely discreet, that no one would know."

"I see," I said. "And then what?"

He glanced up at me briefly and then back down at the tabletop and the pile of tobacco. "It was pleasant. She was a nice girl, if a bit simple."

"Oh, George, how could you?" Vivian said, hurt and disapproval in her voice.

"I'm so sorry, Vivian, I truly am. I have been since the day it happened," he answered, but he didn't look at her.

"And it was more than just a massage," I said.

He nodded slowly. "Yes, Mr. Barrington, that was the understanding. But you must believe, you all must believe, that it was the first time I ever did anything like that, and I felt horribly guilty. I still do."

"You disgust me," Mrs. Verte said.

He looked at her, and he had the expression of a little boy who was just scolded. Then he looked back down at the table again and began moving the bits of cigar tobacco around into little piles as he spoke. "Yes, well, anyway, the next day I stopped in to see Blount again, and he asked me what I thought. I told him that it was just okay, and he asked if I perhaps wanted something more exotic. I wasn't sure what he meant, but I was intrigued, I must admit."

"You'd gotten over your guilt by then?" I asked.

"What? No. I told you, I still feel guilty, but I was intrigued. He had awakened something in me. It's hard to explain."

"I get the impression Mr. Blount could be very persuasive," I said. "I think I can understand."

He looked up at me. "Can you? I hope so. He could indeed be very persuasive. He said he knew a place not far from the hotel where anything goes, and that it could get wild and fun, no questions asked. For a price, of course."

"Of course."

"He gave me the address of an apartment building in a rather bad part of town. I took a cab there, and I must have stood out on the sidewalk for fifteen minutes. At that point, I had changed my mind back and forth probably twenty times as to whether or not I should go through with it. Finally, I reminded myself that nothing ventured, nothing gained, so I went inside. I went through a door into a whole other world."

"In what way?" I asked.

He had moved the cigar bits into three separate piles. "It was a dark world, mysterious, full of shadows, of men, of women, and God knows what else. Presently I felt hands on me, groping me, touching me. I was led to a small chamber with better light. That should have been a clue, but I was too scared, nervous, excited. Mirrors covered the walls, but I did my best not to look at myself."

"What happened next?" I asked. I got the impression that Bennett was relieved to be finally able to talk about this.

"Things happened. They did unspeakable things to me in that room." His voice was almost a whisper as he now destroyed the three mounds of tobacco and spread them flat upon the table.

"I see," I said quietly.

He shook his head violently and his voice raised. "No, no, you don't, no one does, no one could. I couldn't describe them if I tried. When it was over, I went directly home. I got to my flat, took a hot bath, and washed my mouth out with soap. I had a horrible night's sleep, and the next day I called in sick to work. The first time in seven years."

"And what of Blount?"

He shook his head, not looking at me. "I never wanted to see or hear from him again, but of course I knew I would. I couldn't avoid him forever. Still, I vowed never to set foot in his shop again, so I was quite surprised one day when I got an envelope from him at my office here in the hotel, marked private and confidential. Inside was a letter explaining that he expected me to buy clothing from him from now on, at his prices. If I did not, photos like the one he enclosed would be sent to the newspapers and to my employer. I hid the envelope in my desk drawer, wondering what to do next. I was so scared. I'm so sorry, Vivian. Please, I know I've shocked you."

She turned her head away from him, as if she couldn't look at him anymore. "No wonder you hated him so." She almost spat the words in disgust.

"The photos were of you in that building, I presume," I said.

He nodded, slowly. "Yes. They were vile. He said he had a movie, too."

"So you gave him the money."

Bennett looked up at me then, tears running down his cheeks. "I wasn't going to at first, but I felt I had no choice. There was an invoice enclosed in the envelope for some shirts and ties. I wrote out a check for almost a hundred dollars."

I nodded. "He used the clothing as a cover, of course. In case anyone ever questioned where the money was coming from. He could prove you, and others like you, were just purchasing expensive clothing by showing the invoices. It made it all appear very legitimate."

"Yes. The hundred dollars was just the start of it, I'm afraid," Bennett said.

"He continued sending you invoices and having you come in to buy clothes, didn't he?"

He looked up at me and down again, the cigar remnants now spread out in a circle in front of him. "Yes. The invoices kept coming along with more disgusting photos."

I looked again at Mrs. Verte. She was staring at him, her eyes narrowed, a scowl on her face.

"So, Mr. Bennett, you went to his store last night to get the photos back, is that right?"

He shook his head vehemently once more. "No, I didn't go to his store. I didn't kill him. I wanted to, believe me, and I think he got exactly what he deserved, but I didn't do it."

I stared at him hard. "But certainly you had the motive and the opportunity, Mr. Bennett. You knew about the gun. You purchased a suit yesterday and went into the back room, presumably alone, to try it on, which would have given you ample time to search the desk for the gun and to pocket it. Then later, when Mrs. Verte broke her bottle of perfume and asked you to go in search of a replacement, you had the perfect chance.

"You could have easily gone down the elevator, bought the perfume in the lobby boutique, and gone outside around to the alley. A knock at the door, Blount opens it, surprised. You tell him you want to talk to him about future payments. He lets you in, you pull the gun, and demand your photos. He gives you a file, which you mistakenly believe is all of them. You shoot him and then burn the folder in the bathroom sink. Then you hurry back upstairs, winded and disheveled, only to find me, Mr. Keyes, and Mrs. Verte waiting in the hall when the elevator door opened. Surprised, you make up an excuse about having to search up and down Michigan Avenue for the elusive perfume."

He stared at me, wide eyed, wiping away his tears. "Because I did search up and down Michigan Avenue. You must believe me."

"It all makes sense, George," Vivian said at last. "You told me you hated him, and now I understand why. You murdered him. You told me you would get him in the end, and now I know what you meant. I never would have thought it, but then I guess I don't really know you."

He turned to her, his face an expression of shock. "Vivian, I didn't shoot Blount. Please!"

"You're lying," she said, loathing in her voice as she leaned away from him.

"I believe you, Mr. Bennett," I said.

"You do?" He looked up at me, his voice incredulous, shaking, hands trembling.

I nodded. "Yes, I do. It was something Mrs. Gittings said that led me in a different direction."

"Mrs. Gittings again. What did she say? And why isn't she here yet?" Mr. Bennett said, his voice still shaking.

"Mrs. Gittings is a bit unorthodox and keeps her own timetable. I'm assuming she's on her way."

Wilchinski took out a cigarette and lit it. "You certainly like your theatrics, Barrington. Entertaining, I must admit. So, how does this Gittings woman play into all this anyway? You said she's a suspect, and that Bennett, Miss Eye, and Mr. Gillingham are apparently innocent. I'm assuming, then, that you think this Mrs. Gittings did it."

"Mrs. Gittings is indeed a suspect, Wilchinski. She used to work for Blount. She discovered what he was doing, at least some of it, and was fired."

"Gittings. Ah yes, I remember her now. She's that dotty old woman we saw in the lobby Friday night," Mrs. Verte said.

"That's right, Mrs. Verte."

"Well, if George didn't kill Mr. Blount, though it still sounds like he did to me, then certainly this Gittings woman did," Mrs. Verte said.

"Why didn't she go to the police if she discovered what Blount was doing?" Wilchinski asked, blowing a cloud of smoke into the air.

"That's a good question," I said. "She probably was afraid of retribution against her by Blount. She is a widow, all alone in the world, and she probably didn't have any hard evidence. Most likely if she had said anything, people would have put it down to the ramblings of a drunken old woman."

"How sad," Mr. Bennett said, his voice soft, as he wiped his eyes and face with his handkerchief. He looked like he had been struck hard in the face several times.

"Very sad," I said. "So, Mrs. Gittings decided to haunt Blount, figuratively, anyway. She walked slowly by his store every day, staring in at him through the window. I think it bothered him at first, unnerved him as she had intended, but he soon realized people didn't take her seriously, that people laughed at her. She knew about the gun in his desk drawer, of course. She knew all about him, and she felt he was the epitome of evil and that he must be stopped."

"So this Gittings woman shot him," Wilchinski said. "Fine. When she gets here, I'll arrest her. Or maybe she didn't show up because she's guilty. We'll find her, don't you worry."

"No," I answered, looking at him briefly. "She didn't murder Blount." I enjoyed watching the expressions on Wilchinski's face as he alternated between confusion and rage.

"Oh, for heaven's sake, Mr. Barrington," Miss Eye said, exasperated.

"I second that. I'm out of here, Barrington, unless you can wrap this up with something other than games and riddles. The show's just about over," Wilchinski said again, standing up.

I looked at him once more. "Give me five minutes, Wilchinski, please. I really am going somewhere with this."

He looked back at me. "Is this how you do police work in Milwaukee? Guessing games? Drama? That doesn't fly here, Barrington. We don't have time for this." He ground out his cigarette on the bare table top.

"Five more minutes."

He stared at me and then looked at his watch. "Four."

I nodded. "Fine. When Mrs. Gittings was in the back room of his store earlier that afternoon, she stuck her hatpin in the dress form for some reason known only to her, and possibly not even that. She came back last night looking for it. She eventually made her way to the alley and waited for Blount to come out, possibly to harass him as she has done previously, possibly to ask about her hatpin. But it wasn't Blount who came out the back door at about seven twenty-five."

"Who was it?" Mr. Bennett asked, his face now more of a normal color.

"An angel in white, as Mrs. Gittings described it."

"You're joking," Miss Eye said.

"No, it's not very funny, I'm afraid. Mrs. Gittings saw someone she believed to be an angel exiting the back door, leaving it ajar. She looked in and saw Blount dead, smelled the smoke of the burned evidence. It must have been a shock to her. She saw this angel fleeing down the alley, so she followed, just long enough to see the angel enter the hotel and go up, not to heaven, as she described, but just upstairs. She wandered about then, unsure of what to do. The evil she so hated had been destroyed, and it seemed as if it had been an act of God. She was still wandering about when I ran into her just after nine."

"So you're telling us an angel murdered Mr. Blount?" Mr. Bennett said.

"No, just someone Mrs. Gittings mistook for an angel."

"So since I didn't shoot him, and apparently neither Miss Eye nor Mr. Gillingham did, and this Mrs. Gittings didn't, I'd say you're out of suspects," Mr. Bennett said.

"And almost out of time," Wilchinski added, tapping his watch.

"It would appear that way, wouldn't it? Perhaps it was a robber after all," I said.

"Oh good heavens," Mrs. Verte said. "This is all too much. I said from the start it must be a robber, but then you started in on Mr. Bennett."

"Well, I did not kill Blount," Bennett stated firmly. "But didn't you say, Mr. Barrington, that Mrs. Gittings was in the alley about seven twenty-five or so?"

"Yes, I believe that is correct, Mr. Bennett."

"But Blount wasn't murdered until after eight," Mr. Bennett said. "And you said Miss Eye and Mr. Gillingham were there around quarter to eight, and Blount was already dead at that time. Your times don't add up, Barrington."

"You're correct, Mr. Bennett, but I'll get to that in a moment."

"It sounds to me like this Mrs. Gittings is your murderer, as I said before, Detective. She's obviously delusional," Mrs. Verte said.

"Actually, any one of them could have done it, Mrs. Verte. Mr. Bennett, Miss Eye, Mr. Gillingham, or Mrs. Gittings. They all had motive and opportunity, and they all knew of the existence of his gun and its whereabouts. But as I said, it all comes down to the clues Blount left behind. The green spool of thread and the 'W,' as well as Mrs. Gittings's testimony."

"Meaning what?" Mr. Gillingham asked, clearly confused. He reached over and clutched Gloria's hand.

"The green spool of thread. I finally remembered my high school French. Green is *verte* in French, isn't it?"

"I wouldn't know, I took Greek," Mr. Bennett said.

"But *you* know, Mrs. Verte. You speak some French, don't you?" I asked, looking at her.

"Yes."

"Yes what?"

"Yes, I speak some French, and yes, green is *verte*. What of it?" She looked annoyed.

"Because I determined Blount wasn't trying to say 'green' by grabbing that spool of thread. He was trying to say 'Verte.'"

"That's a bit of a stretch," Wilchinski said, rocking back on his chair.

"Perhaps. But if he *was* trying to say 'verte,' then I still couldn't figure out the bloody 'W.' If it wasn't for Walter, what was it for? I even ran through a rather extensive list of French words beginning with 'W,' but nothing made sense."

"So?" Mr. Gillingham asked.

"So it finally occurred to me, it wasn't a 'W' at all. My friend Alan here misread the banner over the stage, mistaking Mr. Henning for Heming, because from a distance the 'N's ran together."

"I don't get it," Walter said, scratching at his eye patch. "You mean Maynard Henning killed Blount? It was a 'M,' not a 'W'?"

"No, Mr. Gillingham, but you're on the right track. I mean it wasn't a bloody 'W' on the floor or an 'M,' it was a 'V' and a 'V' that had bled together, if you'll pardon the expression."

"'V' and a 'V'?" Bennett asked, confused.

"Surely you can figure it out from there, Mr. Bennett. Vivian Verte, VV, Mr. Blount's pet name for her."

"That's absurd," Mr. Bennett said, looking from her to me and back again.

"Is it? Why don't you tell us, Mrs. Verte?"

Her face had gone red, flushed, and she grasped at her throat. "Preposterous, Mr. Barrington. You said yourself we were with you from seven forty until well after the murder."

"That, madam, is quite true, on the surface."

"Oh good heavens. I'm beginning to think you're as mad as that Mrs. Gittings."

"No, not mad, Mr. Bennett. It's quite simple to turn the hands of a watch backward or forward, then smash it against the floor to stop it, making it appear the murder happened later than it did. Blount was most likely shot sometime around seven twenty or so, but the hands of his watch made it appear it was just after eight. That gave Mrs. Verte the perfect alibi. I imagine, Mrs. Verte, you were even congratulating yourself on your good luck of running into us in the hallway and getting to spend the evening with us."

"This is ridiculous, Mr. Barrington. What possible motive would

I have for killing him? I didn't know about all of his disgusting little photos and movies. I only met him a few days ago. I barely knew him at all."

"Oh, but you knew about him years ago, Mrs. Verte, didn't you? I recall you saying your maiden name is Dousman, isn't that right?"

"Yes, so what?" she asked, looking at me suspiciously.

"And when you mentioned your maiden name Friday night in front of Mr. Blount, he looked positively ashen, stricken almost, his face blank. The name Dousman triggered a memory for him. A very unpleasant memory."

"I haven't the faintest idea what you're talking about," she said, drumming her fingers on the tabletop.

"I think you do. You see, there was an empty folder in Blount's little black case where he kept the photos of all the young girls he had photographed. An empty folder between one for a young woman named Ginger Doud and one for a girl by the name of Alice Dove."

"So what?" She had stropped drumming her fingers now and had crossed her arms.

"So, the name Dousman fits in perfectly between those two. And Ginger Doud and Miss Dove were young girls he had taken advantage of. Innocent, naïve girls, trying to break into showbiz, most likely. You mentioned the other day your sister died just before the war ended. What was her name, and how did she die?"

She looked up at me, anger in her eyes. "Rose. Her name was Rose, and she killed herself."

"Rose Dousman. I'm sorry, Mrs. Verte. I know how difficult that must have been. How difficult it must still be. My friend Mike Masterson, the house dick here, told me Blount was mixed up in the death of a young girl just nineteen years old."

"Rose was nineteen years old," she said, her voice suddenly softer as everyone stared at her.

I kept going. "Yes, she was just a child. Rose Dousman, right between Doud and Dove. And Blount took advantage of her, just like he did them. You read about him and his store in the *Tribune* article your uncle sent you, and it angered you, brought up all those old memories. So, you came back to Chicago to meet Mr. Blount, and you feigned delight in him while figuring out how, when, and where to kill him. You pretended to be very fond of him, to be charmed by him, when in fact he disgusted you, didn't he?"

"I don't know what you're talking about."

"Yes, you do, Mrs. Verte. He used your little sister Rose, he took advantage of her. He had her pose scantily dressed, even nude, and then he sold those pictures to a magazine."

"Preposterous. Rose would never do that." Her voice was softer yet as she stared at me defiantly.

"But she did, Mrs. Verte. And he did. Only those photos got leaked, and she was humiliated, ruined. She killed herself, and he was exonerated of any blame. So you decided to get revenge. You bought a gun in New York and came back here. Only your purse was stolen at the train station, and your gun was in it, wasn't it?"

"I told you my purse was stolen, it's no secret," she said.

I nodded. "That's true. But you didn't report it to the police, which I found very odd. Of course, you didn't report it because it had a gun in it."

"Ridiculous."

"Not really. But having the gun stolen really fouled up your plans. Then that night when we were all having cocktails and Mr. Blount mentioned his gun, that was like a gift to you, wasn't it? How simple it would be to buy a dress that needed hemming, bring it to him, go in the back room to try it on, and rummage through his desk until you found the gun. You slipped it in your new purse, and you were off. That's why Miss Eye couldn't find it when she looked for it. You had gotten there before her."

"That's absurd." She had uncrossed her arms and turned her necklace about until it was tangled.

"You went back up to your room and started getting ready for the evening. Blount's closed at seven. You couldn't risk missing him, so you intentionally broke your perfume bottle and sent George out in search of a new one when he came to pick you up. Once he left, you headed downstairs, Blount's gun still in your purse. By the time you reached the alley it was just after seven, maybe five minutes past. You knocked on the service door, Blount answered, surprised.

"You made an excuse, perhaps you told him you lost an earring when you were changing earlier. He let you in to look for it. You pulled the gun and demanded the pictures of Rose. He gave you a file and you shot him. He fell, knocking over the thread rack. You bent down next to him and moved the hands of his watch to two minutes after eight, and then you smashed it against the floor, stopping time, as it were. Then you burned the file in the sink in the bathroom and hurried out into the alley and back upstairs. You probably never noticed Mrs. Gittings out in the alley. With her dark clothes, she most likely blended into the shadows."

"If you insist on making these absurd accusations, Detective, I think I should call my lawyer." She had abandoned her necklace now, leaving it tangled about her throat.

"Go ahead. I think there's a pay phone near the elevators. I'll even loan you a nickel. Or at least Alan will. I'm fresh out." But she didn't move.

"Not up to making the call?"

"I'm amused by your story, that's all. Please continue," she said dryly.

Wilchinski had come forward and was now leaning on the table, listening intently.

"Very well. When Alan and I came out of our room and saw you by the elevator, you weren't waiting to go up, as you had said. You had just come up from downstairs. When you stepped off the elevator, you heard me in the doorway of my room talking to Alan, so you pretended you had just left your room and were waiting for the elevator. Remember, you hadn't pressed the button."

"I forgot."

"Yes, you did, because you had stepped out of the elevator and turned around pretending to be waiting for it when you heard us."

"Why would I do that?" she asked, her voice a bit louder now.

"Because it was seven forty. You needed us to believe you had been in your room waiting for George since six forty-five, when he left. You had planned for him to believe that, too. Your hair was a bit of a mess and you were slightly out of breath, but you made the excuse that you had been dancing by yourself in your room when in fact you had been hurrying through a dark alley, into the lobby and up the elevator. You had hoped to beat George back to the room, but Alan and I disrupted your plans. And when you went back to the room to put the perfume George bought away, you switched to your smaller evening bag."

"Because I changed my mind."

"Because your larger handbag still had the gun it. You went back to the room and switched handbags, putting the larger bag away for safekeeping until you could figure out how to dispose of the gun. What did you do with the gun, Mrs. Verte?"

"I don't know what you're talking about."

"My guess is it's in the lake. I recall you saying you were going to walk down there this morning before breakfast," I said.

"What if I did? That's not a crime, is it?"

"Not in and of itself. You just happened to get lucky in discovering the gun and had to get rid of it. Shooting someone is relatively easy, isn't it?" I asked.

"I wouldn't know, really, because I didn't kill him, and I've had just about enough of this. You're making a fool of yourself with all this talk of green spools, bloody 'W's that aren't bloody 'W's, the ramblings of a drunken old woman as your witness, and a watch you say was altered."

"I forgot to mention a couple of other things, Mrs. Verte."

'What would that be?"

"The fact that you were wearing a lovely white dress last night."

"Yes, I was. I bought it just for this trip. So what?"

"A loose flowing dress you said was easy to move in."

"Because I wanted to dance."

"Because you wanted to be able to move quickly once you shot Blount."

"You're delusional, Mr. Barrington."

"And Mrs. Gittings saw a white angel last night. As I mentioned earlier, she was in the alley, waiting for Blount to come out. But she saw you instead, and mistook you for an angel in white. And then she saw Blount's dead body. She followed you back into the hotel and saw you go up in the elevator, to heaven, she believed."

"Clearly she is delusional as well, as I said before. If anyone murdered him, she did."

"When she gets here soon, she'll recognize you, of course."

Mr. Bennett got to his feet then, his complexion almost purple. "Stop this at once, Mr. Barrington. You were right the first time. I killed him. I did it, and I'm glad."

She looked up at him, surprised and shocked, "You see? He admits it. You all heard it."

"Vivian had nothing to do with this, Mr. Barrington. Blount was blackmailing me, like you said. I couldn't take it anymore. He was driving me mad."

"I find your devotion to Mrs. Verte admirable, Mr. Bennett, especially when she was quick to point the finger at you and still is, but please sit down."

"This is a circus. Unless you have absolute proof, I refuse to listen to any more," Mrs. Verte said.

"There are a few other things," I said. "Of course, we could subpoena the death records of Rose Dousman, search for next of kin, look up the newspaper accounts of her death, find back copies of the girlie magazine, and dredge it all back up, if that's what you want."

"Leave my sister out of this. She's suffered enough."

"I agree. By the way, Mrs. Verte, you were wearing gloves last night, as I recall."

"Of course I was, my evening gloves."

"But you wouldn't have been able to alter the time on Blount's watch while wearing them. They would have been too clumsy. You would've had to take them off. I'm willing to bet we will find your fingerprints on his watch. Yours, Blount's, and no one else's."

Mrs. Verte opened her mouth to speak, then closed it again.

"Oh, Viv," Mr. Bennett said softly, sinking back down onto the chair and putting his hand on hers.

She pulled her hand away. "So what if I did shoot him. So what?

He was a vile, nasty man. If I shot him, and I'm not saying I did, he deserved it. Not just for what he did to my Rose, but for every other girl that had come after and *would* come after her. With men like Blount, there would always be other victims, other innocent young girls, caught in the cross fire."

"What will happen now, Detective?" Mr. Bennett asked, crestfallen.

"Mrs. Verte will be arrested and tried for murder. It's up to the jury to decide her fate after that."

"You can't, they can't. Vivian is innocent in all this. I'll claim I did it, I'll say I shot him."

"But you didn't, Mr. Bennett."

"Your evidence is circumstantial, Detective Barrington. Arrest me if you want to, but I doubt a jury would find me guilty," Mrs. Verte said.

"Not if they find your fingerprint on his watch."

"She can say she handled his watch earlier, when they were together."

"Not likely, Mr. Bennett. I doubt a jury would believe that when confronted with the evidence of Blount and her sister, Rose."

"Please, Mr. Barrington. Vivian's life will be ruined if you arrest her."

"Like Blount's life is over," Alan said.

"He deserved it," Bennett said.

"You two seem to be in agreement on that point, but it's not for either one of you to decide. It doesn't matter if you think her actions were justified, Mr. Bennett. It doesn't matter if I think they were. We are not a jury, we are not the judge, and we cannot sit in judgment of Blount or anyone else. It is not up to you or Mrs. Verte or me or anyone else to try and circumnavigate the law, to be vigilantes."

Wilchinski whistled and looked at his watch again. "Four and a half minutes, Barrington. Not bad. Well, I suppose I should take you downtown, Mrs. Verte, under the circumstances."

"Am I under arrest?"

He shook his head. "Not formally, ma'am, not yet anyway.

Let's go down and just see if your fingerprints happen to be on that watch. If not, well, then we'll see."

"I'll come, too, Vivian," Mr. Bennett said, getting to his feet again.

She looked at him coldly. "No, thank you, Mr. Bennett. It's because of men like you that Blount had his nasty little business in the first place. Men like you who took advantage of innocent young women. For a while, I really thought they were going to pin his murder on you. That, to me, would have been the ultimate justice." She got to her feet, gathered up her handbag, and walked out, followed closely by Wilchinski.

CHAPTER SEVENTEEN

Alan and I picked up our hats and quietly left the ballroom after Wilchinski had gone down with Mrs. Verte. Mr. Bennett had sat back down at the table, looking stunned and hurt. Miss Eye and Mr. Gillingham went back onstage, presumably to rehearse some more or just talk about what had happened. We took the elevator back down to the eighth floor and then to our room.

Alan tossed his hat on the dresser and flopped down on the bed nearest the window, unbuttoning his jacket.

"Gee, I never would have guessed Mrs. Verte killed him. She didn't seem the type, and I thought she was one of the few people who actually liked him."

"That was her intent, of course, to make us think she liked him, that she had no motive."

"What finally tipped you off?"

"When I was reciting basic French words to you, I remembered that green was *verte*. Then you mistaking Henning for Hemming got me to thinking that things aren't always what they first appear to be. And I kept coming back to that blank look Blount had when Mrs. Verte mentioned her maiden name was Dousman. Of course, at first we thought his look was because of Mrs. Verte's off-color joke, but Blount didn't seem the type to be offended by something like that."

"Golly, you put the pieces together well."

"And just in the nick of time. Wilchinski was losing patience."

"He never seemed to have much patience to begin with. So what's going to happen to her?"

I shook my head, putting my hat on the dresser next to his and checking my reflection in the dresser mirror. "I'm not sure, though it's possible she may get off."

"Really?"

I shrugged as I ran a comb through my hair. "Wilchinski still seemed intent that it was an unknown robber."

"Yeah, but if her fingerprints are on the watch…"

I put my comb away and turned to Alan. "If Wilchinski even bothers to check. He said he would, but I have my doubts. I don't think he likes my butting in, figuring things out when he didn't, making him look bad. And in his opinion, Blount was a nasty little man that deserved to be murdered."

"But that's not right, Heath."

"I agree, but I think we've done all we can. People don't always get what they deserve, and they don't always deserve what they get."

Alan started fiddling with his tie absentmindedly. "I suppose that's true."

"Maybe Wilchinski will surprise us. Maybe he'll look for the fingerprint, make the arrest, and press charges. Maybe she'll go to trial."

"And if she does? If she's found guilty?"

"She could go to the gas chamber."

Alan looked away from me. "Wowzer."

"The fact remains she murdered someone in cold blood, with intent. As I said before, we must not, cannot judge."

"What if she's not found guilty? Or if Wilchinski decides to let her go?"

I shook my head. "I don't know. She'll go back to New York and all this will be forgotten, I suppose. She's a strong woman."

"What about Mr. Bennett?"

"Good old Mr. Bennett. I feel sorry for him, but he's relatively young yet. Who knows, he might still find one of those librarians. Since the war, eligible men are in short supply, you know. I doubt there will be any need to disclose what Blount did to him and why, even if Mrs. Verte does go to trial. The prosecuting attorney will focus on Rose Dousman, the fingerprint, and Mrs. Gittings's testimony, along with ours, I imagine."

"Jeepers, you think Mrs. Gittings would testify?"

"Hard to say. The defense attorney may argue she's not a fit witness. Nevertheless, I think Mr. Bennett's career and reputation will be safe. Certainly Miss Eye and Mr. Gillingham have nothing to gain by exposing him."

"I'm glad. He's a good man."

"Yeah, I know. I'm glad, too. He made a few mistakes, but he's learned from them. As for Miss Eye and Mr. Gillingham, their secrets will be safe, too. I wouldn't be at all surprised if they both have long, happy careers."

"Wouldn't that be something? We could say we knew her when."

I laughed. "Yes, and we have her autograph," I said, removing the program from my pocket and setting it on the nightstand.

Alan took his out and set it next to mine for safekeeping. "What about Mrs. Gittings?"

"I worry about her most of all, but I think she will be all right, also. The man she hated is gone. Maybe we can come down here once in a while and visit her."

"I'd like that," Alan said, turning on to his side and propping himself up on one elbow.

"I thought you might," I said, smiling.

"It certainly has been a weekend. Say, you never got the tie for your dad."

"I'll pick one up in Milwaukee when we get back tomorrow, probably get it on sale."

"That's a good idea. This trip sure didn't turn out exactly how I'd pictured it. Maybe my lucky rock isn't so lucky after all."

"Oh, I don't know. We solved the murder, didn't we?"

"Yeah, I guess we did. But still, maybe it's time I place it on a shelf in my apartment."

"You sure?"

"You're all the luck I need, Heath."

I grinned. "You know what? This is our last night in Chicago—why don't we put our tuxes on, and I'll take you to the Pump Room for dinner, and then we'll go clubbing? We'll find some nice girls to dance with and we'll dance close by, pretending we're dancing with each other."

Alan didn't say anything for a bit. He sat up, hands on his knees, and stared at the carpet, his feet on the floor. Finally, he looked at me, his eyes moist. "No, let's stay right here in our room tonight instead, order room service, turn on the radio, and dance. Just the two of us."

I cocked my head in surprise. "But we could do that back in Milwaukee, Alan."

"I know, but I don't want to pretend to dance with you. I want to dance with you. I'll even let you lead."

"Are you sure?"

"Yes. Life's too short to just pretend, and we have to do enough of that every day."

I went over to the dresser and turned the radio on, letting it warm up as it buzzed and crackled to life. A little fine-tuning and soon the sounds of the Andrew Sisters swelled forth. I put out my hands to him. "Then let's do it, Alan. No pretending tonight."

His face was beaming as he got to his feet and came into my arms. "If you're waiting for me, you're wasting your time."

MYSTERY HISTORY

The Edmonton Hotel in *Death Checks In* is fictitious, but is based on a composite of several Chicago hotels of the era.

The Pump Room, the Boulevard Room, Empire Room, Tip Top Tap, and Chez Paree were all well-known, popular Chicago restaurants and nightclubs of the 1940s.

The Brownie camera Alan Keyes uses in the book was first produced in 1900 and introduced snapshots to the general public. It remained in production in various forms up until 1986.

As mentioned in this book, Babe Zaharias really was the first American to win the Women's British Golf Title. She was named the 10th Greatest North American Athlete of the 20th Century, and the 9th greatest by the Associated Press. In addition to golf, she excelled in baseball, softball, bowling, track and field, and basketball. She and Betty Dodd, a fellow golfer, were rumored to be close and loving partners, though Babe was married to George Zaharias.

Alan Keyes is a big believer in horoscopes, which first appeared in daily newspapers around 1930.

Before credit cards, letters of credit were accepted at hotels, and most guests paid by check or cash.

The elevator operator strike mentioned in this book really did occur in 1945 in New York City. It hastened the arrival of automated elevators by bringing business to a grinding halt until the strike was settled.

The fictitious Allegrae Auction House mentioned briefly in this book is also mentioned in *Death Comes Darkly*.

The character of Mrs. Gittings and the incident with Heath in her apartment are based on real-life events that happened to this author.

The movie *The Egg and I* debuted in 1947, starring Claudette Colbert and Fred MacMurray. It was a huge hit and launched the characters of Ma and Pa Kettle, played by Percy Kilbride and Marjorie Main, who went on to star in movies of their own.

About the Author

David S. Pederson was born in Leadville, Colorado, where his father was a miner. Soon after, the family relocated to Wisconsin, where David grew up, attending high school and university, majoring in business and creative writing. Landing a job in retail, he found himself relocating to New York, Massachusetts, and eventually back to Wisconsin, where he currently lives with his longtime partner and works in the furniture and decorating business.

He has written many short stories and poetry and is passionate about mysteries, old movies, and crime novels. When not reading, writing, or working in the furniture business, David also enjoys working out and studying classic ocean liners, floor plans, and historic homes.

David can be contacted at davidspederson@gmail.com.

Books Available From Bold Strokes Books

Death Checks In by David S. Pederson. Despite Heath's promises to Alan to not get involved, Heath can't resist investigating a shopkeeper's murder in Chicago, which dashes their plans for a romantic weekend getaway. (978-1-163555-329-1)

Of Echoes Born by 'Nathan Burgoine. A collection of queer fantasy short stories set in Canada from Lambda Literary Award finalist 'Nathan Burgoine. (978-1-63555-096-2)

The Lurid Sea by Tom Cardamone. Cursed to spend eternity on his knees, Nerites is having the time of his life. (978-1-62639-911-2)

Sinister Justice by Steve Pickens. When a vigilante targets citizens of Jake Finnigan's hometown, Jake and his partner Sam fall under suspicion themselves as they investigate the murders. (978-1-63555-094-8)

Club Arcana: Operation Janus by Jon Wilson. Wizards, demons, Elder Gods: Who knew the universe was so crowded, and that they'd all be out to get Angus McAslan? (978-1-62639-969-3)

Triad Soul by 'Nathan Burgoine. Luc, Anders, and Curtis—vampire, demon, and wizard—must use their powers of blood, soul, and magic to defeat a murderer determined to turn their city into a battlefield. (978-1-62639-863-4)

Gatecrasher by Stephen Graham King. Aided by a high-tech thief, the Maverick Heart crew race against time to prevent a cadre of savage corporate mercenaries from seizing control of a revolutionary wormhole technology. (978-1-62639-936-5)

Wicked Frat Boy Ways by Todd Gregory. Beta Kappa brothers Brandon Benson and Phil Connor play an increasingly dangerous game of love, seduction, and emotional manipulation. (978-1-62639-671-5)

Death Goes Overboard by David S. Pederson. Heath Barrington and Alan Keyes are two sides of a steamy love triangle as they encounter gangsters, con men, murder, and more aboard an old lake steamer. (978-1-62639-907-5)

A Careful Heart by Ralph Josiah Bardsley. Be careful what you wish for…love changes everything. (978-1-62639-887-0)

Worms of Sin by Lyle Blake Smythers. A haunted mental asylum turned drug treatment facility exposes supernatural detective Finn M'Coul to an outbreak of murderous insanity, a strange parasite, and ghosts that seek sex with the living. (978-1-62639-823-8)

Tartarus by Eric Andrews-Katz. When Echidna, Mother of all Monsters, escapes from Tartarus and into the modern world, only an Olympian has the power to oppose her. (978-1-62639-746-0)

Rank by Richard Compson Sater. Rank means nothing to the heart, but the Air Force isn't as impartial. Every airman learns that rank has its privileges. What about love? (978-1-62639-845-0)

The Grim Reaper's Calling Card by Donald Webb. When Katsuro Tanaka begins investigating the disappearance of a young nurse, he discovers more missing persons, and they all have one thing in common: The Grim Reaper Tarot Card. (978-1-62639-748-4)

Smoldering Desires by C.E. Knipes. Evan McGarrity has found the man of his dreams in Sebastian Tantalos. When an old boyfriend from Sebastian's past enters the picture, Evan must fight for the man he loves. (978-1-62639-714-9)

Tallulah Bankhead Slept Here by Sam Lollar. A coming of age/ coming out story, set in El Paso of 1967, that tells of Aaron's adventures with movie stars, cool cars, and topless bars. (978-1-62639-710-1)

Death Came Calling by Donald Webb. When private investigator Katsuro Tanaka is hired to look into the death of a high-profile lawyer, he becomes embroiled in a case of murder and mayhem. (978-1-60282-979-4)

The City of Seven Gods by Andrew J. Peters. In an ancient city of aerie temples, a young priest and a barbarian mercenary struggle to refashion their lives after their worlds are torn apart by betrayal. (978-1-62639-775-0)

Lysistrata Cove by Dena Hankins. Jack and Eve navigate the maelstrom of their darkest desires and find love by transgressing gender, dominance, submission, and the law on the crystal blue Caribbean Sea. (978-1-62639-821-4)

Garden District Gothic by Greg Herren. Scotty Bradley has to solve a notorious thirty-year-old unsolved murder that has terrible repercussions in the present. (978-1-62639-667-8)

The Man on Top of the World by Vanessa Clark. Jonathan Maxwell falling in love with Izzy Rich, the world's hottest glam rock superstar, is not only unpredictable but complicated when a bold teenage fan-girl changes everything. (978-1-62639-699-9)

The Orchard of Flesh by Christian Baines. With two hotheaded men under his roof including his werewolf lover, a vampire tries to solve an increasingly lethal mystery while keeping Sydney's supernatural factions from the brink of war. (978-1-62639-649-4)

The Thassos Confabulation by Sam Sommer. With the inheritance of a great deal of money, David and Chris also inherit a nondescript brown paper parcel and a strange and perplexing letter that sends David on a quest to understand its meaning. (978-1-62639-665-4)

The Photographer's Truth by Ralph Josiah Bardsley. Silicon Valley tech geek Ian Baines gets more than he bargained for on an unexpected journey of self-discovery through the lustrous nightlife of Paris. (978-1-62639-637-1)

CPSIA information can be obtained
at www.ICGtesting.com
Printed in the USA
BVHW09s1749270718
522792BV00001B/29/P